DESTINED TO LOVE

BY
JOURDYN KELLY

JADED
ANGELS

Also by Jourdyn Kelly

CONTENTS

ANALA GEIL

F or the first time in what feels like forever, things were finally going well. Life almost seemed... normal. Graduation was just around the corner. I have friends now. Real ones. People who laugh with me, fight beside me, and trust me. That is new. That is good. Hell, I even have a boyfriend.

For a while, I let myself believe I could have it all: the quiet routine of meditating and training with my Hunters, the fragile peace of nights without bloodshed, the comfort of belonging somewhere—and to someone. I have earned the trust of my Hunters, no small feat considering what I am—what I've always been. A Cursed One. And a Hunter. Both. The line between monster and savior balances on the edge of a blade, and somehow, I'd make it work.

But peace never lasts, not for me. One battle was enough to break the illusion I had so carefully built. Within hours, the fragile world I had stitched together began to fall apart, thread by thread. The lives of my Hunters—my friends, my family—now hang in the balance.

And me? I should have known better. I should have remembered that no matter how normal life seems, darkness always finds its way back. That edge of a blade always cuts.

How did everything go so completely, devastatingly wrong?

CHAPTER ONE
"RANTINGS OF ANGRY VAMPIRE"

I wonder if I could will myself to change and attack Jenna for her incessant gum popping, and if it could be considered an animal attack. I'd make it look like one. I'll be quick; she won't feel a thing.

Rantings of an angry vampire. Maybe that's what I should name my blog. Or memoir. Okay, so I'm cranky. Sue me. I have been sitting here for days, waiting for Zac to wake up. All of my Hunters are here except Sam, who is working. They don't need to be here. They just insist on it. Much to my dismay. Talking, tapping, singing, *popping*. Ugh!

"I need blood."

Amanda's eyes snap up from one of my father's journals she's reading. Her reaction to my thought surprises me, and indicates it wasn't a silent thought at all.

"Sorry," I mumble, lowering my gaze from hers.

"Don't be, Ana. If you need..."

"I'm just irritable." I look pointedly at Jenna, who pops her gum at me. "If you keep popping your gum, I will go all Chicago on you."

Jenna's face scrunches in confusion. "Huh?"

I can't help but roll my eyes. I know, childish, but come on! She's so annoying! "Stop popping your gum. And get some culture."

"Jenna," Amanda interrupts Jenna's comeback - which is bound to be bitchy, since we're talking about Jenna. "Could you get Ana some blood?"

"Why can't she get it herself?"

"Because I need to stay here with Zac," I shoot back. "*You* don't need to be here."

"He's my friend, too!"

I am over 600 years old, and I'm arguing with what is essentially the ultimate 'mean girl.' Sigh.

"I understand that, Jenna. However, I am technically Zac's true Maker. When he wakes up, I need to be here."

"Wouldn't he want all of his friends here?" Jenna counters.

"Jenna, Ana isn't just Zac's friend. He will be bonded with her now."

My boyfriend, Sam, chooses exactly the moment Amanda talks about Zac's bond with me to walk in. I notice his step falter, and his eyes cloud with an emotion I can't quite read as he quickly clears it. Fantastic. As if he wasn't already tired of Zac's feelings for me.

Jenna must have sensed the change in the air because she excuses herself, mumbling about getting me blood - and popping her damn gum. The rest of my Hunters don't move to leave but show enough decorum to at least appear busy doing other things on their smartphones or tablets.

"Any movement, call me back. I'll be right outside," I whisper to Amanda. She nods before glancing at her brother Sam. A look passes between them, and I wish then that I could read minds. With a sigh, I step outside the room with him.

"Hey." He pulls me close, kissing me chastely on the lips. It's not his usual hello kiss, but he just heard that Zac—who had confessed to being in love with me before Thomas turned him—will be bonded to me. I guess I can't blame him.

"Hi. Tough case?"

Sam and I haven't been able to spend much time together since that fateful night we went to fight Thomas and his army of Cursed Ones and Hybrids. He got involved in a big case, and since we're waiting for Zac to wake up before we start searching for Thomas again, he's been focusing a lot on his own investigation. If I weren't so busy with Zac, I'd probably think something was wrong between us.

"They're all tough. I'm a homicide detective."

Or maybe there is something off between us.

"Sam..."

"He'll be bonded to you?"

Sam's voice is steady, but the look in his eyes contradicts that calm. Is he worried that this bond with Zac will bring us closer together?

"I cannot change that, Sam. Believe me, I would if I knew how."

"What does this mean for you two?"

"It means..." I make a frustrated noise that makes Sam's eyebrows quirk. "I do not know what it means. I have never been anyone's Maker. At least, not by choice. If I knew how to be a Maker and use whatever that bond was, I would use it to find Thomas." The idea gives me pause, and I momentarily forget about what Sam and I are talking about. Could it be that easy? I may not have made Thomas myself, but it was my blood. I *am* his Maker.

"Ana?"

Sam brings my attention back to him.

"I am sorry. I was thinking."

Sam's lips curl into a grin. He steps closer when I give him a questioning look.

"Your entire vocabulary shifts when you're thinking as Anala."

"Does it?"

"Mmhmm." Finally, Sam wraps his arms around me without any of the stiffness or reluctance I felt earlier. "It's sexy."

I snort. Not exactly sexy, but it's what happened.

"You just think my accent is sexy."

He had told me before that, along with my long, raven hair, translucent eyes, and awesome body (his words, not mine), my English accent turns him on. I accused him of being biased and insisted I didn't have an accent. What can I say? I don't always take compliments very well, especially when they come from someone who looks like Sam.

"I think all of you is sexy," he responds, touching my cheek softly. Thank God I can't blush.

My response is to kiss him. And not just a chaste kiss like he gave me before. I've missed this. I realize that if we had finished the job with Thomas, I wouldn't be here. Or I *shouldn't* be here. I had given Zac instructions to kill me after Thomas was dead. Things didn't go quite as expected that night.

It's been almost a week since then, and as I run my fingers through Sam's wheat-colored - and oh-so-soft - hair, I can't help but think that this is the first time Sam and I have had more than just a quick kiss in that span.

"I miss you," he whispers, echoing my thoughts.

"Are you off tonight?"

He sighs, pressing his forehead to mine. "No. I'll be late."

"I don't care. Come to me when you're done."

He seems like he has more to say, but he nods and kisses me again.

"I have to go, baby."

The endearment began a couple of weeks ago, and I still haven't gotten used to it. However, I must admit that I enjoy it quite a bit.

"Be careful."

"Why hasn't he woken up, Ana?"

Amanda's voice cuts through my thoughts, and I look up at her. Jenna came through with her grumbling about getting me blood, and I've been sipping it slowly, trying to figure out where to start looking for Thomas.

I honestly don't know, Amanda. This has never happened before, and it hasn't. I staked Zac after he was turned. Don't judge me. He tried attacking me, and I believed I had no choice. Besides, I'm a Hunter. If I had followed the Society's rules, Zac would be dead. Usually, when the stake is removed, the awakening is immediate—painful as hell but instant. I know this firsthand. Unfortunately.

"Will he?"

All of my Hunters' eyes turn to me, waiting for the answer.

"Yes." Of course, my voice sounds more confident than I actually feel. He should be awake. It makes me nervous that he isn't. "Amanda?"

She glances up from that always-present journal with a questioning look.

"In any of those journals, was there anything specific about the bond?"

"Is Sam worried about it?"

I hold back the sigh that forms on my lips. I wish I didn't have to worry about my relationship with Sam. But this concern extends far beyond Zac's connection with me. It even reaches as deep as my desire to stay alive. For the first time in centuries, I want—no, I need— someone in my life, specifically Sam. And I'm not sure if what I desire is even possible.

"You know the answer to that. But *I'm* curious about this. I know that I can feel their pain, and they have a loyalty to me. Is there anything else?"

"Not that I've read. I mean, it's not like your father had a lot of Cursed Ones to study... oh God! Ana, I'm so sorry!"

Just as mine did, Amanda's thoughts turned to the last time my parents were alive. Papa was studying a Cursed One, hoping to find a cure for me. It was Bernard who betrayed him, but I still felt responsible. I will always feel responsible.

"It's okay, I thought the same thing. Papa wouldn't have had Cursed Ones to experiment with until after me. And I've never turned anyone." My eyes slide to Zac. I didn't turn him, but he was mine. I didn't turn Thomas either, but my blood did.

"Do you hope you can use the bond to find Thomas?"

I study Amanda for a moment before answering. The change in her still amazes me. When I first met Amanda, despite my liking her, she seemed a bit shallow. I knew I might have been overreacting, since I've been alive for many lifetimes, which means I've had more time to mature. But Amanda had always been more interested in clothes and boys than anything more meaningful. The complete change in her over the past few months surprised me just as much as it pleased me. I know I should feel guilty about feeling that way, but honestly, I think Amanda has surprised even herself.

"I think it's a possibility that we should explore." I tip my head to the journal. "You'll need a fresh one of those."

"You want *me* to write about it?"

"Yes."

"But why can't you? I mean, you would know more about what's happening."

"I can tell you. And you can continue writing if there are any more incidents after I'm..."

"Ana."

"No arguing, Amanda. We had a deal."

"I hate your deal." Amanda snaps the journal shut and focuses on Zac.

"Yeah, well, I'm not ecstatic about it either," I mumble. "But it's..."

"If you say it's the code, I will scream." Amanda glances at Zac. "Maybe if I did, he would wake the hell up."

I take another sip of my blood - with traces of Zac's blood in hopes it connects me to his thoughts again - and set it aside. I take Zac's hand in mine, focusing on him while I block everyone else out.

Zac? Can you hear me?

I focus harder when I get nothing.

It's time to wake up.

Nothing. Damn it. I sigh heavily and lean back in my chair. Why in the hell aren't you awake, Zac? I try to recall if there's anything I might have done that could have prevented Zac from waking. I didn't use a splintering stake, I'm sure of that. The only difference in what happened with Zac is that we used my father's elixir in the hope that it would help him retain his humanity. I had to force it down Zac's throat before we removed the stake. Could that really be it?

"I need to look at Papa's formulas."

Amanda shuffles through the stack of books until she finds the one she was looking for and hands it to me.

"What are you looking for?"

"Answers."

I flip through the pages until I find the formula for the "humanity elixir." It's what Papa called it. I had laughed at him at the time, but I suppose it's as good a name as any. I examine each of the ingredients, all of which are easy to find today, except maybe the Blood Orchlips. The beautiful flowers were created centuries ago by medicine men of the Medieval era. They were believed to have healing properties when mixed with other specific ingredients. The things Papa combined with it certainly affected the mind. I wasn't beyond thinking it was a hallucinogen, but I try to think positively. The elixir itself was running low, and if Zac needed it to keep his humanity, I was in trouble.

"There's nothing in the elixir that should keep him in a sleeping state. I'm not speaking to anyone in particular, but I hear Amanda grunt in agreement. "You've already looked at this, haven't you?"

"Yes." She gives me a little shrug accompanied by a sheepish smile. "I looked it up when I saw we were low. I don't know what Blood Orchlips are, though."

"Flowers." Okay, so there's a little bit of surprise in my voice, but I think I cover it well. "They were created by medicine men centuries ago. Papa learned how to cultivate them, but I can't imagine I could find them these days."

"Sometimes I forget you're so old."

My eyes snap to Jenna, who throws out that little nugget.

"I wish I could forget what a bit..."

"Ana."

I hear the laughter in Amanda's voice and can't hide my scowl. She could have let me have my fun at Jenna's expense. Wow. I really need a break from my Hunters before I lose it.

"Go train," I order. "All of you."

"What if he wakes up?" Emily asks softly.

"Then I'll call for you. You need to train and keep your skills and stamina sharp."

Eric stands up and slaps Jeremy, who is sleeping, on the shoulder.

Jeremy bolts up in his chair, looking around wildly.

"What! What happened?"

I can't help but laugh at him. I needed that more than I realized. I watch as they all file out of the room, leaving me alone with Zac. Finally. No popping, no talking, nothing. Just the fear that Zac won't wake up. Or, he will, and the elixir doesn't work, and I'll have no choice but to kill him.

CHAPTER TWO

"INHUMAN"

My head is resting on Sam's chest, our legs tangled together. He is sleeping and snoring softly, in that quiet way that always makes me smile. When he told me he would be late, I didn't think he meant past two in the morning. Still, he kept his promise and came to me.

Sam had been working so much lately that I didn't mind waiting for him, but he would never talk about the case with me. Every time I asked, he would change the subject or try to distract me in other ways. I'm not sure how that makes me feel.

That's a lie. It doesn't make me feel good at all. When we're together, I can feel how much he loves me. I don't think that has changed. But he certainly isn't being open about his work with me. It makes me wonder if the case was dangerous and he doesn't want me to worry. Maybe it's time to tell him that hiding things from me worries me more.

"Ana?"

My body involuntarily flinches at the sound of his voice, breaking my train of thought.

"I thought you were sleeping."

"I was. Your fingers are digging into my chest, baby. What's on your mind?" Sam takes my hand in his and kisses my knuckles.

"I'm sorry." I'm about to tell him that I was just worried about Zac, but think better of it. Mentioning Zac only makes things worse. Maybe I should try honesty. I prop my chin on Sam's chest to look at him. "You're on my mind."

His smile is beautiful. Perfectly white teeth contrasted with the stubble on his strong jaw.

"I enjoy being on your mind," Sam says as he leans down to kiss me on the forehead. "But I'm not sure that's such a good thing if it agitates you so much."

I'm not agitated. I trail a finger down his cheek and across his bottom lip. "I just feel like you're pulling away from me." As soon as the words leave my mouth, I want to take them back. It makes me look—and feel—weak.

Sam's beautiful smile vanishes. He grabs me by my arms and pulls me up until my face is level with his.

"I'm not pulling away from you, Ana. I'm just not sure how to handle this anymore."

"Handle what?"

"I find myself torn." He sits up, leaning against the headboard of my bed. Sam scrubs his hands over his face, and I take the time to sit up with him, bringing the sheet around me. "I want to find Thomas because it's dangerous having him out there," he continues. "On the other hand, you've made us promise to kill you after that is over."

Of course, I know he never wanted to agree to the stipulation I set in order to give my consent to keep Zac alive. Hell, the more I think about it, the less I want to agree to it either. But I can't help feeling responsible for everything that's happened. The murders Thomas and his crew committed, the Hybrids they created, Zac, and honestly, the lost youth of my Hunters - all of that is my fault. If I had just paid more attention that fateful day, I wouldn't be here now. Nor would Thomas. These kids I have trained to be killers would be graduating from high school, and their biggest problem would be deciding which college to attend.

If my parents had killed me after my mistake of being turned, they wouldn't have been murdered because of me. I shiver when I think of finding their bodies in Papa's lab. Sam pulls me closer and holds me tighter.

"You know I'm in love with you, right?" he whispers.

"I love you, too."

Sam turns to me, holding my face in his hands. "No, Ana. I'm in love with you. Meaning I don't want to live without you. Don't make us do this."

"Sam."

Whatever else I'm going to say is completely forgotten when Sam kisses me. I don't want to leave him. I don't think I have a choice.

Anala.

I break the kiss abruptly and frown.

"What is -?"

I press my fingers to Sam's lips to stop his question, quieting him.

Anala.

"Zac."

I register the flash of anger in Sam's eyes before rolling off him.

"Sam, I think Zac is waking up." I hurriedly get dressed, hoping Sam will understand. With a sigh, Sam dresses and walks with me to check on Zac.

"He's still sleeping. Why did she send for us?" Jenna, sans the gum, thank God, whispers to the others. They are sleepy and grumpy. Not that I blame them. I had made them train for much longer than they were used to. It kept them from getting on my nerves, which really saved their lives. Irritated vampires are probably not a good thing.

"I don't know. She said to get you all, so I did," Amanda whispers back.

"Quiet." All chatter stops at the authority in my voice. I lean in close to Zac, taking his hand in mine as I did earlier. *Zac, I'm here. Wake up.*

I'm afraid.

I frown. "Why?"

None of my Hunters answer. They must understand that I am communicating with Zac.

I tried to attack you.

You remember that? I know my surprise shows on my face. It might seem strange to the others, who don't know what the conversation is about, but they stay quiet.

I remember everything. I don't want to be like this.

Tell me what to do, Zac. The others made me promise to spare you. At least until we find Thomas. Wake up, and we'll discuss this with everyone.

What if I hurt them?

I won't let you. Do you feel like hurting them?

I don't know.

Even though his answer was in my mind, I could hear the anguish. He hated what he had become. What we are. Zac might have crossed the line regarding the Society's code, but he was fiercely loyal to humanity. Now a monster, a Cursed One, he didn't know how to handle that.

"Wake up, Zac," I say softly so that everyone can hear. "Whatever happens, we'll deal with it."

I stand up, releasing Zac's hand, and move next to Sam. He slips his arm around my waist, and even though I know it's a possessive gesture, I don't mind. Amanda hands me one of my swords, and I hold it close as I watch Zac wrestle with himself. The others step back, relaxed but alert. They understand the risks, but they're Zac's friends. They will stand there for him, as one of their own.

"What did he say?" Amanda's mouth is close to my ear, and she is pressed against me. I feel her tremble. Whether it's out of fear or anticipation, I don't know.

"We'll talk about it as a group when Zac is awake. Do you have the blood?"

Amanda nods, slightly moving away from me before stepping behind me. She isn't afraid of Zac. She knows, like the others, how to defend herself from the likes of me and Zac. I'm willing to bet that's what she's worried about—having to protect herself and hurting Zac in the process.

Zac's body moves almost imperceptibly, and all my Hunters tense. I take a moment to feel pride swell within me. Their skills and perception have certainly improved greatly. When Zac's eyes open, I immediately notice the color—or lack of it. They are now translucent, like mine, with a blood-red ring around the iris. Only Zac's is much more prominent since he's in the Cursed state.

"My eyes burn," he growls. Good news, he is coherent. Bad news, his voice is that of a Hybrid. Rough and raw. Inhuman. "So do my teeth. What the hell?"

He raises his hands to his face, rubbing his fingers over his longer teeth. He growls another curse as they easily bite into his skin. That is the only movement he makes until he lifts his eyes to mine. "Is this what you go through every time you change?"

CHAPTER THREE
"MY CONNECTION IS WITH YOU."

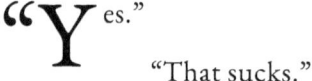es."

"That sucks."

Zac had been brooding up until then. Suddenly, he starts to chuckle, and my other Hunters join in. Zac and the others are laughing at his pun. Vampire, that sucks. Get it? If I weren't so worried about his voice, I would have laughed too — even if it was cheesy.

"Good to know you haven't lost your sense of humor," I say dryly, and walk toward him. "Other than the discomfort, how do you feel?"

"Hungry."

"We'll get to that in a minute. Since you're hungry, do you feel like tearing any of them apart?" I jerk my thumb toward the others. That my thumb is pointed directly at Jenna is purely a coincidence. I swear.

"I don't want to hurt them."

I nod, signaling Amanda to bring the blood. Zac's eyes stay fixed on me the whole time, as if he's concentrating, fighting not to make any sudden moves. When Amanda hands over the blood, she goes back to the others.

"Drink," I order.

Zac hesitates, scowling at the red liquid. "It smells good. Looks gross."

"It tastes better than it looks," I tell him softly, ignoring the disgusted sounds behind me. He studies me for a minute longer before deciding to trust me, bringing the bottle to his lips. I notice his pupils beginning to dilate. "Everyone out."

"But Ana!"

"Jeremy, out. You all can come back after he's done."

"It's not like we haven't seen this before, Ana. I mean, we watch you drink."

I turn to face Amanda. "And it's still uncomfortable for me. The first time having blood is not something that needs to be witnessed by everyone."

"Let's go." Sam begins ushering the others out before they can protest again. I catch his eye and mouth a *thank you* to him before he gives me a curt nod and closes the door behind him. Sigh. You would think that being a 600-year-old vampire, training vampire Hunters, having to hunt down someone you used to care about, and trying to figure out if you'll have to kill one of your own because he was changed, would be enough drama. But no. I have to add a boyfriend who is jealous of those I have to kill or should kill.

"You didn't need to make them leave. They should see what I am now."

As much as his voice concerns me, I manage to keep my emotions in check. "Drink, Zac."

He has been holding the bottle to his lips, taking deep whiffs but not drinking. Finally, he tipped the bottle, and the first drop hit his tongue. The savage sound that came out of Zac rips through the room.

"Stay out there!" I shout to the others as they scramble to get back in.

"Ana!"

"Everything is fine, Sam. Stay out there. Please." I refocus my attention on Zac, watching him closely. When I see him flare his nostrils and glance at the door, I move to position myself between him and the exit. "Fight it, Zac. Remember who you are and all of your training. Fight it."

I can remember, as vividly as if it were yesterday, Papa saying those words to me. Telling me that I was stronger than the urge.

"You said yourself that you did not want to hurt them. Use that, and everything I have taught you, to fight this."

Zac's chest lifts and falls in a fast rhythm, and I can almost see the struggle inside. It is the same thing I had felt all those years ago. He grips the bottle of blood so tightly that I am afraid he will break it. Finally, he focuses back on the bottle, upending it and chugging down what is now his life.

"How is he?"

"Resting." I quickly glance at Emily, noticing her slight blush when she asks about Zac. Interesting.

"He just woke up. Why does he need to rest?"

It was the pop of the gum. That's what broke the proverbial camel's back. I change. I didn't stop it, but then, I didn't really want to. I am on Jenna in less than a second, my hand grabbing the front of her shirt and holding her at least an inch off the floor.

"Would you like to find out for yourself why he needs more rest?" I growl.

"Anala!"

"Back off, Amanda! I am sick of your attitude, Jenna. I am sick of you popping your damn gum. And, most of all, I am sick of the way you talk to me. Like it or not, I am your leader. You will treat me with respect. If you cannot do that, then get out!"

"I'm sorry." I feel Jenna tremble, and what I see in her eyes makes me feel horrible for my outburst. It isn't fear. It is sadness. Shit. Once again, I let my emotions get the best of me, and I lashed out at my Hunters. Papa would not approve, which is fine since I don't approve of myself. I gently release Jenna and take a deep breath. I feel the effects of my change return to normal, and I wait for my irritation to ebb before addressing my Hunters.

"I apologize." I lower my head in shame. I yelled at Jenna about being her leader, and I acted like an ass. "I should not have done that, and there is no excuse for my behavior. Jenna." I force myself to face Jenna. "I cannot tell you how ashamed I am of what I did to you. I do not expect you to forgive me, but I hope you will. I also hope you will consider staying with the group, as you are invaluable to us. To me."

When Jenna says nothing, and the others stare at me as if I had just grown three more heads, I leave them. What more could I say, really? I've already done the damage. Now I have to wait and see if I have ruined everything.

"Ana?"

Sam jogs up behind me and grabs my arm.

"Sam, I need some time."

"Talk to me about what just happened in there."

Sigh. What kind of leader am I? No one listens.

"I lost my cool." I shrug. As I had said to Jenna and the others, I have no excuse.

"You never —"

Lose it?" I laugh bitterly. "Have you been here the whole time? Apparently, I have moments of uncontrollable outbursts." I hold my hand up to stop Sam's rebuttal. "I'm going to go sit with Zac for a bit. You guys are free to leave or train."

Fury flashes across Sam's face, and I roll my eyes. Totally a teenage move, and definitely the wrong one, based on Sam's reaction.

"Sam, he's going through a difficult situation right now."

"Aren't we all?"

"Not like him."

"Are you falling for him? Is it easier for you to be with him because of what he is now? He's like you, and now you have someone who knows what you're going through? Is that it?"

I blink. And I blink because I can't believe what he just said to me. I have no words. Then I feel the anger, which has done nothing except get me into trouble so far. One. Two. Three. Four. Five. And that's as far as I get before I grab Sam's shirt and drag him into an empty room.

"Is that what you really think? No! You know what, don't answer that. Let me answer your ridiculous questions," I say before he can speak. "No. I am not falling for Zac. I love you. No, it wouldn't be easier for me because of what he is now. I don't want him. I don't care if he's like me. I want you, Sam. But you're the one who is pulling away from me because of your damn jealousy. And, honestly, it's starting to piss me off."

"He has a connection with you, Ana."

"No, Sam. He has a bond with me that I have no control over. My connection is with you. You feel that as much as I do, I know you do."

Sam closes his eyes and pulls me closer. When I struggle, he holds on tighter.

"I do. That's why this is driving me crazy, Ana. If I had been the one Thomas turned, we could be together. You wouldn't be leaving me."

I gasp. "Don't say things like that, Sam. You don't want to be what I am."

"If it meant being with you forever, I do."

I study him for a while and see that he is serious. He would consider being a monster to be with me. At least that's how he feels now. If it had really happened, he would feel differently, I'm sure of it.

Sam, we have more immediate concerns than our future. If we don't find Thomas, many people's lives will be at risk. I notice him tense up, and I don't want him to think I don't care or that I'm not thinking about what happens after Thomas. I just can't focus on that right now—mainly because I have no idea what to do after Thomas. "Hey. I love you. When the time comes, we'll deal with whatever must be done."

As he did when I spoke to him earlier, he seems like there's more he wants to say. But he just kisses me and tells me he loves me, too, before letting me go.

"Is everyone freaked out by me?"

Sam had left for work, and the others were training, so I took some time to spend with Zac. His voice seems to be improving, but it still doesn't sound quite human enough to me. I also don't know if the improvement is just wishful thinking on my part or if it's really true. I feed him more blood and give him regular food to help him get used to it. I am determined to do whatever I can to make this easy on him—and as normal as possible.

"They're worried about you."

"You should have made them kill me, Anala."

I watch Zac take a drink of blood, favoring that over the burger I got for him.

"Eat the food, Zac."

He sighs but takes a bite of the burger. Then he takes another bite as if he had forgotten just how good Jake's burgers are.

"How pissed is Sam?"

I frown at him in confusion. I haven't said anything to him about Sam or his problem with Zac being bonded to me.

"I can feel your unhappiness," he explains. "All of these feelings I have inside are so weird. I don't know which are mine and which are yours. Or if they're ours at all."

"What do you mean by that?"

"I don't know yet. There's so much going on, I can't focus." He takes another bite of the burger, washing it down with blood like it's a chocolate shake. If I didn't know for myself how normal that was for someone like us, I would have laughed - or gagged - at the combination.

"Take your time, and sort it all out. What we have to figure out is whether you can use this to find Thomas."

"Do you think he's still here? He could be halfway across the world by now."

It occurs to me that as we speak, Zac's voice continues to change. It's almost as if talking as though our topics were normal helps him (at least that's what I'm hoping).

"He could be," I agree. I just don't think he is. Something tells me he is still close. I don't know if being around Zac makes me feel that way, or if I've become aware of the blood bond. "Once you're up for it, I want to try some things. See if we can connect with Thomas through your bond."

"I thought you were my true Maker."

"I am. But a part of Thomas is there as well. Maybe the other feelings you feel are his?"

Zac narrows his eyes. I can feel him focusing on trying to distinguish the thoughts in his head. It's starting to give me a headache; I can only imagine how he feels.

"Zac, we don't have to do this right now. You have to learn how to control all of this before we can delve deeper into it."

"But, if I could just..." Zac changes abruptly, as do I. Whatever he felt or thought hurt us both enough to cause the change.

"Zac, just stop. You don't know how to control this now, and it's doing nothing but giving me a headache."

Zac sighs heavily, muttering under his breath about almost having it. He didn't, of course, but I admire his tenacity.

"We'll work on it. I'm also going to have you train with the others."

"Are you sure that's a good idea, Anala?"

I glance up at Zac when he calls me by my given name. He hadn't liked calling me that before. I assumed it was because it reminded him of what I was.

He shrugs. "It's how I think of you in my head now."

Hmm. That's interesting. I shake the thought away and focus on Zac's question. "Yes, I think it's a good idea. You need to see if you can be around them without wanting to kill them. They could use the training with a Hybrid."

He scowls at the name. Like it or not, that's what he is now. Zac will just have to learn to live with it. I scoff silently at the irony of that. Once Thomas is dealt with, my Hunters will have to deal with Zac and me. And, of course, with that thought, my mind automatically shifts to Sam.

"How is he taking this? Us being bonded, and having to say goodbye to you soon?"

"Don't do that," I scold. I am not going to like having someone around who can read my mind. "Stay out of my head unless I invite you in. In *that* sense, be a damn vampire."

"I can't always tell exactly what you're thinking, but I feel your feelings. Especially when it's about Sam." He clears his throat and looks a bit uncomfortable. "Why him?"

"Zac, please don't start this."

20

"No, that's not what I meant. I can... feel now how important Sam is to you. But, honestly, Anala, this all happened pretty quickly."

Sigh. I wonder if this is how everyone feels.

"Yes."

"I said don't do that." I notice his smirk before he hides it. Fantastic. "I have lived many lifetimes, Zac. To someone like me, what happened with Sam wasn't quick. Maybe it is or was to the others, and obviously you." I pause. I'm not even sure why I'm trying to explain this. I don't owe anyone... I cut my thoughts off when I see Zac narrow his eyes.

"They would probably understand more if they thought it had to do with Thomas. Sam is Thomas's descendant, right? That would explain the connection."

"It doesn't matter, Zac. What is happening between me and Sam is just that. Between me and Sam. It's no one else's business." I eye him as I catch one of his thoughts. Or feelings. Whatever. "She asked about you."

"I... I don't know... who?"

I can't help but chuckle at his embarrassment. "Doesn't feel good, does it? I didn't know you and Emily were..."

"We're not! Especially not now," he mutters. "Why get involved in anything you know has no future?"

Sometimes you have no choice.

CHAPTER FOUR
"BLOOD ORCHLIPS"

"Again! Zac, you're holding back! You have to go at them!"

"Anala!"

"Do as I say! Trust in their abilities. If you don't, they can't either."

I know what I'm doing is risky, but we've already lost more than a week with Thomas. I don't understand why he would still be here in Los Angeles when he knows I'm here, with Hunters, and on a mission to find him and kill him for what he did to Zac. But Zac insists he can still feel him, though I can't be sure he truly knows what he's feeling. I'm not certain if proximity affects the bond, but I do know that I didn't have cravings until Thomas and his army were nearby. That's about the extent of my knowledge on the subject.

I shift my focus back to my group and watch them spar—or fight. That seems to be the better description. Finally, they are pulling no punches. Zac has stopped holding back, and after having just fed, he is a force. I keep a part of my mind focused on Zac's thoughts. If I sense he can no longer control himself, I will step in. Not that I don't have faith in the others, I just don't want to have to pick up the pieces after they kill him.

I see Emily hesitate for a brief second before executing a series of flips over Zac as he lunges at her. It's a good thing they're using wooden swords; otherwise,

Zac would be toast. I feel a small smile form on my lips before Zac glares at me. I shrug and cross my arms as I watch more of the show.

My Hunters sit in a circle around me and Zac. Even Sam is here - which isn't awkward at all. We're in the meditation room, and the goal is to try to control this bond. I noticed throughout the day that Zac's voice was beginning to change again. And, this time, not for the good. I gave him another dose of Papa's elixir and made a mental note to find some way to get Blood Orchlips. How? Hell, I don't know. But I've lived long enough to gather some intelligence. I can figure it out. I have a lead, I'm just hoping it works out.

"Close your eyes." Zac complies, and I glance over his shoulder at Sam. Now, there's a mind I would like to read, but his expression reveals nothing.

"Why don't you hear all of this that's going on inside my head?" Even with the rough, growl of a voice, Zac was perilously close to whining.

"Because I've had years of meditation to learn how to clear my mind of irritations."

Jenna picks that exact moment to pop the gum I specifically told her not to chew. I slant a look at her, trying to conceal my annoyance. Or at least most of it. She immediately stops chewing and bows her head.

"Now, I continue, both of us will learn to focus our energies on weeding out what is unimportant and concentrating on what we need. Are you ready?"

"Yes."

Let's start by focusing on something we can control—my thoughts. Once you're used to that, you can learn to shut them off when they're not needed. And, Zac, they will never be needed unless we're in combat.

Zac smirks, and so does Sam. I roll my eyes and give Zac a look he will definitely recognize as mine. He quickly loses his smirk.

"Really, Anala?"

Ha! That'll teach him. It's my turn to smirk, even though Zac's eyes are closed and he won't see it. Giving him a clear and precise thought about Sam will hopefully keep Zac out of my mind unless absolutely necessary.

"You know my thoughts. Now, turn them off."

"How?"

"Concentrate on blocking them. Whatever you feel when my thoughts are present, block it."

I keep my thoughts running so Zac can filter them out.

"Could you please think of something else?"

"No. Thinking of Sam lets you know it's me. Block it." I see a slight flush creep up Sam's throat, and he lowers his head to hide the smile. Zac, on the other hand, just sighs and focuses harder.

"Okay. I think I've blocked you out." He mutters a 'thank God', which causes the others to giggle.

"Good job. What else is there?"

Zac's brows furrow. "Nothing that I can make out. It's not clear." He opens his eyes and shakes his head. "There's nothing concrete."

"It's okay. We'll work on it. For now, I need you to keep doing these exercises." I turn to the others and address them. "The rest of you will continue to train, with both me and Zac. We'll be more than ready for Thomas when we find him."

Ana? What about the elixir? Amanda glances quickly at Zac. I know she heard his voice as well. If we lose Zac completely now, we wouldn't have enough elixir to bring back his humanity. I'm hoping that having Zac work on his meditation will stop - or at least slow down - the process of his regression. Hybrids and Cursed Ones are increasingly becoming more evolved, but it's not hard to tell them apart from innocents - humans. If Zac loses his humanity, his craving for blood will overwhelm him, and he will become a murderer. And I can't let that happen.

"I've been looking into it. I've got a lead on someone who may be able to help me. I'll go tomorrow and see if it's possible."

"And if it's not?"

"We'll think of something, Amanda." My gaze stays level with Amanda's. She needs to see how much I rely on her. The look of surprise and happiness shows she gets it.

The day is beautiful. One of those days that makes you feel lucky to be alive—even if you are a vampire. To me, it is a day that makes me glad those vampire folklore stories were just that: stories. I mean, seriously, could you imagine not being able to step out into the gorgeous sun without bursting into flames—or something else that draws attention to you?

I am alone today, and I value the time. As much as I love my Hunters - and Sam - I am starting to feel a bit claustrophobic. Yes, I know my estate is large, but when you're the leader of a small - yet very opinionated - society of Hunters, the walls feel like they're closing in fast.

I check my phone for the address of the flower shop I'm looking for and examine my surroundings. What a charming little village. I don't have high hopes of finding what I need, but at least I came across this hidden gem. The aromas wafting from the diner I passed were mouthwatering, even for me. Distracted, I think about having a date there with Sam. The thought makes me sad, because I realize that Sam and I have never had a real date. Given how things are going, I doubt we ever will. I clear my mind of the thought since it doesn't help my situation right now. The flower shop is two doors down, and with a sigh, I walk over and step inside.

The scent of a variety of flowers immediately hits me, competing for my attention. My heightened sense of smell is on overload, but it's not unpleasant. Of course, I don't smell what I need, not that I expected to. That's something I will have to discuss with the owner.

"Hi! How can I help you?"

The woman-or girl, rather-who almost skips up to me is probably not much older than I am. Well, the me before the change.

"I'm looking for the owner."

"Oh. Sure." She hesitates for a moment, locking eyes with me. I'm used to that after centuries. Lately, after feeding from Sam and ingesting blood more often, my eyes have a brighter red ring. During outings like this, I take a little of Papa's elixir to dull the ring enough to avoid drawing attention. If I run out of it, I can always use contacts as a backup.

I clear my throat, and the girl jumps, apologizes, and runs off to find the owner. I take a moment to look around. The plants and flowers here are truly amazing. Unlike anything I've seen before—and, believe me, I've seen quite a bit. This is the work of someone who clearly has talent, and I cautiously allow myself to feel a little more hopeful.

Excuse me? I hear you're looking for me?" I immediately notice a New Zealand accent. One of my favorite accents, actually, because I find it charming. I turn to her with a smile and assess her freely. What I need will require someone knowledgeable, and preferably not nosy.

She appears to be in her early thirties, if my guess is correct. I would have expected someone a little older, given her level of talent. But who am I to judge a book by its age? Her brunette hair, subtly highlighted, is pulled back into a loose ponytail, and her warm, nearly golden eyes look friendly.

She grins, letting me examine her. Probably because she's doing the same to me. Again, I think, it must be the eyes.

"You were looking for the owner, correct? My name is Blaise Knight."

I take her outstretched hand and smile.

"Ana. I read on your website that you cross-breed?" No need to procrastinate. I don't have enough time for that.

"I do, yes. Are you looking for anything in particular?"

"Um." I pause. How do I explain this? The flower I need has been extinct for centuries. My earlier hope is fading because I don't even know how to describe something this woman would not have even heard of.

Blaise frowns at my hesitance. "Why don't we go to the back for more privacy?" She turns suddenly and begins walking. I have to take a few quick steps to catch up. "You're from England?" she asks conversationally.

"Yes."

"How long have you been in the States?"

Um. About a century. "A while now."

"Not much of a talker, are you?" She chuckles. "I've been here for about four years."

"Do you miss New Zealand?"

Blaise turns to me in surprise. "Not many people place the accent. They usually confuse me with being an Aussie."

"Perhaps it's because I'm a foreigner myself."

"Hmm. Please sit." She gestures toward a chair in front of her desk, then sits, leaning back comfortably and waiting.

"What I need may be impossible," I start.

"Nothing is impossible," she said with a smile.

"Even if it's been extinct for a long time?"

She leans forward again, completely captivated. "Well, that may be tough, but not necessarily impossible."

"I'm looking for a flower that was developed in the 1400s."

"Developed? I'm to assume that it wasn't a product of nature?"

"Correct. Medicine men of that time created the flower to assist them medicinally."

Blaise tilts her head. "Many flowers, plants, and herbs were used medicinally. Which one are you looking for?"

"The Blood Orchlip."

I notice Blaise's pupils dilate infinitesimally. I'm sure a normal human wouldn't have caught it, but I do. Her eyes widen a bit before she smiles.

"I didn't think anyone other than myself knew of that flower."

Okay, it's my turn to be surprised. "You know it?"

She pops up from her chair and walks over to the bookcase behind her. She runs her finger along a few books before finding the one she's clearly looking for. Blaise flips through the pages as she carries it back to her desk. To me.

"I have what many say is an unhealthy obsession with the history of plant life. I've read pretty much anything I could get my hands on, going back as far as...well, the era you speak of." She finds the page, flips the book around, and pushes it towards me. Pointing at the section she wanted me to read, she left me to it.

It is the history - albeit a very brief account - of the Blood Orchlip. That's a good sign, right? I look up at her with hope.

"Can you recreate them?"

"I don't see why not. I can at least try. May I ask why you need them?"

Sigh. Maybe I was too hasty to assume she would not be nosy.

"You know what? It doesn't matter," she says suddenly, filling the silence caused by my hesitation. "It'll be a challenge for me, and I look forward to it."

"Ms. Knight?" The young girl who greeted me first peers through the doorway. "Mr. Steele is here to see you."

"Ugh. Tell him I'm busy, please, Mer." I watch Blaise shake her head and notice the faint blush and quickening of her heartbeat.

She takes my information and tells me she will let me know how the process is going. If she finds she is unable to recreate the flower, she won't charge me, arguing that it is a thrill just to be able to try. Of course, I'm going to pay her, but I appreciate her enthusiasm. I thank her—quite profusely—since if she is successful, she is literally saving a life—and I take my leave. I am in such a hurry to get back and tell Amanda that we may be lucky that I almost run into a couple, and what I assume is their daughter, as I am rushing out the door.

"Excuse me. I am sorry."

The woman looks at me as if she's memorizing my face. It's a look I'm sure someone as beautiful as her gets quite often. I just lower my head and keep walking.

"She can do it?"

Amanda stops in the middle of making herself a sandwich and looks up at me.

"She seems to think so," I answer before popping a strawberry into my mouth. "Even if she can, it'll take a while to develop. We're going to have to do whatever we can to keep Zac with us."

"Do you think the meditation will work?"

"I hope so. I also think that if you and the others keep talking to him as though he's still Zac, it will help."

"He is still Zac," Emily interrupts as she walks into the kitchen. The intensity in her voice surprises me. I didn't mean to imply that Zac was lost, but let's be honest. He has changed, just like I did when I was Cursed.

"She didn't mean anything by that, Emily," Amanda continues building 'the world's best sandwich,' giving Emily a small smile.

"Of course I didn't. I just —"

"Did your voice sound like that when you were changed?"

Clearly, Emily isn't interested in my excuses. Still, I'm unsure she'll like my response to her question.

"No."

"So, you didn't go through what he's going through now?"

She is angry, which isn't an emotion I would normally associate with Emily. Is she angry at me? It definitely sounds like it, though I don't understand why she would be. Unless she blames me for what happened to Zac, and why wouldn't she? I do.

"I went through the cravings and disorientation. It was confusing. My parents didn't understand why I didn't lose my humanity, but it was the main reason they didn't kill me."

Emily stares at me for a moment, and if I could hear her thoughts, I wouldn't be surprised to hear her wish my parents had killed me. I know she likes me, respects me, and even cares about me. But I also know Zac would be normal if I didn't exist.

"I don't blame you."

Well, hell. Can everyone hear my thoughts?

I know it sounds like I do," Emily replies in her usual quiet voice, which makes her accent harder to understand. "I'm just frustrated."

"We all are, Emily. I'm doing everything I can to help Zac."

"Just to kill him after we've finished with Thomas?"

I decide to keep my customary "it's the code" to myself. I'm here, which means the code of the society had already been broken. How do I convince my Hunters that this is what is right when I don't know if I believe it myself anymore?

CHAPTER FIVE
"SARA"

I find Sam pacing in my bedroom when I finally decide to call it a night. His scent hits me before I actually see him, and I am surprised because I thought he was working tonight.

"Sam?"

He moves toward me, and I see the outfit I hunt in lying across the foot of my bed.

"What's going on?"

"Ana." He pauses in front of me and runs a hand through his hair. "We need to talk."

Damn. Nothing good ever starts with 'we need to talk.' Sam is either breaking up with me— which would hurt badly — or he's about to tell me something that will piss me off royally. I walk past him and sit next to my cloak. I pick at the fabric and briefly think about the last time I went out as the Cloaked One. That was not a good night.

"So talk."

Sam looks as if he wants to run away instead of telling me what he has to say. I wait.

"My recent cases... they've been baffling."

Totally not where I thought this conversation would start. "Baffling?"

"To my colleagues, yes."

Shit. "But not to you?"

"It seems as though your theory about Thomas still being around here could be correct."

"Why are you just now telling me about this, Sam?" I feel the fury rise low in my stomach, and I struggle to keep it in check. How would Papa handle this? The question helps me stay calm.

"You were dealing with Zac. I thought if I could just find Thomas…"

"You went hunting by yourself?!" So much for keeping my cool. "Are you insane!"

"Ana, I was careful."

"No, Sam, you weren't. You were by yourself. Have I taught you nothing?" I stand, unable to stay still any longer. Taking a page from Sam's book, I start pacing.

Sam exhales in frustration.

"You hunt by yourself."

"I'm a damn vampire, Sam! Cursed. My strength and reflexes are far beyond yours! Not to mention, I've been doing this for a hell of a lot longer than you have!"

"I know what I'm doing, Ana." Sam's voice is icy. "I'm not only a Hunter, I'm also a cop. I'm perfectly capable of taking care of myself."

"That same arrogance is what got me turned, Sam! If I had just… oh my God!" The thought hits me like a semi-truck. "Is that what you're trying to do? Get yourself turned?"

"Of course not!" Sam stands in my path, effectively cutting off my pacing path. "Do you really think I would do that?"

"I don't know. With everything you've been saying to me lately…"

"*If* I wanted to be turned, I would want *you* to do it, Anala. I want *you* to be my Maker. I certainly wouldn't seek out my ancient ancestor to do it."

I'm speechless. The words alone were enough to do that, but it was the look in his eyes when he said he wanted me to be his Maker that broke me. I push the thought away, focusing on the immediate issue at hand.

"What have you found?" I'm going to be reasonable. I don't feel reasonable, but the thing I have drilled into my Hunters' heads from day one was to have faith in their abilities. I do not doubt Sam's abilities. Just his motivation. And sensibility.

"Hybrids. Obviously, Thomas is trying to build a new army, but starting over must be difficult for him," he says wryly.

"He'll have trouble controlling them," I agree. "However, if the Hybrids keep evolving the way they have been, it might not be that way for long." I sigh, sinking onto the bed. I run my hands through my hair, and that's when Sam catches them. He pulls my hands to him and kisses my knuckles. I'm angry enough to want to yank them away, but I don't.

"I should have said something earlier, but I thought with Zac... your attention was needed here."

"We are a society, Sam. A family. If I'm not available, your fellow Hunters are."

"I couldn't put them at risk."

"Do you hear yourself? You're thinking of them as kids instead of Hunters. You're not giving them enough credit. Surely you've seen the growth in them, especially Amanda."

Sam mutters an oath, dropping my hands.

"You're right."

"Always a good thing to say to your girlfriend, especially when she's particularly angry with you." I smile slightly at him. I'm still pissed, but at least he sees his mistake. I gesture to my hunting gear. "I take it you're ready for me to help with your...case?"

"I can't keep going off to kill Hybrids while I'm on duty. And I can't keep doing it after I'm off."

"This is why you're never here?"

Sam averts his eyes. There's my answer. He's been sacrificing our time together to hunt alone, putting himself in danger when he could have asked the others for help. Yeah. I'm definitely still pissed.

"Tell me where, and I'll go out."

"I'll show you."

"No. You're going to stay here and brief the others as to what's been happening. Then, I want your assessment of Zac. He's been a Hybrid for more than a week now. If I'm right about the evolution, he could become a full blood soon."

"You would know better than I would if that was happening."

It's your instinct I'm interested in. I'm too... I want him to be normal so badly that I'm afraid I might not be seeing things clearly. I reach for his hand, squeezing it gently. "Please don't read anything into that. I care -"

"I know. And I know I've been an ass about all of this lately. I apologize for that."

"Another thing that's always good to say to your girlfriend," I chuckle. Silently, I thank him for not voicing excuses for his behavior.

He smiles for the first time since I walked into the room.

"I'll visit Zac tomorrow morning. I'll also brief the others. In the mean-time,..."

I stand and press my hand firmly on Sam's chest as he approaches me. "Go and see Zac now. The others can wait until later. I need to hunt."

"Non-negotiable?"

"Correct. Give me locations, then go. I have to get ready."

"At least let me stay for that."

I gave him a wicked smile. "Some things should remain a mystery. Me getting into that," I jerk my thumb at my outfit, "is one of them."

I chose one of the locations Sam provided, and I am currently hidden in the shadows, even more concealed by my cloak. My Hunters know who I am now, and so does Thomas. Maybe I don't need my cloak, but it's been part of me, of who I am as a Hunter, for so long that it feels second nature to put it on.

I roll my shoulders, trying to loosen the tightly coiled muscles that are hell-bent on giving me a headache. I know it's tension, not an actual headache I feel, but I tell myself whatever I need to in order to feel even the slightest bit of normalcy. It has been about thirty minutes now, and I haven't seen or felt a Cursed One yet. At least it's a beautiful night, and the park I'm in is serene. The closely cut grass is a lush green, and I long to kick off my thigh-high boots just to feel the blades under my feet. It's deserted at this time of night, but I can imagine couples taking a stroll, holding hands, stealing soft kisses...damn it! Six hundred freakin' years old, and I still haven't learned to keep my mind on where I am and what's important! Obviously, getting bitten and turned taught me nothing. I kick the tree I'm standing next to hard enough to make it shake.

"Your life will never be normal again, Anala. It's time to get over it and accept who you are and your limitations." My whispered reprimand to myself depresses me enough to put everything out of my mind except my surroundings and the situation my Hunters and I are in.

My eyes stay alert, capturing every small movement. What I don't see with my eyes, my ears pick up, or my body feels, and I focus all my heightened senses on the area. I would smell or feel a Cursed One long before it gets close enough to notice me. I don't let my attention slip, but I do allow myself to consider Thomas and his motives. If he's really building an army, I can't understand why he wouldn't keep his Hybrids close. He would need constant contact to control them, especially during the early stages when they are completely unpredictable. Letting them wander the streets is reckless. Or maybe, smart. Thomas could be making enough Hybrids to keep with him while also turning some loose to create chaos for me and my Hunters. If we're occupied fighting his expendables, we won't be looking for him right away. It's a solid theory, and I realize with a shudder that it's what I would do if I were in Thomas's shoes.

"Damn it." My whisper sounds loud in the quiet, empty space around me. He's distracting us. The murders Sam has been investigating, me hunting, and now the others will be getting involved. He's drawing *us* out.

Before I can fully digest that thought, I catch the scent I had been waiting for. Fresh. Maybe an hour or so since the Hybrid was turned. Thomas is selecting his spots, choosing from the 'crop' and then replanting them. Why? What's so special about the locations Sam gave me? That's a question for Sam to answer. He's the detective.

I crouch and wait for the approach of the Cursed One. I've learned since the first battle with Thomas not to question why other Cursed Ones cannot sense me. Even my own Hunters, who are born and trained to sense those like me, can't. As the Hybrid creeps closer, looking for someone to prey on, I thank whatever entity is responsible for that fact.

The Hybrid looks like a gang member, probably in his mid-twenties if I'm right. I'm starting to think that's becoming Thomas's MO. Maybe he finds them easy targets. Or he believes they might be tougher for my Hunters because of their size. I hesitate as my thoughts drift to another possibility. I make a mental note to discuss my suspicions with Sam and Amanda, then refocus on Bob. The name I give the intimidating-looking, 250-pound, tattoo-covered, bald, snarling Hybrid makes me chuckle. I consider letting him live and following him to see if he would lead me to Thomas, but the more I think about it, the more convinced I am that these Hybrids were specifically created to be decoys. Anyway, a young woman, clearly unfazed by her surroundings, has apparently decided to take a walk through the park. In the dark. Alone. Honestly, I question the mentality of some humans.

As I prepare to take the Hybrid out, he lunges at the woman, and I'm so stunned by what happens next that I'm momentarily frozen. I watch in complete awe as the woman employs a series of defensive moves to fend off the Hybrid. She can't weigh more than 120 pounds, yet she has the Hybrid flying over her shoulder. When he slams to the ground, she spins quickly and kicks him hard in the groin. Even a vampire would feel that pain, but it won't stop him.

He scrambles up, snarling and snapping at her, and I see her eyes widen in surprise and fear at what she sees. I force myself into action, releasing my swords as I sprint towards them. Hunters should never have an audience. Innocents are not supposed to know that Cursed Ones even exist. That's our job. To keep them safe and feeling secure. Unfortunately, I won't be able to avoid this unwanted spectator.

I spring from the ground just as he makes a grab for her and tackle him. I somersault into a crouch, my swords ready. I don't have to wait long, though I notice he hesitates for a fraction of a second before attacking. Later, I'll stop to analyze that. Right now, I slice my swords across his neck, feeling a bit of pain in my own, as it rolled once before turning to dust.

"Oh my God!"

I look up at the woman and see her take a breath to scream. At a speed she wouldn't expect, I am behind her, covering her mouth with my hand.

"Don't." I disguise my voice, and I know it sounds threatening to her. It's rough, almost growling, and I can feel her muscles tense. She is about to start defending herself any second, which means she will get hurt. She slams her foot down on mine and whimpers slightly when it doesn't affect me. "I'm going to let you go, just don't scream."

She nods, and I loosen my grip on her, cautiously stepping back. If she screams, I'll have to knock her out. I might even take a little pleasure in it since my foot is throbbing a bit.

"You killed him," she whispers.

"Who are you?"

I don't think she's a Hunter, but even being trained in martial arts couldn't have given her the strength to best a Cursed One.

She looks back to where the Hybrid was, her eyes darting as she tries to find any sign of her attacker. Shaking her head - or maybe her whole body is trembling - she refocuses on me. She can't see me because my cloak hides my features, but she tilts her head and takes a deep breath.

"I saw him. I know he was here. You cu - " She shivers violently, turning pale.

"Who are you?" I repeat impatiently. I may have even raised the intensity in my voice, though I know it won't be as effective as making eye contact.

"S-Sara. Sara Ramos." Her accent makes her automatically trill the r's in her name.

Ramos? I try to remember any Hunters who resemble Sara. Silently, I observe her Hispanic features—dark hair and almond-shaped, rich brown eyes that are now filled with fear and uncertainty—framed by dark arched eyebrows. Her full lips appear pale compared to her warm toffee-colored skin. While she holds a sense of familiarity to me, I will need to know her ancestry to be sure, and that will be tricky. It won't be easy to introduce her into society. Trust is fragile, and my Hunters are fiercely loyal to one another.

"Do you know what he was?"

She frowns.

"A gang member? I know this city has a lot of them, and that's why I trained in self-defense. But I never thought the park…"

"That's how most people get hurt. They don't think about the danger lurking everywhere. No matter how nice your surroundings are."

Sara loses her pallor and flushes instantly. With the fury in her eyes, I can tell it's not embarrassment she's feeling.

"I don't know who you are, but I don't need you to lecture me. *Yo no necesito tu ayuda.*"

"It seemed like you needed help, to me." I ignore her surprised look and circle her like a predator. She tenses up, keeping a close eye on my movements. Her fists clench at her sides, a sign to her attacker that she's ready to defend herself. "You saw his eyes, his teeth. What did you think?"

"That people will go to any length these days to be unique," she says dryly while looking at my outfit.

"Where are you from?" I ask, ignoring her blatant insult.

"I don't need to tell you anything. You just killed a man!" Sara turns and starts to run away. "Stay away from me!"

"Sara!" She stops abruptly at the sharp tone in my voice. I can't let her go after everything she's seen. I either have to compel her to forget or face my Hunters when I take her back to the compound to figure out who she is. Crap. "I need you to come with me."

It took a bit of compelling to get Sara to come with me. It took a little more explaining when I brought her in to meet the others.

"She's an outsider! How could you bring her here?"

Amanda - apparently the spokesperson for the 'Committee Against Anala Making Any Important Decisions' - paces irritably in front of me. The others grumble, and Sam watches me intensely. Ah, how I've missed that. I doubt Papa ever had to go through this with his Hunters.

"First, she fought the Hybrid and held her own. If she's not a Hunter, I will be surprised. Second, she saw me kill the Hybrid. I had no choice but to cut his head off right in front of her. Was I supposed to just leave her there? Or let her go to tell someone?"

"You compelled her to come here; couldn't you have just made her forget?"

Well, at least Amanda is a little less irritated, as in not yelling at me anymore.

"Yes, I could have. But, if she's a Hunter –"

"Do we really want to bring someone else into this, Ana?" Sam's voice is quiet, but I hear the disappointment. I'm not sure if I'm more hurt by his disappointment or his questioning of my authority and ability to make good decisions.

"*If* she's a Hunter," I continue, "we could use her help."

"It would take too long to train her," Emily interjects.

"I saw her with the Hybrid. I don't think it will take much to train her. Besides, with all of your help, it'll be easier."

"Will you tell her?" Jenna had been quiet throughout the whole conversation until then. The timid question shows she's still cautious around me. "About you and Zac?"

I give Jenna my full attention, softening my gaze. "Would it have helped you to know from the beginning? Or do you think it's too much for her?"

Jenna appears surprised by how genuinely I seek her opinion.

"Could we speak to her first? Maybe if we get a better feel for who she is, we'll know what the best course will be."

Every Hunters' eyes turn to her in astonishment, and Jenna blushes under the scrutiny.

I break the silence and draw everyone's gaze.

"I think that's a great idea, Jenna."

CHAPTER SIX

"YOU ARE DIFFERENT."

I am in the dark corner of the dining room while my Hunters sit around the table, questioning Sara. She is seated at the head of the table, but with everyone interrogating her, it feels more like the hot seat. Amanda is on her left, with Emily and Sam next to her. Jenna is on Sara's right, followed by Eric and Jeremy. For obvious reasons, Zac is not present.

I haven't revealed myself to her, so she wouldn't know who I was even if I had sat in on the questioning — though I still haven't changed out of my hunting gear — but I want to give my team the space they need to get to know Sara. I need them to give me their honest opinion about her. They know I'm there and hold nothing back.

"Do you know why you're here?" Amanda asks. Her tone is steady, but I can hear her heartbeat pounding.

Sara regards her with confusion. She is coming out of the compulsion, and I know it must be difficult for her to understand where she is and how she got here.

"I don't even know where here is," Sara answers.

"Do you remember how you got here?" Jenna's approach is surprisingly delicate.

Sara's eyes cloud over, and her brows furrow as she concentrates on remembering.

"There was a man," she begins slowly. "I was attacked, but I fought him off. I thought... but he got up. Someone else was there. I don't know who. I couldn't see their face."

"Go on," Sam presses when she hesitates.

"That's all I really remember."

Sam studies her. She is lying, and he knows it just as well as I do. Maybe she doesn't want them to think she's crazy. Or perhaps she feels some responsibility to the one who helped her. That would be interesting.

"Sara, you need to be honest with us."

"Tell me where I am. Who are you?"

Everyone looks at each other, but it's Sam who speaks up.

"My name is Sam Logan. I'm a homicide detective with the LAPD."

Every muscle in Sara's body becomes tense.

"Did someone call you? Maybe the person who helped me?" Her expression is a mix of hope and fear. "Can you tell me who they were?"

"If you expect things from us, you must give us something," Emily states firmly. "The truth."

"I-I don't know what happened," Sara's words start tumbling out in a rush, making her accent thicker. "The maneuvers I used should have incapacitated him, but he got up like all I did was slap him. His eyes," she shivers once before composing herself again, "they were scary. Unreal. His teeth, long. I know what you're going to think, but he had ... vampire teeth. Estúpido."

Even though Sam can't see me, he glances in my direction before turning back to Sara.

"Continue."

She looks dumbfounded for a moment, probably because none of my Hunters reacted to what she said. Sara takes a deep breath and continues.

"After he stood up, I was scared. A movement caught my eye, and I thought he had brought friends. I didn't have time to think about what was going to happen to me. Everything is such a blur." Sara hesitates again, but only for a moment. "A figure, completely covered, came out of nowhere. Tackled him to the ground and then..."

She stands abruptly, and I quickly get to my feet too. If she's going to bolt, I'll need to use extreme compulsion to make her forget everything she just told my team.

"His head," she says quietly with a laugh that sounds almost like a sob. "They used a sword. It just disappeared." She makes a small 'poof' sound and gestures with her hands.

Amanda stands and walks cautiously toward Sara. She gently places a hand on Sara's arm and speaks softly.

"Are you okay?"

"What does it say about me that I am?" She turns to Sam then. "I don't know whether to be grateful to the person, or so scared that I should be running to someone like you and giving them as much of a description as I can. All I know is that I'm alive because of whoever that was. And when they spoke to me, I wasn't afraid of them. Freaked out by the situation, yeah, but not scared."

"Ana?"

I walk forward into the light at Amanda's request. I still have my cloak on, but my hood is down so Sara can see me clearly this time. She notices the cloak first, then her eyes move up to my face. She gasps slightly, and I can only guess it's because my eyes are so similar to the ones she saw on the Hybrid.

"You?"

"Yes."

Sara slumps heavily into her chair.

"Someone please tell me what's going on before I think I've gone completely *loco*."

We leave Sara pacing the length of the dining room while we gather on the deck outside the French doors.

"Well?" I glance at Amanda first, then turn to Jenna. "Do you think I should tell her the truth?"

Jenna stares at me for a moment as if she's unsure if I'm actually asking her.

"I think she already knows something is different about you. It could only help us train her if she knew everything."

I pause for a moment to consider that, then nod.

"Is everyone in agreement?"

My Hunters voice their approval, and we walk back inside to Sara. She spins around and walks straight up to me.

"You saved me. You killed a man. Then, you bring me here to this..." she gestures widely, "place. Please? Tell me what is going on."

"He was not a man," I begin quietly. "Not anymore. You were right, what you said before."

"Vampire?"

"Yes."

"*They're real*," she whispers reverently. "*Mi abuela* told me stories of monsters that existed long ago. I thought they were just her way of keeping me in line. *Tu sabe*, scare me enough to keep me from running too far from her protection."

"Did she mention Hunters in these stories?" My voice is steady, but honestly, I'm stunned to realize that stories about a time long, long ago are still being told.

"*Si*. She spoke of those born to protect humans." She studies me for a minute, then reaches toward me. "May I?"

I nod, and she cautiously reaches behind me to pull my hood up over my head.

"She spoke of you. Called you 'The Cloaked One'."

I hear the collective gasp from my Hunters. I don't blame them. I'm as floored as they are.

"Your grandmother? Is she still alive?"

The pain in her eyes is sharp but brief. In a moment, Sara let herself grieve before taking a deep breath and straightening up.

"No. She passed away last year. It's why I'm here now. Nothing was keeping me in Girona. I wanted to go to University here in the States."

"Girona. You are from Spain."

"*Si*," she answers, even though it wasn't a question.

"I knew Hunters from Spain."

"*Mi familia?*"

"Perhaps. I would like you to sit with Amanda. She knows the history better than anyone. Tell her what you know of your family, your ancestors. We'll get a greater idea of everything with more information."

"I could be a *Cazador*?"

"Yes."

I feel her hand grip my arm as I begin to turn.

"You are Cursed?"

Well. Sara Ramos's family did not stick to the tradition of never speaking of Cursed Ones as generations passed. In fact, they seemed to ensure all information was shared, even if it was in the form of 'bedtime' stories.

"I am."

My Hunters surround me in a show of solidarity and support. Feeling their energy, loyalty, and love gives me a rare moment of raw emotion, and I feel the tears trying to fight their way out. I force them back, but I can't entirely suppress the small smile.

"You are different."

"She is," Sam says quietly.

Sara nods slightly. "Thank you," she says softly.

She is thanking me for saving her life. The guilt for bringing her here, for dragging her into this battle with Thomas, brought on a stab of pain.

"Do not thank me. I cannot make you stay here. My Hunters will tell you what is expected of you and what we are up against. You will make your decision then. Whatever that decision is, we will honor that."

"If I am a Hunter, it is my duty to be here."

"And the others thought it was a good idea to bring someone new here?"

I would have taken offense at Zac's scowl, but it has been the norm since he woke up. I choose just to ignore it. I also choose to ignore his questioning of my leadership. Otherwise, it would just piss me off.

"Have you been meditating?"

Zac's voice still isn't where I want it to be, and I have to refrain from calling Blaise to ask about the flowers I need for the elixir. When she knows something, she will call.

"Yes. You didn't answer my question."

"Because I don't have to. I am the leader of this society, Zac. I don't need permission to bring anyone else in."

It was a snarky thing to say, but seriously, questioning my authority makes me cranky.

"I didn't say you needed permission, Anala. I know you trust us... the others' opinions, that's all."

"I trust you, too, Zac."

He scoffs, which comes out almost as a snarl.

"I've jumped the gun, tried to go rogue, tried to kill you after telling you I loved you, and then tried to bite you. I wouldn't trust myself."

"We're not perfect, Zac. We all have flaws."

"Not you."

I laugh. "I am one huge flaw. A vampire hunter who *is* a vampire and *in love* with another vampire hunter. Can't get much more flawed than that."

"Do you think any of us, especially Sam, think that makes you flawed?"

"You do recall that Sam staked me when he found out what I am?"

Zac opens his mouth to say something, then stops and smiles ruefully.

"I would have done the same thing, Anala."

"I know. But I would have expected it from you." I punch Zac lightly on the shoulder. It was the truth, but I also want him to know that I understand.

"It must have been extremely hard for him," he says quietly.

I stand and pace away from him. I don't want to discuss this with Zac. When Sam had staked me, it broke my heart. Literally. It shouldn't have. I should have been happy that he made his decision with his head, not his heart. Okay, perhaps happy isn't the right word. Understanding of his decision, at least.

"Let's set some ground rules, Zac. First, my relationship with Sam is off limits. You and I don't speak about it. Second, you don't get to question my authority. And, finally, your main concern is meditating and trying to keep from becoming a murderer."

It's unfair to Zac to take out my frustrations on him. I understand that, but he's the easiest target. Since Zac is bound to me, he has no choice but to listen, even if it pisses him off.

"Yes, ma'am," Zac growls, stalking off toward the meditation room.

Damn it. If I want Zac to keep his humanity, I need to do a better job of not making him mad. The problem is, I'm getting just as restless as he is. The longer Thomas is out there, the more death there will be. Now I have to figure out whether I'm stalling because I need Zac to be okay, or if I'm just scared of what might happen when it's all over.

CHAPTER SEVEN
"THE REAL ME."

"How is Sara doing?"

"Jesus! Ana! I don't have your nifty sensing power. Do *not* sneak up on me like that! I mean, I could have cut your dang head off."

I stare at Amanda for a moment before a laugh escapes me.

"Amanda, you do realize that you're holding a wooden sword, right?"

"That's not the point," she mutters.

"I'm sorry I scared you..."

"Startled. I wasn't scared," she clarifies haughtily.

"My mistake." I smile at Amanda and give her a gentle bump with my shoulder. No matter how much she's grown these past few weeks, she's still young. I need to keep that in mind about her, as well as the others. "So? Sara?"

"She's definitely well-trained. Apparently, she's a black belt in multiple forms of martial arts. I've been looking into her background after she gave me information to work with. She's clearly a Hunter." Amanda pauses and looks at me. "She knows a lot about the history of Hunters. I get the feeling she didn't exactly believe everything she was told until the other night."

"You think she believes completely now?"

"Completely? No."

"What are you not saying?"

Amanda turns to me, giving me her full attention. Her wheat-colored hair, slightly lighter from hair dye, is pulled into a ponytail, and she looks as young as she is. However, now her golden eyes—so much like Sam's—hold more wisdom from everything she's experienced over the past months. Over her shoulder, I see the others taking turns sparring with Sara. My Hunters are incredibly skilled. That Sara is holding her own, and quite impressively, is a true testament to her competence.

"You couldn't show us who you were when we first started this. I understand why. But Sara knows about Cursed Ones. I mean, she already knows about you. She needs to *see* you. The real you."

The real me. Most days, I try to forget what I truly am inside. I don't feel Cursed. When I'm around friends, I don't believe I'm Cursed. When I'm with Sam, all I feel is blessed. However, with each passing century, as others around me grow old and die, I'm reminded of the real me. Immortal. Eternally alive. Eternally alone.

I shake off the horrible feeling. "And you feel that will...expedite things?"

"Ana? Are you alright?" Amanda studies me, concern clear in her eyes.

"Yes. Why?"

"You just seem sad. I didn't mean anything by the 'real' you comment. We all know who you really are."

I smile even though I'm shocked by her observance. "I know, Amanda. It's just that for years, I've hidden what I am. It's still difficult bringing that part of me to the surface." I glance at Sara. "However, I think you're right. Gather everyone in the meditation room after dinner."

I believe I've done it! :)

I read the text from Blaise at least three times before texting her back.

You're sure?

If Blaise really has figured out how to recreate Blood Orchlips, my stress over Zac's humanity would be far less, and I'd be able to focus more on Thomas.

As sure as I can be. Which is pretty damn sure.

I can almost see Blaise's triumphant smile, and can't help but smile myself. My smile, however, fades when I think about how long it must take for the flowers to actually be ready for me.

Is there a way to expedite the process?

Sensing how knowledgeable Blaise is on everything having to do with plants and flowers, I had no doubt she would know what I'm asking.

Yes. Sound waves. It would take me too long to explain in text. You could come see me and I can explain, or call.

I hear my Hunters settle in the meditation room, chattering softly with each other about graduation. A pang of guilt shoots through me. Graduation is so close. If I could just find Thomas...

I trust you. Please keep me informed.

I catch Sam's scent before entering the meditation room, and it makes my step falter. For once in my many lives, I'm not alone, and as much as it scares me, it exhilarates me. Ugh, enough. There are many more pressing concerns to worry about right now.

"Sara," I begin as I walk in, glancing at Sam. "Come join me in the middle, please."

I sit down, crossing my legs, waiting for Sara to settle in. She looks comfortable, expectant, and not at all nervous. I wonder if her training is what gives her the confidence. The others surround us, all still in their workout clothes. They trained right up to dinner and then immediately gathered here. Only Sam is dressed in black slacks and a dark gray button-up shirt, sleeves rolled to his elbows.

That's his usual work attire, and it always catches my attention. Deliberately, I focus on Sara.

"I apologize for thrusting you into this life."

"I was born into it," Sara interrupts. Her tone is clear, but I can still detect a hint of disbelief. I don't blame her. I'd feel the same if someone told me one day that the Boogey Man was real. Or maybe I am the embodiment of the Boogey Man. I shrug off that thought and keep going.

"In any case, you've decided to stay with us, and we respect that."

When I brought the others in, they didn't understand what was happening or why they had been chosen. None of them thought they had anything to contribute until I made it clear to them exactly what they brought to the table. However, when I look at Sara and see her confidence in herself, I don't feel the need to give her the same assessment.

"You know what you bring to us. Your training has spoken for itself. But I have a feeling you need something different from me." My eyes find Amanda's, and I give her a slight nod.

"I don't understand," Sara frowns.

"You need to know what you're up against. What it was that attacked you."

"Cursed Ones, no? I know about them."

Them. Sara might know I'm Cursed, but she can't quite wrap her head around it. I can only imagine she still sees Cursed Ones as the scary monsters in her grandmother's stories.

"You know what your grandmother told you." I ensure my voice remains gentle and non-threatening. "You need to see the truth."

"Sara, just relax and know that nothing will hurt you here," Amanda places a hand on Sara's shoulder.

"You're safer here than anywhere else," Sam says quietly.

"Ana would never harm you," Jenna adds.

Sara looks at all of them. The fear is in her eyes, but so is the curiosity when she turns back to me.

"*Show me,*" she whispers.

I hold her eyes for a moment, then lower my head and will myself to change. I don't want to scare Sara, so I take my time lifting my gaze to hers. The familiar burn of my eyes and teeth tells me what Sara will see, and I can only hope she doesn't run from me screaming.

Sara regards me with what can only be described as fascination shining in her eyes.

"You are nothing like what mi abuela told me. I thought Cursed Ones were."

"Anala isn't like the others," Emily interjects. Well, good. She may blame me for Zac, but at least she knows I'm still different.

Sara gasps. "Anala? Your parents were the leaders of Hunters. *Mi abuela* said - well, I guess they're my ancestors - were trained by them."

"Yes."

"That makes you how old?"

"Old enough," I mutter, glowering at the others for laughing. "That's not important. What's important is that you know we still exist. Now you're part of our small society to help handle this problem."

"Amanda gave me journals to read, and I know the rules of the Society." Sara tilts her head, studying me. "How are you still here, in a house full of Hunters, if the rules clearly state you shouldn't be?"

I can feel the tension fill the room. Sara is new to this group, and they are fiercely loyal to me. To have her question my presence is not going to sit well with them, even if she isn't trying to be cruel. I quickly hold up my hand to stop everyone's objections.

"I am here because my parents saw something different in me," I start slowly. Truth is, my parents *should* have killed me, whether I could speak clearly and hold on to my humanity or not. I was Cursed. They listened to their hearts instead of their heads. "They chose to... study me instead of kill me."

"Or they loved you too much," Sara counters.

"Sara, if I had lost my humanity, Mum and Papa wouldn't have hesitated to cut my head off. In fact, they drew their swords on me." I raise my eyes to Sam. "Love does not give me a pass. I am needed right now. When it comes time for me to...move on, that is what will happen."

"I have been training in martial arts for most of my life, but I'm nowhere near that good."

"You're what? Early 20s? I'd say Anala has quite a few years on you."

I maneuver my body into a flying spin kick, nearly taking the head off the sparring dummy as my foot connects solidly. From Amanda's laughter, I know she realizes I can hear her conversation with Sara while they watch me train. It's silly. I've never been self-conscious about my age, probably because no one knew who or what I really am and just saw me as an eighteen-year-old girl. I wonder now if I weren't with Sam, if I would care this much. But I am with Sam, and as much as I never worried about death before, it now seems to loom over me. If I let it, it will consume me, and I won't be able to do what I need to.

"Will you teach me that kick?" Sara marches up to me with a determined look on her face. She seems to be daring me to tell her she can't do it. Yeah, she'll fit in just fine with my Hunters. None of them lacks self-confidence these days. And, as long as the arrogance doesn't get them in trouble, I'm okay with that.

"I'll show you the mechanics." I eye her, judging her height and weight. She is a little shorter than my 5'9", and her figure isn't as muscular as mine. With her Hispanic background, she has curves. I decided that, with practice, she could do the kick well enough. It wouldn't come as easily to her as it does to someone like Emily, who is at least four inches shorter than I am and slim. Or Amanda, who is around the same height as Sara, but with her training, she has built up an impressive core. With Jenna's cheerleading background, it took her very little time to master the maneuver, despite being chest-heavy. Any one of them would be able to help Sara as much as I could. "You can work on it on your own time, or have the others help you. However, I need you to be trained in swordsmanship more. See Eric or Emily for instruction."

"Why can't I work with you?"

I notice Amanda's frown and know she isn't happy about Sara's reluctance to work with the others. Perhaps she doesn't see them as accomplished as she is. Well, that will change soon.

"All of my Hunters work with me. But I can't be there all the time. You will learn to work with the others and know that they are well-trained." I step closer. "Do not doubt their abilities. You need to trust them as much as they need to trust you in order to hunt together effectively. Get to know them. Let them get to know you. It's important."

"Will I meet this new girl?"

Damn it. Zac's voice is harsh, and the rims around his eyes are getting a deeper shade of red. I hope Blaise has something for me soon.

"In time."

"Have you shown her what you are?"

"I have."

"But you don't think she's ready to see me."

It's not a question, and I can hear the bitterness in Zac's voice. I know he knows he's deteriorating, and I desperately wish there was more I could do.

"Zac..."

"Just kill me and get it over with, Anala."

"We will get through this."

"What does it matter?" he growls. "You want to be killed after Thomas is dead, anyway."

My mind automatically shifts to Sam. Each day, it becomes increasingly difficult to accept leaving him. I know it's what's right. I understand that the code must be followed. I realize I shouldn't let the fact that I have ignored the code for centuries influence my decision. And, most importantly, I know I shouldn't let my love for Sam interfere with what is right. Now, if only I could take what I know and override how I feel.

"I don't want to live like this, Anala. And you have no right to force me because you can't control your human emotions!"

My eyes snap to Zac, and I realize he has read my thoughts.

"You do not have permission to be in my head." Feeling threatened, I let the heat of my anger and the pure authority behind it seep into my words. "The next time you read my thoughts, I will compel you to forget you are able to. Am I clear?"

Zac looks at me for a few moments. His eyes show he's struggling. Whether he's struggling to obey me or to defy me, I don't know.

"Yes. But it should be my decision if I want to live like this. And I choose not to. I don't want to be like you."

It is petty. Everything inside me is begging me not to say it, but my lips move of their own volition.

"You're not."

CHAPTER EIGHT
"MY HEART BEATS."

"We need to hunt," I say as I sit with Sam and Amanda at the kitchen table. The others decided they were tired of being at the estate and went out to eat. Since they were willing to take Sara along, I thought it was a good chance for them to get to know each other. They would be at Jake's, and it reminded me of when I first approached my Hunters with the Society. We went to Jake's that first night, and I was pleasantly surprised to see that my eclectic group could be cordial to each other despite running in such different circles at school.

"I agree. The number of deaths is rising. We've been attributing it to gang wars, but I don't know how much longer we can keep going like this." Sam passes a bottle of water to me, and I drink it even though it's not what I want. When gangs are mentioned, I remember my theory about what Thomas was up to.

"About the gangs," I begin, then pause, waiting for Amanda to come back from the fridge. "I think I know why Thomas is using them."

"Because they're mean?" Amanda asks flippantly.

"Simply put, yes. If you think about it—and not to sound like I'm stereotyping—a lot of gang members are willing to kill without remorse. Turf wars, messing with their girls, and so on. They've done a good job of losing their humanity themselves. Thomas is using that to his advantage. The closer they are to the edge, the easier it is to fall."

"So, he's just making strong killers."

"Exactly. They are also more susceptible to being controlled by their Maker. Almost mindless."

"He just goes out and finds gang members?" Sam asks.

"I really think he received help earlier. If you remember, he had innocents assisting him before. Each one had a unique tattoo."

"I remember." Sam suddenly stands up and starts pacing. I wonder if he does this every time he works a case. "The circles with the blood drops."

I nod and turn to Amanda while Sam keeps pacing and is obviously lost in thought. "I'm beginning to think that the speed of the loss of humanity depends on the person themselves."

"Like, if they're good in life, they'll try to be good in – are...are you technically dead?"

The question is so unexpected that I can't help but laugh. I sober just as quickly when I see Sam's pained expression.

"I never died," I answer softly, and I step forward to meet Sam in mid-stride. I take his hand in mine and press it over my still-beating heart. "My heart beats. My skin is warm. I feel. I love. I'm alive."

Somewhere in the back of my mind, I hear Amanda excuse herself quietly, and Sam and I are alone.

"I can't grow old," I continue, "but I can die. I can't give life. I can't be everything that you deserve. You will never have a family with me. You will never be able to stay in one place or keep friends. Things will never be normal for us."

"Who says I want normal?" Sam murmurs. "If it's not with you, I don't want any of those things. And if I can't have them with you, then I will be happy just to be with you."

"You say that now, Sam. What happens in five years? Or 10? You'll be growing older, perhaps wanting more out of your life."

"Ana, is it me you're worried about, or are you worried you'll want something different in five or 10 years?"

I sigh and attempt to step back, but Sam keeps me in place.

"I don't want to watch you die, Sam."

"Then change —"

"Stop. Please. We can't do this now. Thomas is out there killing people. Zac is losing his battle with humanity and wants to die. And we have a new Hunter."

"Will it be too late to discuss this after all of this is over?"

I cup Sam's cheeks in my palms. "I promise I will not do anything without us talking about it. Deal?"

Sam smiles sadly but nods. "Deal," he agrees, and kisses me.

"Sam is working on cases that could intersect with our objective." I stand before my Hunters, who are dressed in their hunting gear. It will be Sara's first time out, and I know I'm throwing her into the proverbial deep end, but as it was with the others, it's unfortunately necessary. "He'll text me with a location that we should begin hunting in; then, for Sara's first time, we will go out together."

"Will Zac be coming, too?"

I see Sara regard Emily curiously. "Who is Zac?"

"Not tonight," I say quickly. We haven't introduced Sara to Zac, and I haven't yet determined how trustworthy she is. "We'll get to that soon, but tonight, it's just us."

"Is this really all of the Hunters that are left?"

"No," Amanda answers Sara before I can say anything. "We're fairly certain that they reside all over the world, but Thomas is here. And we're here."

"Why did Thomas come here?"

I struggle to keep my patience with all the questions right before a hunt. I'm about to, hopefully, answer in a nice way, when Jenna jumps in.

"Amanda and I have been trying to figure that out." She pauses and looks at me. From her slight smile, I can tell she notices the confusion on my face. It's astonishing to me not only that they have been trying to figure it out, but also that

Amanda and Jenna are working together. "From what we can tell, we just think he was drawn here. It may be because Ana is Thomas's..."

"Jenna!" Amanda hisses with a pointed look at Sara. Apparently, Amanda isn't very trusting of Sara yet, either.

Sara is about to argue, and then hunting would become awkward and possibly dangerous. Time for me to take charge.

"It's fine, Amanda. If Sara is to trust us, and vice versa, she needs to know the truth." I focus my attention on Sara. "I am Thomas's true Maker."

"You! But –"

"She didn't know," Eric says quickly. "She didn't even know Thomas existed all the years later."

"That's the truth." Jeremy steps closer to me, ready to defend if necessary. "We were there. We know what it was like when she found out Thomas was still alive. Umm..."

Jeremy frowns, and I can tell he has the same question Amanda had about the state of living of a Cursed One. I place my hand on his shoulder and gently push him back in line.

"All of this can be discussed later. Right now, we have a mission, and we need to be focused. Grab your gear, and let's head out."

I chose another one of the locations Sam had texted me to bring the others to hunt. If Sam's cases revolve around these areas, clearly, this is where Thomas is focusing on building his army. Or, at least, his foot soldiers. It's another peaceful spot, like the park, this time a beautiful retreat into the traditional aesthetics of a Japanese garden. If I'm not careful, I could lose myself in the simple beauty and forget why I'm there. That's when I start to think about Thomas's reasons for his choices.

People here aren't worried about their surroundings, at least not the danger. They're captivated by the peacefulness around them. That's why they come here, tuning out anything that might bother them. It makes them easy prey. Thomas is definitely putting a lot of thought into this. It makes me wonder if I was wrong about Thomas's growth. While his humanity might be compromised, his ability to plan - and plan well — doesn't seem to be.

"Ana?"

Amanda's hand on my forearm jolts me out of my thoughts.

"Do you see it?" At the questioning look in Amanda's eyes, I continue. "Do you see why Thomas is choosing these sites?"

I watch as Amanda and the others take in their surroundings. I can almost see the peace settle over their faces. The deep calm here has nearly eased their alertness.

"Well, damn," Amanda whispers. The realization sharpens the alertness in her eyes, and I have no doubt she shares the same thought I do. A glance at the others shows they feel the same, except for Sara, which is understandable.

"No one who walks in this park is going to feel like danger is lurking around the corner," I explain. "They'll be caught off guard, especially with the speed and strength of a Cursed One."

"So, Thomas, is it? He's choosing these areas for that reason—easy prey?" Sara inquires as she looks around again.

"All innocents are easy prey." I don't like pointing that fact out, but it is a fact, nonetheless. "However, it could be because he feels it's easier here. Or he's trying to tell us that there are no safe and serene places anymore. Whatever his message, it pisses me off."

I catch the stench of a Hybrid then, mixed with sweat and booze. Very new, I surmise. One doesn't make sense, though. Why send one at a time when Thomas could create more panic with more? Something about this doesn't feel right.

"Amanda, take Sara and a couple more for back-up and get rid of the Hybrid. He'll be coming in on the north side. Be careful."

Amanda nods, pointing to Jeremy and Jenna, and the four of them take off, leaving Eric and Emily with me.

"Are there any more?" Emily's voice is tight with fury and frustration. Not emotions you would expect in a place like this. Fleetingly, I think of how Thomas is already getting what he wanted.

"Not yet. We'll patrol here for a while and then move on."

"It doesn't make sense," Eric mumbles. It makes me wonder—more than once—if by drinking small doses of my Hunters' blood, we are more connected than I originally thought. Either that, or my Hunters are embracing the society with fervor.

"I was just thinking the same thing."

"Perhaps he means to split us up? Have smaller groups go to the different locations that Sam has supplied?"

"To what end? Thomas must know we can overtake any Hybrid. You guys are extremely well trained."

Both Emily and Eric reward me with a small smile of satisfaction at my compliment. Before we can say more, the others join us once again.

"Everything go well?"

"Too well," Amanda responds. "Too easy, Ana. I mean, one Hybrid won't be much of a challenge for us. Thomas has to have something else in mind."

We stay hidden among the trees, alert and prepared. I wanted to see how Sara was handling the Hybrid, but I trust Amanda to let me know if there's anything to worry about. For now, I have a much more pressing concern.

"Yes, but what?"

It's 2 a.m. and my Hunters are getting restless. This is our third stop on the list Sam gave me, and just as the others, it is calm and beautiful. And extremely quiet. No one is here, innocent or Cursed.

"This is ridiculous," Jenna complains. "If Thomas is going to build this stupid army, why not bring it out?"

I am just as frustrated with the situation as Jenna is, so for once, her whining doesn't bother me. Before we raided Thomas's hideout weeks ago, he had built a strong army that included innocent people. My Hunters faced humans armed with guns as well as full-blooded Cursed Ones. I know we've taken out Thomas's Cursed army, but where are the humans he had compelled to help him? What the hell is he waiting for?

"Do you think he's playing us?" Emily's voice is soft, and if I didn't have heightened hearing, I seriously doubt I would have heard her. But, damn, what she lacks in vocal skills, she definitely makes up for in hand-to-hand combat skills.

"What, he plans on boring us to death?" Jenna scoffs.

"Perhaps."

Emily's affirmative answer almost makes me laugh. I can't imagine Thomas trying to bore us to death. It seems to me that when Sam is out working, there are plenty of deaths...

"*Oh my God.*"

"Ana?"

"What if it's not *us* he's drawing out, but Sam?"

"Why would he?"

Amanda's small cry of alarm interrupts Jeremy's question. I replay it in my mind, trying to figure out what Thomas hopes to gain by exposing Sam. Clearly, he must know that Sam is just as trained - or maybe even more so, as he's a cop - than the rest of my Hunters. He's been out alone, either working or hunting - which still pisses me off. So, why wait? If Thomas really wants to draw Sam out, he's had plenty of chances. Why would he wait until we all find out what's going on?

"Ana, do you think that's what's happening here?"

I turn to Amanda, whose eyes are filled with fear. I wonder briefly if my own eyes reflect the same fear.

"I don't know. It still doesn't make sense, does it? Why would he delay?"

"He wants you to be aware of what he's going to do," Jenna says softly. "What's the point of killing Sam if you - the one who loves him - are not out here thinking that what you're doing is going to save everyone?"

"*That's it.*" My legs buckle beneath me, and I have no choice but to either sit down or fall down. "It's not just Sam. He's spreading everyone out. He's going to make me choose who to save."

CHAPTER NINE
"FOR YOU, MY MAKER."

W e decide to call it a night—or rather, morning since it's past 4 a.m.—and I immediately retreat to the sanctuary of my bedroom. Amanda and the others sensed my 'impending doom' mood and tried to reassure me that Thomas obviously didn't know them well enough if he thought his plan would work. Unfortunately, as much as I know they can take care of themselves, if there's an influx of Hybrids and my Hunters have to split up to stop the killing of innocents, they could very well be overpowered.

There are only so many of us, and the list Sam gave me of the crime scenes will take all of us to patrol. The problem is, we can only be one Hunter at each scene. Hunters do not hunt alone. It's too dangerous. We may be highly trained, and our abilities are, of course, heightened, but we don't have eyes in the back of our heads.

"Damn it."

I loosen the clasp on my cloak and let it slip off. Then I do my best imitation of a falling cloak and flop onto my bed. Turning up my heightened senses, I make sure no one is around before I do something I have never done before. At least not as a Cursed One. I have a temper tantrum.

"Damn it, damn it, damn it, damn it!" Each curse is shouted with my arms and legs flailing, pounding on my bed. I'm not proud of this. But I am too angry to care. Finally, with my anger exhausted—at least as much as it can be, just by hitting my bed—I take a deep breath and sit up.

"Time to think, Anala. You can't let Thomas do this to you and the ones you care about."

And... I'm talking to myself. If I didn't know better, I would think I was going just as crazy as Bernard did. Of course, living so long off vampire blood but not being a true vampire probably would drive anyone mad. Having survived all those years, witnessing wars and plagues, watching everyone you know die while you keep living—hmm, maybe the fact that I haven't gone insane shows I might not have all my humanity left after all. Before I can dwell on that thought, I detect my favorite scent approaching my room. I stand up, smooth my hair, and walk to the door to greet my visitor.

"Hi." I allow myself a moment of weakness and wrap my arms around Sam's neck. "Hold me."

"Amanda filled me in," Sam murmurs close to my ear. "We'll find a way to get through this, baby."

I struggle with myself. Part of me wants to give in to the weakness and let Sam take over. The other part of me needs to be the strong leader my father believed I could be. Is this what love does to you? I'm not sure I like the effect, but I can't deny how human Sam makes me feel. I sigh and take a step back, yet keep my arms wrapped around Sam.

"There's not enough of us, Sam. And, as fast as I am, I can't be in seven different places at once." I release Sam this time and run a hand through my hair. "I don't think Zac is ready to face other Cursed Ones. He wants to die."

Sam's body tenses so much that I can almost physically feel it, even though I'm not touching him.

"Perhaps you should let him."

I stare at Sam. Deep down, I know he's right. Zac should be able to decide for himself when and how he dies. What makes me so important that I can make that decision for him? Of course, the only reason he's alive now is because my Hunters begged me to spare him. But when I think about that, I wonder if I would have had the strength to kill Zac if I had refused the others.

"Are you saying that because that's truly what you believe now, Sam? Or is it because he's bonded to me, and you don't like it?"

"Do you really think that's how I am, Ana?"

Sigh. "No, of course not. Sam, you and the others are the ones who asked me to let him live. You even agreed to my stipulation." He winces but quickly pulls himself together. "Why the change of heart?"

"Baby, he wasn't conscious when you wanted to..." Sam hesitates for a moment, then continues. "He is now. He's made his decision."

"I did, too." I remind him. "You weren't so quick to comply with my wishes."

"I'm in love with you." Sam wraps his arms around my waist and pulls me close. "Before you retreat from me again for saying that, let's discuss what's going on with Thomas."

"Why do you think I would retreat?" I ask, ignoring his change in conversation.

"Because you always do when we have this discussion."

"I'm not retreating, Sam. We have things..."

"Yes, Ana, I know. Important things. But this is important to me, too."

It hurts me that Sam doesn't think this is killing me as much as it is him. "Let me see if I can put this in perspective for you, Sam. I have lived many, many lifetimes, and not once has anyone gotten as close to me as you have. Never once have I been in love, because I never allowed it. Never once have I considered –"

"Considered what, Ana?" I hear the tremor in Sam's voice. Was it caused by excitement? I don't know. I'm too distressed and completely baffled by my almost confession. Surely, I wasn't about to say that I'm considering *turning* Sam. The thought alone of Sam being what I am makes me sick.

"Nothing." My voice is soft, and I hope I've hidden the shock and fear. Sam searches my eyes for any indication, but after 600 years, I'm very good at hiding my emotions. "Let's get some rest, and tomorrow we will sit with the others to discuss what to do about our situation."

As the others sleep, I sit in the middle of the meditation room. I clear my mind, becoming fully aware of my surroundings. The silk Zabuton beneath me is soft and relaxing, making me feel serene. The aromatic candles around me emit a light fragrance that helps me relax even more. I choose one candle that stands in front of me and focus on its flame, letting it occupy my thoughts. I know this is dangerous for me—allowing my mind to be open and vulnerable. As much as I don't want to do this, I've realized I have no other choice. I could wait for Zac to learn how to connect with Thomas. But in reality, I am the best link to Thomas. I am his Maker. There's no one between us. My blood, and only my blood, created Thomas. It's time I use that to my advantage, no matter how risky it is for me.

I start to lose focus on the flame, and I know subconsciously that my mind has begun reaching out, searching for the one bonded to me like no other.

"Thomas?"

I know he can hear me. I can feel him trying to resist me. Does he have enough power to do that? To not obey me?

"Thomas, answer me."

"How are you doing this, Anala?"

The heavy Irish brogue was unmistakable, even with the rough growl of being Cursed.

"You are of my blood, Thomas. We are bonded."

I hear a feral growl that makes my head pound from the sheer force. Thomas begins to resist even harder, and I push to keep the connection.

The contact with Thomas is fading, and I rush to ask what I need to know. "Thomas, where are you?"

"Get out of my head, Anala!"

"Tell me where you are, Thomas. As your Maker, I command you."

Hell, I don't know if that's how it works, but I saw it once on some show, so why not try? The only response I get is more resistance. Apparently, Thomas is strong enough to resist me. Either that, or I'm not using this bond correctly. Before I can make another attempt at commanding him, a sharp, almost unbearable pain shoots through my head.

"Son of a –" I bury my head in my hands, trying to keep it from exploding. I can feel the change taking over, and I welcome it. If there's a chance it can help me with the pain, I'm OK with it. But the inexplicable hunger I felt—I'm not OK with *that*. I could taste blood in my mouth, and it took me a moment to realize that my nose was bleeding. Tentatively, I touch my nose, coming away with the warm wetness. "This can't be good."

The last time my nose bled, I was about 15 years old, and Thomas had accidentally hit me during a friendly sparring match. That was three years before I became Cursed. Since thinking hurt, I stopped trying. The pain—despite my changing—didn't go away; it pounded with every beat of my heart. I wished for the old saying about vampires not having hearts to be true. I close my eyes to the flickering candles and try meditating. The vision came almost immediately.

Thomas's wheat-colored hair shimmered under the dim light that barely illuminated the alley, casting only shadows. His eyes, white except for the thick red line circling the iris, were wild with anticipation. His long teeth were bared, ready to sink into the woman he held against his body. For a moment, he appeared distracted and confused. His movements seemed paused in an almost amusing way. Then, as if a switch had been flipped, he blinked once, snarled, and sank his teeth into the woman, who was no longer resisting.

I feel her blood rush into my mouth, taste her as though I had been the one to bite her. I also feel her life drain from her, her body limp and lifeless. I feel that loss deep within my soul - if I have one. I was in Thomas's head as he killed an innocent. The knowledge of that rips my heart apart.

My Hunters sit around the dining table, our makeshift meeting spot since they found the actual conference room in the house to be too formal. Teenagers. I've been 'eighteen' for so long, yet I still don't understand their logic these days. I'm sitting at the head of the table—my usual spot—but after last night's episode, I feel less commanding than usual. I struggle to keep the weariness out of my voice and maintain a blank expression. I didn't do that great of a job this morning when Sam woke up, instantly asking me what was wrong. I chalked it up to him being a trained investigator, rather than my own ineptness. I managed to convince him that I was just worried about Thomas's plan—or our theory, at least—but I'm not sure I can keep my experience a secret from the others. It wouldn't be fair to them.

I can't hold back the small sigh that escapes on its own, and Sam's eyes immediately lock with mine. I give him a barely perceptible shake of my head, noticing the concern that darkens his golden eyes.

"We all know what the theory is," I begin softly. "So, let's focus on solutions."

"I still think we will be fine on our own," Jeremy says confidently. He puffs his thick chest out, making his 200-pound muscular frame seem even bigger.

"You cannot fight multiple Hybrids alone, Jeremy." I'm not naive enough to believe that my Hunters will be reasonable about their abilities. Especially after I've drilled it into their heads to be confident in themselves.

"There's no other choice, Ana. We have to divide." Though Amanda's voice is firm, I notice her heartbeat quickening and see a sheen of sweat on her forehead. She's scared. Good. Fear is healthy.

"There *is* another choice," I say softly.

"You can't honestly think we could just ignore one place and let all of those innocents die," Jenna interjects passionately. I hide a smile. It's clearly not a joyful moment, but I'm impressed that Jenna has figured out my idea.

"If we all die, Jenna, more innocents will be lost. Infinitely more."

"Casualties of war," Eric murmurs. I dislike the term, but he's essentially right. Thomas is waging a war against us, and sadly, we won't be able to save everyone. Hell, we've already lost so many. I don't want to lose more. I just don't see any other way.

"That's bullshit!" Jenna abruptly stands and spins around to storm off.

"Sit down, Jenna." My tone is even, my voice quiet, but there is no mistaking the power behind it. Jenna immediately sits back down, clamping her mouth shut. "It is not something I want. In fact, it hurts me. But I cannot risk your safety. You are all too important to join this fight. *To me.*"

"You would spare them...us, over potentially hundreds of other victims?" Sara asks. There was no censure in her voice, just pure curiosity.

"As I mentioned before, if the Hunters are lost, no one is safe. It's a lose-lose situation. No outcome is particularly ideal, but we must choose the one with the best odds."

"You have fought many at one time by yourself," Emily points out. "You're still here."

"Yes, and I am Cursed. My abilities—sorry to say—are far beyond yours. And even I struggled. If I hadn't escaped from that place when I did, I wouldn't be standing here."

"What do you suggest, Ana?" It's the first time Sam has spoken since we began. He has been listening intently, as always, weighing each person's opinions with scrutiny.

"We pair up at the least —" I gasp sharply as pain sears through my head like a splintered stake.

"For you, my Maker."

Thomas's scathing voice fills my brain seconds before the taste of blood fills my mouth, causing me to change. Once again, I feel the life drain from Thomas's current victim - my victim - and I cry out in pain that isn't physical.

"Ana!"

I can sense the others rising to come and tend to me, and I push back in my chair, toppling it over.

"Don't! Stay away from me!" The hunger is so intense that the smell of their blood, the beat of their hearts, floods me, and for a brief, terrifying moment, I fear I will attack them. I feel the warmth of blood running down from my nose into my mouth, and just that taste sends me into a frenzy. With immense strength, I run from my Hunters before I lose self-control.

CHAPTER TEN

"WHAT'S DONE IS DONE."

"She made me lock her in there."

Zac's voice carries through the thick, impenetrable glass of the holding room that I had built specifically to hold Cursed Ones like me. Though I am not chained to the silver chair with silver chains, I sit there with the chains draped over my arms. I didn't want Zac touching the chains, so I compelled him to lock the doors behind me and not let me out.

"Give me the keys." Amanda's eyes lock with mine as she extends her hand to Zac.

"I can't."

"Zac, give me the damn keys!"

"I can't! She won't let me!"

"He is compelled, Amanda."

Amanda whirls in my direction, and she looks extremely pissed. I'm almost glad I'm locked in here. Not that I think she could overpower me, but I'd rather not have to fight her.

"Undo it!"

Sam touches Amanda's shoulder as he passes her to walk up to the glass.

"Why are you doing this, baby?"

The endearment nearly pushes me to the brink of despair, but I swallow the tears and depression and meet Sam's eyes.

"I have been compromised and can no longer trust myself around you all."

Sam places a hand on the glass. "What do you mean? What happened?"

The others step up next to Sam, their faces showing curiosity and disbelief.

"I tried using my bond with Thomas last night to find him. I let him in." I continue to explain everything that happened, keeping my tone flat and emotionless.

"You should have trusted me to do it, Anala," Zac growls, gesturing to the others with a jerk of his thumb. "You're too important to them to handle this yourself."

"It is my responsibility. Besides," I continue over the scoffs and arguments of the others, "Thomas is mine, completely. There is only my blood in him. My bond is stronger than yours."

I notice Sam's eyes darken ominously, but I say nothing.

"Your nose," Emily begins. "Has it done that before?"

"No."

"So, it's because of this?"

I nod.

"Can you get him out?"

I focus on Emily, needing to get the pain and anger in Sam's eyes out of my head.

"I'm trying."

"Let us help you," Eric says desperately.

"You cannot, Eric."

"How about you give us a chance," Jenna grumbles.

I sigh and take a deep breath to steady myself.

"*I wanted to hurt you*," I whisper. "The hunger was overwhelming me. It took everything in me to restrain myself. I cannot take that chance."

"But you did, Ana. You stopped yourself," Amanda tells me softly. "That's what matters. I mean, you made yourself run and do this. You're still you. Let us help you. Let us in."

I lower my head and shake it slightly. Almost immediately, a warmth spreads through me. Confused, I look up and see all my Hunters with their hands pressed against the glass. I know it's impossible for me to feel anything through it, but I sense the sentiment as if a warm wind is swirling around me.

"If I cannot control myself, you must –"

"You won't hurt us."

"Amanda, please. Promise me you will not let me hurt you. Or anyone else."

"I promise."

"*Zac, I release you.*"

Zac immediately hands Amanda the keys and steps away. Some part of me notices that Sara is watching Zac curiously - and, perhaps a little warily. She's careful, and that's good. On the other hand, if my Hunters can't trust *me*, I'm not sure what I'm going to do. I'm not even sure I trust myself.

Amanda rushes to the door and unlocks it, walking inside without hesitation, with Sam following her. They know that the silver will weaken my strength, so they quickly remove the chains from my skin. I can instantly feel some of my energy returning, which had been drained by the chains.

"You need to feed," Sam murmurs close to my ear.

"I'm fine."

Sam places a hand under my left elbow, and Amanda does the same under my right, helping me stand.

"Why is she so weak?" Sara asks, watching me closely.

"The silver drains their strength," Jenna explains.

I realize that Jenna is talking about Cursed Ones in general, not mentioning me by name. I wonder briefly if I've lost even more of Jenna's respect. Then, I push it out of my mind because I wouldn't blame her. I straighten up, shrugging off Sam's and Amanda's hands.

"I'm fine," I say again, with more conviction. Sam is right, I need to feed because I'm hungry, and that is not good for a vampire in a house full of innocents. "You all should go and spend time with your families."

"I'm not leaving you," Sam says with frustration.

74

"I need time, Sam. I'm going to meditate and rest. You need to rest, and the others need to be kids for one night, at least."

Amanda moves in, nearly between Sam and me, effectively halting Sam's argument.

"You can't be alone, Ana, especially while meditating. If Thomas gets back in, you'll need someone here."

"If Thomas gets back in, Amanda, I might do something that will kill me. I need all of you to leave."

"Trust us to take care of ourselves." Amanda's voice starts to rise with frustration. The change in Amanda over the past few months almost makes me forget she has a short temper. It doesn't take much to calm her down, but when she's pissed, she can burn you in an instant.

"It's not you I don't trust, Amanda. But I am not like the others you have fought. I am stronger, faster...more lethal." I pause for a moment. "And I also know you would hesitate to kill me if you needed to."

"I wouldn't." The soft, Spanish-accented voice causes everyone to turn their attention from me and focus their anger on the newcomer. In an instant, everyone starts yelling, cursing, and saying things teenagers shouldn't say, all of it directed at Sara. They're ganging up on her, and although I can see a slight fear in her expression, she doesn't back down. Not even when Zac bares his teeth at her. It takes a moment for me to stop being appalled at Zac's reaction toward one of his fellow Hunters, then I shake myself into action.

"Enough!"

Everyone stops abruptly, but the anger doesn't fade from their faces.

"Zac, go feed, then meditate. I don't want you around the others again unless you can control your change."

Zac glances at Sara, then turns and storms off. It must be his bond that angered him, since he was the one who offered to kill me earlier. Granted, he was compelled, but compulsion can enhance your true feelings if used properly.

"The rest of you, take off. Go home and spend time with your family and other friends. The time is coming when we have to start this fight again. We don't know what is going to happen, so don't take this time off for granted."

"I am *not* leaving, Ana." Sam crosses his arms defiantly, spreading his legs a bit in a powerful stance.

"I don't want you here, Sam."

The pain that flashes in Sam's eyes breaks my heart. I curl my fists to stop myself from reaching out to him.

"She doesn't mean that," Amanda tells him softly.

"Yes, I do. Amanda, if he doesn't leave, he will insist that I..." Sara is still watching me, and for some reason, I don't want her to know the intimacy of me feeding from Sam. I walk to Sam, tugging his arm so he will follow me. "I'm not trying to hurt you. But I can't feed from you. Not when I feel like this."

"I trust you."

"Well, I don't. Please, baby, do this for me." The endearment slips from my mouth, and I hope I say it genuinely, not just because I subconsciously believe it will make Sam do what I ask. But I notice the flicker of fire in his golden eyes.

"I can't leave, but I promise to stay away from you. Please," he continues when I begin to protest. "You can't ask me to leave you when you're vulnerable."

"It's because I'm vulnerable that I'm asking this of you."

He sighs heavily, scrubbing his hands over his face in frustration. "Fine. I'll go, but only for a little while. I'm coming back, Ana. That's my compromise."

His tone leaves no room for discussion or disagreement, so I nod in agreement. "Make sure Amanda goes, too."

"And Sara?"

"No."

"Ana, I will not leave her alone here with you."

"You said you trusted me, Sam. Show me that you do."

After the others left, I forced myself to drink two bottles of blood. Immediately, I taste the essence of my Hunters. They've done this before, mixing drops of their blood in with my supply, after they found out the effects on me were powerful. Just a hint of their blood connected me to them. To the point where I could communicate through thought alone. My strength was also heightened, as well as the rest of my abilities. Hunters were apparently a super food for me. I toss the bottle in the trash and head for Zac's room. Judging by the look on his face, he's not happy with me. Well, join the club, mister.

"You baring your teeth at a fellow Hunter is unacceptable," I start without any preamble.

"She threatened you," he growls in return.

"No, she didn't. She stated that she would be able to do what must be done if needed."

Zac immaturely mutters a 'whatever' and walks to the other side of the room.

"Are you really that hypocritical, Zac?" Ironically, I'm just as hypocritical. Hell, just me being alive is against everything the Society of Hunters believes in.

"She is new. She doesn't even know you. What gives her the right to make that decision?"

I can tell that even he isn't fully accepting of his explanation.

"So, it would have been better if one of the others offered to kill me?"

"Maybe," he mutters. "Don't let him back in, Anala."

The sudden shift in conversation makes me hesitate. I quickly follow his train of thought. It's time to put an end to this.

"He's too powerful for you. If he can jeopardize my humanity..." I let the unfinished sentence hang in the air, not wanting to make Zac feel worse than he already does.

"I can handle it. And if I can't, it won't matter. I'm not needed here. You are."

"Stop. I will not put you in danger. This is my fight."

"It's ours! Maybe if you hadn't thought you could do everything on your own all those years ago, you wouldn't *be* in this mess!"

Well, he had me there. My arrogance certainly was my downfall. Though, in my defense, I wasn't alone until Thomas left me to take his sister back home. Granted, I should have gone with him, but that doesn't matter anymore. What's done is done.

"Under no circumstance will you leave this room to help me," I begin, putting the power of our bond and a bit of compulsion behind the words. "No matter what you hear, you cannot come to me."

"Don't do this, Anala." His words falter slightly as my order seeps in.

"*It is done, Zac,*" I whisper and walk out, closing the door behind me.

I find Sara waiting for me in the mediation room, her dark eyes filled with questions. But I'm not in the mood to give her answers.

"You need to leave, too."

She looks up at me, her face showing surprise.

"I thought..."

"You are not trained to handle me. If I become compromised, there will be nothing you can do to save yourself."

"If you knew this, why did you tell the others I could stay?" The curiosity gives way to defiance, mixed with a hint of insult. It's not my intention to insult Sara, but the truth is the truth.

"They never would have left if they thought I would be alone."

"Do you always deceive those you lead?"

I hear the judgment in her voice, and I feel the anger start to boil in the pit of my stomach.

"I do what I must to keep them safe. That includes you."

"And, if I refuse to leave?"

"You have no choice."

"What's to keep me from going to the others and telling them what you're doing?" She's got a spine; I'll give her that. I see the stiffening of that spine as I stride towards her.

"You will leave here and go straight home. You are not to come back until tomorrow afternoon. Do you understand?" I see her eyes glaze over, and her pupils dilate before she nods and walks away without another word. I close and lock the door before settling in to either lose myself to Thomas or beat him at his own game.

CHAPTER ELEVEN
"I THINK OF HIM ALWAYS."

Before I attempt to connect with Thomas, I meditate for a long while, centering myself. I draw from the strength of my parents and my hunters whose blood flows through me. If I have any chance of bringing Thomas to me on my terms, I'm going to have to go back to the beginning. To a time when Thomas loved me. With my eyes closed, I block out the present and focus all of my energy on a time long ago.

England, 1403

"Anala, this is Thomas. He will be training with you." Papa pushes the skinny boy closer to me, and I can see his face redden. I wonder if he is feverish since it is not warm enough outside to be hot.

"Hello." I stick my hand out in a polite gesture, and he hesitates before taking it. His hands are cold and clammy, and I think maybe he is sick. Great. I do not want to miss any training, so if he is sick, he will just have to sit out and watch me. I am 15. I am so close to being able to go out and hunt with the others. No one will keep me from that, no matter how charming he is. Oh God, I did not just think

*that. 'What does Papa always tell you, Anala?' I silently scold myself. Focus!
I do not have time for boys—even ones with wheat colored hair that somehow
brings out the golden flecks in his eyes.*

*"Hello, Anala." His voice is deeper than I would have thought for him being
so young, and his Irish brogue brings me out of my thoughts.*

"Are you sick?"

He frowns slightly, glancing at Papa before answering.

"No."

*"Then let us spar." I toss him a sword and crouch in my fighting stance. I
can hear Papa laughing with someone I assume is Thomas's father.*

*"We shall leave them to it, then," Papa says. "Anala, remember, they are
here to train. Take care."*

"Yes, Papa."

*I flash Thomas a cocky grin, and he returns one of his own, obviously
thinking he can take me. He is in for a surprise. He lunges for me, and I spin
away quickly. Taking advantage of his being temporarily off balance, I sweep
my leg close to the ground, taking his legs out from under him. He lands on his
backside with a thud, and I smother my need to laugh.*

"Lucky," he mutters, rising and brushing the dust off his trousers.

"Luck," I snort. "That was not luck. That was skill."

"Again!"

*This time, he circles me a few times, trying to find a weakness. Perhaps he
is looking for me to get distracted enough to make his move. Too bad for him
that is the one thing Papa works on the most with me. I do struggle to keep my
frustration at a minimum. I want to spar, not dance in circles.*

*"Are you intending to make me dizzy?" I ask, unable to keep the bite out of
my voice.*

*"Is it working?" he answers with a grin. I will deny it if it ever comes up
anywhere, but it is the grin that distracts me. He finds his moment, and in
doing so, unfortunately, finds my nose. I hear the crack as my head snaps back
from the force, then I feel the sticky warmth of blood flowing down my face.*

"*Shit!*" *My eyes pop open from the curse word as much as the pain. Papa would disapprove of me speaking in such a way, but the pain has my mind making its own decisions.*

"*I am sorry!*" *He comes to me, holding his hand out with a handkerchief.* "*Anala, I did not mean...*" *He looks downright chagrined, and I cannot help but feel a little sorry for him. Even though I am the one who is bleeding.*

"*I am fine.*" *I bat his hand away.* "*I will live, it is not that bad.*" *So, my head is pounding, and I have to fight to keep the tears out of my eyes. Who cares?*

"*Anala!*"

I groan inwardly when I see Papa running towards me. Perfect. He will think Thomas got the best of me when all he really did was get in a cheap shot. If Thomas tells him I was distracted, Papa will be so disappointed in me. I silently curse again, not willing to say such words in front of my papa, my leader.

"*What is this, Anala? How are we here?*"

I felt Thomas's presence before I saw him materialize beside me. Together, we watch the scene from centuries ago. We observe Papa tending to the bleeding nose of my 15-year-old self, and I can sense fury in Thomas. I don't understand the reaction to such an innocent time in our lives.

"*Do you remember this, Thomas? The day we first met?*" *I pause, hoping he'll answer. When it's clear he's not going to cooperate, I keep going.* "*You were so nervous. I did not understand it back then. I was too naïve to know why you would be anxious around me, but now I get it.*"

I turn to look at Thomas, just a shadow of the person he used to be. I know he's not physically there with me, but I don't let that keep me from addressing him as if I could reach out and touch him.

"*I noticed you, too. I was so confused by the way you made me feel that I didn't know how to react.*"

"*I do not want to be here.*" *His voice is low and rumbles through me.*

"*What happened to you, Thomas? This,*" *I gesture to the scene in front of us,* "*is who I remember.*"

"*Do you want to know what I remember, Anala?*" *he growls, and then the setting of my memory—that is supposed to help Thomas remember his humani-*

ty—shimmered. I lose my hold on controlling the scene, and the next thing I know, I am watching Thomas with Bernard.

"They are using her, Thomas. Her own parents are using their daughter to try to cure Cursed Ones," Bernard tells the young Thomas, his voice filled with contempt. "As if there was a cure!"

"I do not believe they would do that," Thomas replies unbelievingly.

As I watch the two of them converse, I realize Thomas has taken control of the memories. I observe Thomas with Bernard, pacing around his small room - I guess pacing really runs in the family. He looks to be about twenty, which would mean I am eighteen and have been Cursed.

"You do not know Henry, my boy. He is greedy and seeks fame. If he finds the cure, the king would give him anything he desires."

"But Anala is his daughter. You cannot expect me to believe he would…"

"You are young!" Bernard interjects sharply. "You do not understand the minds of men. I am telling you money is what is important to Henry and Eleanor Geil."

"What do I do?"

"Do you love young Anala?"

"Yes," Thomas whispers.

"Then save her. Or if she cannot be saved, avenge her."

"How? They are the leaders of the society, and much stronger than I am." Disbelief still shines in Thomas's eyes, but I can see sparks of anger beginning.

"That is why I am here, my boy. To help you." Bernard produces a bottle of what I imagine is my blood from his pack. "Drinking this will give you an advantage over them."

"What is it?"

"Blood of a Cursed One."

"I do not want to become Cursed!" Thomas steps back, holding his hands out in front of him.

"You cannot become Cursed from drinking a bit of the blood," Bernard lies.

He is purposefully lying, and it pisses me off. The entire conversation is one lie after another, all to use Thomas as his pawn.

"Thomas, you trained with us. You trained with my parents. Did you really believe they would use me like that?"

"I had not seen you in months, Anala. It made sense what Bernard told me."

"I was Cursed, Thomas. They were trying to find a cure for me."

"You will say anything. They are your parents. Even after what they did to you, you will still protect them."

I spin around to face him. "It is the truth!"

The image shimmers again, and I take control once more. This struggle between us was becoming tiresome, but I have to do everything I can to stop Thomas from whatever he is planning. When the image clears again, we are at the spot where I had been bitten.

"Do you remember this, Thomas? The last day we patrolled together?"

"I will be right back," Thomas calls to me as he pulls his young sister, Emma, along with him. She had been hiding in the bushes, wanting to be near her big brother. It had scared the hell out of me when we almost cut her head off, thinking she was a Cursed One.

"Whatever." I watch as my younger self mutters moodily. Then I see the moment I forgot about my surroundings. I recall thinking about Thomas and how he made me feel. And then it happened. The Cursed One moved silently up behind me, grabbing me and whispering in my ear. I remember what he said clearly, as if it had happened yesterday. 'A Hunter's daughter. You could be helpful to us.'

I turn away, watching Thomas. I did not want to see the moment my life changed.

"Do you see, Thomas? I was Cursed. My parents did not do anything to me except try to help me."

"You're lying."

"Look, Thomas! You can see what happened!"

"You are tricking me."

"I cannot trick you, Thomas. I cannot change what happened. This is the truth. What Bernard told you was lies."

"I have had enough of this, Anala. You will say anything. I know what the truth is. Your parents took you from me, and now my own descendant is doing the same thing."

I shiver at the mention of Sam, and the memory shifts again as if it were connected with my shudder. I soon realize that I am standing in Papa's lab. Even though I know it's impossible, I smell the familiar scents of my Mum and Papa. The tears threaten, but I refuse to let Thomas see me cry.

"Why did you bring me here, Thomas?"

Before he can answer, I hear my father's voice. I turn in the direction of the sound and see Papa, his hands lifted in surrender, addressing Thomas.

"Thomas, let us try to help you. We are working on a cure."

Thomas snarls at Papa. His eyes were white and ringed with red, his teeth long and sharp. And he is circling my mother and father with three other Cursed Ones. My parents are unarmed and look worried about Thomas more than fearful for themselves.

"Thomas, fight it. You don't want to hurt us. Anala wouldn't want..."

I turn away quickly when Thomas and another Cursed One lunge at my father while the other two go for Mum. I don't want to watch what I know will happen, so I focus on the Thomas that is showing me this horrible memory.

"You." Fury, sorrow, disbelief, and unadulterated need to kill Thomas battle for first position in my brain. *"You killed my family."*

"They should not have taken you from me. I have spent my entire existence avenging you. Killing every Hunter I came across because I knew they helped your father. The only one I didn't get was the Cloaked One." He faces me then, his lips in a thin line. *"But when I found it out it was you, you refused to stand with me. Because you love someone else. I will not let anyone have you."*

"You killed my family," I repeat, my tone filled with rage. *"Bernard lied to you, and you killed them. For nothing. You killed all of those Hunters because of lies."*

"You should have come to me. After all these years, you could have come to me, but you chose another."

"I didn't even know you were alive!" I scream.

"You do now, and still, you refuse me."

85

I take a deep breath, trying to calm my temper. It's not working. I fear nothing will work after finding out the truth. When I discovered Bernard had betrayed my parents and ordered their deaths, I killed him. Without remorse. It didn't stop the hurt, but I did feel better knowing what happened. Knowing it was Bernard's fault as much as it was mine. But this. Learning that Thomas was the one who actually took my parents away from me has destroyed me.

"You expect me to stand with you now?"

"I never stopped loving you, Anala. You belong with me."

"You are delusional, Thomas. We never had a chance to see where our feelings would take us. I was infatuated with you, but it never became more. I cared, Thomas. Now, all I feel for you is hate."

"Because of the one that stole you from me."

"No! Because you tore my heart out, Thomas! You stole my family!" I need to escape this mind game I'm playing with Thomas. I struggle to control my thoughts, and immediately, Sam floods my mind.

"You think of him now!"

"I think of him always," I shoot back. "What I feel for Sam is more than I ever imagined feeling for anyone. I was young when I knew you, Thomas. I have lived lifetimes now and know what it means to be truly in love."

"Then you will know how I felt when you were taken from me."

I ponder his meaning, wondering how he could have possibly felt for me what I now feel for Sam when we never had a chance to explore. I don't even notice the change of scenery around me until a car catches my eye. Cars did not exist in... we're no longer in memories. We're in the present. His scent filled my senses.

"Sam."

"It is easy for me to get to him, Anala."

"Leave him alone."

Thomas laughs, the rough noise making him sound as evil as I now know him to be.

"Stand with me, and I will leave your precious Hunters alone."

Sam's scent is so strong, I can only imagine how close Thomas is to him. Sam, please be careful. Thomas is near. *I can't be certain if my warning can reach Sam, so I turn back to Thomas.*

"If you hurt him, any of them, I will rip you apart with my bare hands."

"Do you think you can find me before they're gone, Anala? Before I tell those who do stand with me to kill them all?"

"They are strong, Thomas. Your Hybrids can not harm them."

"Ah, but will they kill an innocent if they need to?"

Thomas's laugh follows me out of my dream state, and I find myself in the meditation room, alone. I immediately reach for my cell phone and hit speed dial.

This is Detective Sam Logan. I can't answer your call right now..."

"Damn it."

I tap another number and wait impatiently.

"Ana?"

Thank Christ!

"Amanda, where is Sam?"

"Um, he said he was going to the station for a while before he headed back over there. What's wrong?"

"He's not answering his phone. I need him to answer."

"Ana, you're scaring me. What's wrong?"

"Thomas was near him."

"*Oh God.*"

"Call the others. Meet me at Griffith. Now!"

After quickly changing into my hunting gear, I race to Zac's room.

"Time to put you to the test."

He looks up from his iPad and glares at me. I honestly don't have time to explain, so I grab his gear and toss it at him.

"Get dressed. Grab what you need from the training room and get to Griffith."

I don't give him a chance to argue or respond. Briefly, I consider stopping by Sara's to free her from compulsion, but I dismiss the idea. Too much time. I organize my daggers, swords, and stakes in their places on my outfit and flip my cloak around me.

I arrive at the park before anyone else and focus. I put every ounce of concentration into my heightened senses. I can hear bugs burrowing under the soil and animals scurrying at the sound of what might be a predator. I can smell the dew gathering on the blades of grass, the aftermath of a young couple who recently had sex in the park, but not Sam. For a moment, I question myself. Did I get the right place? I remember Thomas's image as clearly as if I were still with him. This is it. Sam was here, I'm sure of it. But he's not here now. Still, there are Hybrids nearby, and they're getting closer. Good. I'm in the mood to kill someone.

"Ana?"

"Shh." I motion for my Hunters to gather closer, and notice they have all dressed for the hunt. I let my pride in them linger for a moment before tamping it down. "Hybrids coming in on the west and south."

"*Sam?*"

I shake my head and glance at Amanda. I see fear in her, but she's holding it in. If I understand her correctly, the anger is fueling her more than the fear.

"Be aware that the Hybrids may have innocents with them."

"As hostages?" Emily asks quietly.

Again, I shake my head and hear groans.

"Where is Sara?"

"If Anala had any say, she probably compelled her to leave the compound before going under for Thomas," Zac growls his answer to Jenna.

I spare a moment to glare at him.

"We have work," I say and walk away, effectively cutting off anyone else's response. They follow me, then follow the directions I send them with a flick of my hand. Jenna and Jeremy take off in one direction, Emily and Eric in another. That leaves me with Amanda and Zac. I don't know if I can trust Zac alone with Amanda, but I don't think I'm going to have a choice. Amanda can't hunt on her own, but I can.

"Amanda, take Zac and head down to the path. If there are innocents, incapacitate them. Zac, do *not* kill anyone unless they are Cursed."

He simply snarls in return and stalks off with Amanda.

Thomas? Stop hiding from me.

I'll come to you when I'm ready, Anala.

I am your Maker, Thomas. I command you to stop this and come to me now.

I feel the hesitation deep inside, along with the epic battle he's fighting within himself to disobey me. He's so strong, it's a wonder I can even communicate with him. And just like that, my connection with him was broken. Damn it. With Thomas out of my mind, I focus on Sam.

Sam? Baby, talk to me.

Nothing. Damn it.

I pull up my hood, grasp my swords, and release my blades. In one smooth motion, I do a back flip in the air, landing behind the Hybrid that was trying to 'sneak up' on its prey. My swords cut through him before he even turns around. I pause briefly to check if the others are okay, then turn to the innocents approaching me with confidence.

Their smirks alone make me want to slap them, but I let them come to me without a word of warning. I see the gleam of guns sticking out of their waistbands and knives—switchblades, because apparently that's the gangster thing to do—in their hands. Baggy clothing and dark blue bandanas worn in various ways almost complete the look. The small tattoo on their necks is what draws me the most. They're fresh tattoos. So fresh, I can see the tiny droplets of blood that haven't yet scabbed over. Big gang members—three in all, but their size is enough to give them the strength of five or more. Of course, they're no problem for me, unless I consider that I shouldn't kill them. Damn it.

"What is this? Halloween?" one of them says, sizing me up with a mix of curiosity and disdain. His friends chuckle, patting him on the back to praise his cleverness.

"Trick or treat?" I ask, not bothering to hide that I am female. That piqued their interest even more.

"I think we'll go for the treat," the obvious spokesperson replied. "How about you show us the goods?"

I'll show you the goods. I resist my urge to punch their teeth down their throats and lift my hood.

"Woo hoo hoo! Look at this, boys! We got us a hot one!"

The others made approving grunts as they surrounded me.

"This is going to be fun!"

"Yes, it is," I agree, and I smile sweetly at him.

"If you don't struggle, we'll make it easy on you," he responds casually. I wonder if that ever works for him. Unfortunately for him, it won't work tonight.

"I'm sure you say that to all the girls."

He snorts, and the others follow suit, but still don't say anything. "I like them a little feisty. Like you."

"You've never had someone like me."

"Oh, pretty sure of your abilities, are you?"

"You have no idea," I answer with a small smile.

"Ana, are you done playing with these young men?"

Amanda's voice, strong and confident, makes me smile even wider. She knows they're innocents, and I'm biding my time with them.

"Well, now. Seems like we have one for you now, Snake."

This time, it's my turn to snicker. "Snake? Really? Were all the original nicknames already taken?"

"I guess you're not," Amanda mutters.

"What's going on?" Jenna steps up next to Amanda, jutting out her hip, placing her hand on it, and tapping her fingers.

"This just keeps getting better!" Mr. Spokesman says appreciatively.

I know what he sees. Three women, attractive women - if I say so myself - all dressed in black, skin-tight body suits. Easy and quite tempting prey for them all.

"Ana is messing with the gangsters," Amanda replies. Her voice was bored and accompanied by an overly dramatic sigh from Jenna. Honestly, if I weren't so worried about Sam, I would let this continue because it's entirely too entertaining. I sense the others approaching, along with Zac, and I know now is probably a good time to stop this charade.

"Put the knives away," I say without threat. "Let's have a chat."

"We're not interested in chatting with you... ladies." He sucks his teeth and sneers at me. "How about you get on your knees. You can talk to him." He grabbed himself between the legs.

"Sorry, I didn't bring my magnifying glass."

I see all three of them tense, preparing to attack as the presence of the rest of my Hunters fills the air around them.

"I would rethink what you are planning," Zac says quietly, his voice rough and menacing.

Part of me is annoyed when the humans falter at the sound of a male voice. I certainly do not need Zac, Jeremy, or Eric to save me, nor do the other ladies with me, but I tamp down my pride.

Zac, please keep an eye on these two goons while I talk to their friend.

Zac nods almost imperceptibly, nudging Jeremy and tilting his chin toward one of the guys. In seconds, the two humans are restrained, and I focus on the one who did all the talking. If he wants to talk, that's fine with me. Right now, he looks totally confused about what's going on around him, barely noticing when I move closer.

"What is your name?" I study his features closely and notice that his eyes are cloudy. He's compelled. It will be more difficult for me, but not impossible.

He tilts his head like a puppy, a crease forming between his dark brows. I change, needing the extra strength in my compulsion, and try again.

"What is your name?"

"Cruz." His voice is hesitant and quiet—a strong contrast to just moments before.

"Who sent you here, Cruz?"

If past experience has taught me anything, Cruz won't know who sent him here. Thomas would have made sure Cruz forgot him. A memory wipe that strong isn't reversible. But it doesn't hurt to try and see if Thomas messed up. Unfortunately, Cruz's silence tells me that's not possible. Sigh.

"What are you supposed to do?" I ask instead. At least he should know what his orders were.

"Kill."

"Kill who?"

Cruz shrugs, telling me that Thomas just issued the order to kill anyone who gets in his way. One more way for Thomas to keep Sam busy.

"How many of your kind are there?"

He frowns again, considering my question, then shrugs once more. Jenna and Amanda both groan in frustration, and Emily stomps away. From a quick look, I see she took a spot near Zac, and he didn't seem bothered by her being close. I grab Cruz by the shirt and pull him over to his friends.

"Cruz, you and your friends can no longer kill anyone." I turn up the heat in my eyes, making sure to look at all of them. I drill into their heads what will happen if they kill anyone else. Honestly, if Thomas keeps this up, I will have to look past the oath not to harm innocents. I don't know what else to do. I cannot tolerate senseless killing, and I cannot continue to compel people. It takes too much time and energy.

"You're just going to let them go?" Zac growls. Ugh. I'm quickly tiring of hearing his inhuman voice. Especially when it's dangerously close to sounding like a whine.

"Yes, Zac." I watch Cruz and his buddies run from the park before turning to my Hunters. "We need to find Sam."

Every five seconds, I am hitting redial, hoping Sam will finally answer. Each time his voicemail comes on, my dread grows. Fear has me by the throat, and I don't know what to do about it. I'm almost sorry I didn't feed from Sam when I had the chance. It would have strengthened our connection, and maybe I would know where the hell he was right now.

"Any luck?" Amanda plops down beside me on the couch.

I should be out looking for Sam, but I don't know where to start. The image Thomas took me to revealed no Sam, and so I sit here now in my home, trying not to go insane with worry.

"No, you?"

"No. I mean, he could be on a case. He wouldn't answer if he were in interrogation or something." She tries to sound hopeful and reassuring, but it doesn't quite resonate. Probably because she knows I've already called the station, only to hear Sam isn't on shift tonight.

"Mmhmm." I bring my knees up and rest my chin on them. "I would know if he was hurt, wouldn't I?"

"Of course. He's fine, Ana. He'll come through the door any minute, and you can kick his ass for not answering our calls."

If he walks through that door, I'll be doing more kissing than kicking.

"The others went out again," Amanda continues quietly. "Don't worry, they're staying in a group. They just wanted to look around some more."

"Why didn't you go?"

"They can handle things. They didn't need me."

"Translation: I need you in order not to fall apart?"

Amanda sighs. "Or maybe I thought we could help each other make it through this waiting. He *is* my brother, Ana."

I wince slightly at my insensitivity. Of course, she would be just as worried as I am. I reach over and squeeze her hand. "We would both know if something was wrong. I'm sure of it."

Only, I'm not sure. Yes, Sam and I share a strong connection, but what if my encounters with Thomas have weakened that?

Sam? Sam, please, come home. Call me. Something. I love you.

I catch Amanda studying me curiously.

"Anything?"

I realize then that she figured out I was trying to communicate with Sam. I shake my head, sadly.

I can't sleep. I can't sit still. I can't go out to find Sam until I have some idea of where to look. The others have been back for hours with nothing to report except a few Hybrids and 'innocents.' Zac tried out his compulsion skills and was vaguely pleased with the result. At least he controlled himself enough not to kill anyone he wasn't supposed to. Now they're all locked away in their rooms, avoiding me and my mood swings, while I wander the halls like a restless spirit.

I consider meditating to reach Sam, but I'm scared of another confrontation with Thomas. Emotionally, I'm not prepared for that. So, instead, I go to the gym—wearing my workout gear—and plan to crush the equipment. After an hour and a half and destroying four sparring dummies, I'm still far from feeling calm. Damn it.

I try taking a steaming shower, soaking in the whirlpool bath with relaxing bubbles, and watching TV. Nothing can keep my mind off of Sam, and the worry hurts more than a splintering stake. Believe me, I know. This is exactly why I never allowed myself to feel emotions for anyone. I lost my parents, and it devastated me. The thought of falling in love with someone held no appeal because I believed there could never be a good outcome. But with Sam, it wasn't a choice. I don't think I could have fought it, even if I wanted to. And, for once, I didn't want to. That's how powerful the feelings Sam brought out in me were. Yes, it was shocking, of course. Hell, I knew how it looked to the others. A relationship emerging out of nowhere between Sam and me, when fighting was our typical dynamic. The fighting, at least on my part, was a direct result of the fear I felt at the immediate attraction I had for him. But I couldn't deny it for long, and apparently - thankfully - neither could he. Only now, when I'm miserable with uncertainty, do I allow a little regret and self-criticism to seep in.

He would have called. There's no way he wouldn't call. Sam was worried about me and everything going on with Thomas. He didn't want to leave me, but I made him. Now I have no idea where he is. But I do know that if there wasn't something extremely wrong, he would be here or at least call. My stomach sinks, and my heart breaks even more at the thought.

Chapter Twelve
"Because You're Chosen?"

As the night turns into day and then back into night again, my hope fades even more. I can't stay cooped up inside anymore with the others hovering around me. Part of me wants to be there for Amanda as much as she wants to be there for me. I just don't have it in me. Selfish? Yes. I just can't bring myself to care right now. Sam is missing. That's my only concern at this moment, and I'm tired of waiting for answers.

"Ana? Do you think it's a good idea for you to go out hunting feeling the way you do?"

"What do you want me to do, Amanda? Sit around here and bite my nails?"

"No. But you can let someone go with you."

"You and the others need to patrol the other places on Sam's list." My voice cracks slightly when I say Sam's name, and I clear my throat.

"There are enough of us to –"

"No!" I say it much sharply than I mean, and Amanda flinches. "I'm sorry. I know this is hard for you, too. Please, Amanda. Do this for me? Hunt with the others, and have Zac try to get any answers he can out of innocents." I hesitate for a moment. "And don't let him kill anyone."

My hood is up, and I move stealthily through the shadows, fully aware of my surroundings. I'm in the worst part of town I could be in, and I can feel the adrenaline rush through my veins. Gangs, drug dealers, and all kinds of riffraff gather here. It's exactly what I need to distract myself from everything else. Plus, if Thomas is using places like this to "recruit," I might be able to learn some information.

I survey my surroundings and my outfit. I decide to lose the cloak to seem more approachable. Not that my hunting attire is casual, but I'm sure people will at least be curious. I find a cubby to tuck my cloak and most of my weapons into. I make sure they're safely out of sight before walking away - I definitely don't want to lose anything. The age of the swords alone makes them worth a fortune.

My bodysuit is made specifically for me, and I know that it hugs my body in a way that - if I am honest with myself - is sexy. The thigh-high boots alone were enough to turn men's - or even a few women's - heads. I pull the zipper down just enough to reveal some cleavage, silently giving thanks to Mum for the generosity in my chest area. Distractions for others, I muse.

My gait is purposeful, yet unintimidating. Though I doubt these jokers will be smart enough to be intimidated by me. Yes, I realize I am stereotyping, but I shake off the slight sting of guilt and focus. Why would they be intimidated by some random chick walking down the street in one of the toughest neighborhoods in the city?

"Hey, baby!"

The man's voice interrupts my thoughts, making me cringe. He sounds nothing like Sam, so when he calls me 'baby', it feels wrong.

"How about you come over here? Let's get to know each other."

I turn towards him, taking my time. I make no secret of the fact that I am letting my eyes roam over his entire body. He's tall—when I guess, I'd say around

6'2"—and lanky. His jeans hang loose off his nonexistent hips, held up only by a belt. His white T-shirt is tucked in the front and left untucked in the back. His hair is long, brushing his shoulders, and shaggy—almost dirty—as if it hasn't been washed in a week. When my eyes meet his, I can tell my blatant staring amuses him. Even from across the street, I see his pupils are dilated, though I'm not sure if it's from drugs or arousal. I do smell the distinct odor of marijuana in the air, but it could be coming from anywhere, considering where I am.

"Like what you see?" he asks in what I imagine he thinks is a seductive voice. My initial assessment of him as a man has shifted. He can't be more than nineteen or twenty. Old enough to be called a man, I guess, but still young enough to be naive and easily manipulated.

"Maybe," I respond lightly, but I don't move toward him.

"Well, I totally like what I see." He shifts his weight, hooking a thumb in his front pocket. I figure he thinks it's a sexy stance since he curls his fingers toward the front of his jeans, almost cupping himself.

"Do you now?" I allow a slow, sensual smile to form, and his eyes dilate even more, nearly eclipsing the blue irises. He stands up straight and takes a step toward the street, toward me.

"Leo!"

The young man actually winces at the sound of a girl's shriek. It was the best way to describe how she sounded, and the undisguised hatred in her eyes when she looks at me doesn't surprise me in the least. At first glance, she appears to be the typical gang member's girlfriend. A colored bandana keeps her dark hair back, and huge hoop earrings hang from her ears.

"S'up, Gia?" Leo grunts, slanting a look at me before turning back to the girl.

"You were supposed to meet me ten minutes ago. That's what's up."

He shrugs sheepishly as she smacks him in the chest the moment she gets to him.

"We had an important meeting, remember? And you're here flirting with this slut?"

Slut? I scowl at her, and she returns it right back to me.

"I wasn't flirting," Leo mumbles.

"No?" Gia plunks her hands on her generous hips and turns to me. "Hey, bitch! Why dontchu keep walking?"

"Public street," I call back.

"Actually, it's not. This is my street. You wanna stand there, you hafta pay me."

I make a show of looking around me.

"I don't see your name anywhere, *Gia*." I intentionally draw out her name, and her eyes flash with fury.

"Maybe I should show you," she spat.

"Gia, come on. Let's just go." Leo reaches for Gia's arm, and she snatches it away from him.

"You need to learn how to defend what's yours," she tells him scathingly. "I'm gonna hafta let Cruz make a man out of you. A little beating would do ya good."

Cruz? Sounds really familiar. I guess I've uncovered Thomas's recruiting spot.

"Whatever," Leo mumbles again. The quiet mumbles show me he's really scared of both Gia and Cruz. I get the feeling Leo here doesn't really want to be in a gang.

"You don't want the beatin'? Then show me you're a man." Gia juts her chin out, indicating me. "Show her you know how to defend your territory."

I laugh, and the death stare she gives me is impressive. Not frightening, but impressive.

"Why don't you defend your territory?" I toss to her.

She wastes no time stalking across the street toward me. I notice that Leo looks a bit nervous and turned on at the same time—typical guy, excited by the thought of two women fighting.

"Bitch, you think I'm afraid of you in your stupid whore outfit?"

"Do I think you're afraid? No. Should you be? Probably." I smile sweetly at her, only serving to infuriate her even more.

Gia pulls out a butterfly knife, efficiently swinging it open with a flourish. Not bad.

"Wanna rethink being here on my street?"

Her hesitation to attack me outright is confusing. From what I've observed so far, Gia is hot-tempered and appears ready to fight at the drop of a hat.

"No."

Yes, I'm baiting her. I don't know why. She's not a match for me, not even close. Still, here I am, smiling sweetly at the increasingly agitated Gia.

She lunges at me with the knife, and I dodge her easily. My quick move momentarily confuses Gia. I assume she thinks she's a badass with that knife, and she probably has been before. But she's never fought someone like me. I see her shake her head just a little, then she refocuses on me. When her eyes meet mine, they widen slightly. Then I notice the tattoo on her neck—two small holes with a drop of 'blood.' Definitely one of Thomas's.

"Tell me about this meeting you have." My tone is smooth and inviting, and she falters again. By this time, Leo has crossed the street to be closer to us.

"Bitch, I ain't gotta tell you nothin'!" She slashes at me with the knife. She was so adept at opening the knife that the clumsy move surprises me.

"No, you don't have to tell me anything," I soothe. "But you want to, don't you?"

Out of the corner of my eye, I see Leo's head tilt the same way Gia's does. Wow, he is really susceptible. No wonder he's part of a gang he doesn't want to be a part of.

"Wh-who are you?"

I keep my focus on Gia as she stammers.

"The person you want to tell about this important meeting."

"We've been chosen to be a part of something big," she tells me, her eyes were glazing over as my compulsion begins to take effect.

"What have you been chosen for?"

"The city is going to be ours. We ain't gonna hafta worry about cops or anything anymore. He promised us."

My heart begins pounding in my chest.

"Who promised you?"

"Our leader."

"What is his name?"

Gia shrugs almost imperceptibly, and I realize Thomas won't tell these pawns anything as important as his name.

"Are you meeting with your leader?" I ask hopefully.

"Yes," she nods. "He's going to make us stronger."

I fight the bile back down my throat.

"How?"

"He has some kind of drug. I tried tellin' him it would be all the rage on the street, that it could be worth thousands if he would sell it. But he says it's reserved for those who are chosen. So, he's givin' it to us."

"Because you're chosen?"

Gia nods again, a small smile appearing on her round face.

"Take me to him."

Gia stumbles back a step as if I slapped her.

"I can't."

"Why?"

"I'm not allowed."

I glance back at Leo, noticing his completely dazed expression. I shift, unleashing my Cursed side in all its glory, then turn back to Gia.

"Take. Me. To. Him."

I make Gia and Leo take a detour through the alley where I hid my cloak and weapons. After putting everything back in place, I follow the duo, who are walking stiffly in front of me. I know they have no conscious awareness of their surroundings; they are simply following orders—my orders. Thomas's influence is strong. It took me longer than I wanted to break through, but I succeeded. It confirmed that I am still the stronger one between us. That realization helped calm me down. If it comes down to a battle of wills, I am now confident I can win. That was my biggest concern with Thomas. Physical strength wasn't a worry—I could defeat Thomas with my swords or fists without any trouble. I'm almost eager at the chance to prove it. My current anxiety stems from how long it took to convince Gia to take me to this meeting, and I worry Thomas might become suspicious.

Gia's steps slow, and I know we're at the meeting point. I touch her shoulder to get her attention.

"You will forget me," I say, my eyes boring into hers. "You will not remember bringing anyone except Leo here. Do you understand?"

"Yes."

I nod and turn her toward the door again. I don't worry about Leo. I'm pretty sure that even if he wasn't influenced by my words, he would be too nervous to say anything about me to the 'leader.' I wait until they disappear inside and look for an alternative entrance. I immediately sense Hybrids, but not Thomas. At least not yet. I scale the side of the building, thinking I could find a way in from the roof undetected. I take a moment to watch the street, noticing a few more 'chosen' ones heading to the meeting. Damn it. Thomas is seriously pissing me off. He's a damn Hunter, and it should be ingrained in his being not to harm innocents. He's not a Hunter anymore, I remind myself silently. He lost his humanity long ago.

I drop down from a skylight, landing silently behind the group of humans waiting "patiently" for their leader. Meaning, they've all been forced to be here to bow to Thomas. Okay, so I don't know if he actually forced them to bow to him, but somehow I don't doubt it.

My hood is once again pulled low over my face as I take in the scene. There are twenty people here. Sizes range from huge to Gia, who is around 5'2" by my calculation. Male and female alike, so Thomas isn't selective, other than the fact that they all seem to be hardened gang members. Well, and Leo. The Hybrids are not attacking, and I wonder if they're compelled as well. It's the only thing that makes sense, because I highly doubt they have the humanity it would take to keep them at bay. Unlike Zac. I take a moment to wonder about the Blood Orchlips and how Blaise is doing with them, and then I catch his scent. Thomas.

CHAPTER THIRTEEN

"TRASHCAN PING-PONG."

The humans—I'm not even sure I can call them innocents at this point—line up eagerly, their eyes shining with the promise of power. I'm almost curious to learn how Thomas actually creates his Hybrids. A simple drink of blood won't do the trick. He would need gallons upon gallons to transform all these humans. He doesn't have that. The only other option is to bite them, to feed from them. All of these live bodies... I shake myself mentally when I realize my mouth is watering. Damn it. Focus, Anala!

Thomas walks in front of the crowd, full of power and purpose. Even I am mesmerized for a split second by the sheer confidence he exudes. This is so different from the nervous, flushed boy I met so many lifetimes ago. He points to the first person in line to receive him.

"Come."

It is all he has to say before the young man, once again covered in tattoos, bounces happily toward the last day of a life without cravings. I'm pretty sure he won't mind being a killer, but just wait until he finds out how much it hurts when he's hungry. Thomas turns him to face the others, as if he's about to make an example out of him.

"You all have been chosen to stand beside me," he calls out, his Irish brogue echoing in the warehouse-like space. "You deserve to be able to live your lives without someone telling you how to be, or who to be. We *will* take over this city!"

He bares his teeth, and not one of the humans flinches at the sight.

"Thomas, stop!"

At the sound of my voice, Thomas freezes just inches from his subject's neck.

"Anala." Thomas's voice is tinged with disbelief and anger.

I see his grip tighten on his victim, and the young man whimpers in pain. The others in the room shift their eyes from me to Thomas, but they are so entirely under Thomas's spell that they do nothing without his permission.

"Are you here alone, Anala?"

I can see the smirk and hear the amusement in his taunt. I can almost hear Papa's disappointed lecture: "Never hunt by yourself, Anala. Make sure someone always has your back." But no one has had my back since I was Cursed. I've spent most of my life alone. Even before my parents were killed, I had to hunt alone because none of my fellow Hunters would understand what was happening to me. None of them would believe that, although I am Cursed, I still have my humanity.

So, here I stand, alone in a room with twenty innocents, a few Hybrids, and Thomas. Not exactly terrible odds for me. But the chances of killing an innocent have now risen exponentially. A little help would have been great. Too late to worry about that now.

"Let him go."

Thomas laughs, and it honestly sounds evil. Could it be possible that someone as sweet as Thomas once was could have lost every bit of humanity he had? I get my answer when Thomas sinks his teeth into the young man standing in front of him. There is nothing I can do for him, but I can try to help the others here if I don't end up killing them first.

"She is trying to stop us!" Thomas points at me as his victim slumps at his feet. "Are you going to let her?"

I feel the anger radiating off everyone in that room as they turn toward me. *Shit.* I can't lose sight of Thomas, and if I have to plow over these humans to get to him, I will. He knows where Sam is. I'm sure of it.

I jump over the bodies that come rushing toward me, gripping my swords in midair. I slice the head off one of the Hybrids sprinting toward me as I descend.

I keep an eye on Thomas, momentarily wondering why he isn't running. Maybe he's waiting to see if I will kill an innocent. Fine. Let that curiosity keep you where I can see you, I think, as another Hybrid grabs me from behind. I quickly flick him up and over my back until he's standing in front of me. I see Thomas begin to move, and I push the Hybrid into the group of innocents who have regained their path to me. Like a bunch of bowling pins, they fall over as the Hybrid crashes into them with the force of my shove.

"Thomas!"

His step wavers at the commanding tone in my voice. I seize his hesitation to make my move. With a speed even Thomas can't match, I have him within my grasp.

"You cannot win, Anala," he sneers. "Kill me and you will never find out what happened to your precious love." The way he says the word love makes the hair on my neck stand up. When I found him and realized he was behind all the Cursed Ones, he asked me to join him. He declared his love for me. But now, I can't even imagine he still knows what that word means. I sense rather than see Thomas's gang of misfits following us as I drag Thomas toward the back door. At least I hope it's the back door; I wish I had taken a moment to check the exits. Damn it. Worry for Sam throws me off so much that I skip the steps necessary for a Hunter to stay safe. Screw it, I'm Cursed. I can do this.

"I am not going to kill you, Thomas." I kick open the door, relieved to find out it actually led to the back alley. I step outside, clutching tightly to Thomas's neck, my fingernails digging into his skin. He knows that with any sudden move he makes, I could simply tear his throat out, effectively killing him. I slam the door shut, and with a quick shove, I block the exit with the rusted blue trash receptacle filled with what seems like months' worth of accumulated waste. I shove Thomas up against the brick wall of the building, causing my fingers to dig even deeper into his neck. For a moment, Thomas actually looks scared and in pain. I try to find an ounce of regret within myself, but with a quick flash of Sam's face in my mind, it never comes. "But you will tell me what I need to know."

Thomas's eyes bulge with disbelief at the pain, right before he slumps into my arms. The silver stake protrudes prominently from his chest, and I swear I can see it move as if his heart beats around it. I reason that it is the beating of the Hybrids and humans on the other side of the exit, trying to get out. I rub at the intense pain that still grips my own chest. I was expecting it, knowing that since Thomas is bonded to me, I would feel it. But I wasn't prepared for how severe it would be, leaving me... weak.

The pounding continues, and I can't stop myself from wondering why they don't just go around. I am half expecting to have to fight my way out of the alley, but no one is blocking my path. I shove a second trash can in front of the other to buy more time, and find my phone in one of the hidden pockets of my outfit.

"Stupid," I mutter as I punch in Amanda's number. "Doesn't take a rocket scientist to figure out there's another way to reach me."

I am still muttering about the ignorance of the "*chosen*" when Amanda answers.

"Ana?"

"I need you all here. Now." I spout off the address and hang up before she has a chance to respond. The damn ache in my chest won't alleviate, and it's pissing me off. Not to mention the constant banging against the door and trash bins. But each time they manage to move the bins, I shove them back into place. It takes quite a bit of willpower not to yell at them for being so incredibly dense. I should be happy they're not finding a way to get to me. "*So much for total evolvement,*" I whisper grumpily. I have no excuses for the humans.

It takes the others less than fifteen minutes to reach my location and find me playing trashcan ping-pong with the geniuses inside. I had contemplated just walking in there and putting them all out of my misery, but I am still feeling weak. I also won't risk leaving Thomas's body out in this alley alone.

"Oh my God, Ana. You found him?"

I nod and shove the trash bins back in place.

Jenna observes the absurdity of the situation with a genuine smile, turning her head back and forth between the actions as if she were watching an actual tennis match. "What's going on in there?" she asks, jerking her head toward the door.

"Weekly meeting of the Idiot's Club," I deadpan, getting chuckles all around. It's a welcome sound that hasn't been heard since Sam's disappearance. Zac, however, isn't chuckling. He's rubbing his chest, and pain flashes in his eyes, making them brighter. I can tell he's fighting the change. I don't blame him. Entering Cursed mode significantly blurs your sense of right and wrong.

"Why didn't you just kill him?" he rasps, looking down at Thomas. "And, seriously, what the hell is going on in there?"

"He knows where Sam is."

I push the bins back in place before updating everyone on the situation, leaving out how weak I'm feeling right now. The simple truth is that I won't risk losing Thomas's body.

"So, I need you all to go in there. Take care of the Hybrids and try not to hurt any of the innocent."

They groan in protest.

"Fine. Try not to kill them." I eye Sara. "Are you okay with this?"

Sara looks at Thomas's completely still body, then at me, then back at Thomas. Finally, she fixes her gaze on me and nods. I give Amanda a questioning look when Sara turns away to follow the others.

"She's fine. She made her first kill tonight. Three, actually. Sara can hold her own." Amanda then heads off to join the others, and I roughly push the garbage-filled containers against the door again.

"Don't, Zac."

I know he hasn't gone with the others, sensing his presence before seeing him slip back out of the shadows toward Thomas.

"He did this to me." He's trying to reason with me about why he should kill Thomas right now. I see his hand move toward the hilt of his sword.

"I understand that. But I cannot let you kill him. Not yet. He knows where Sam is." I face Zac, knowing - feeling - he shares the same fierce pain I do. "I will not let you jeopardize my finding Sam."

If Zac is reading my mind right now, he will understand the true meaning of what I told him. He will realize that his life is not as important to me as Sam's is. It's harsh, I know. But it's the truth.

Just a moment. That's all I need — one moment to gather my thoughts so I don't end up killing either Zac or Thomas - or both. Zac's constant brooding and overwhelming desire to kill Thomas are incredibly annoying and hard for me to handle. I tell him to go to his room and not come out until I say so. I feel like his mother for punishing him. Honestly, though, staying away from me is probably saving his life.

After strapping Thomas into the silver chair in the holding room, I take a moment to study him. His features are more hardened, even in "sleep," than I remember. The years haven't seemed to favor him as they have me. Of course, he still appears to be a typical, extremely attractive twenty-year-old. But now, upon closer inspection, the lack of humanity, the killing, the plotting—they all seem to be taking a toll on Thomas. Still, I find no sign of remorse in my desire to rip his head off with my bare hands. So, to prevent myself from doing that, I take a moment for myself.

If anyone thought it was strange that I would just walk away when I finally have Thomas in my hands, they don't show it. Maybe they realize that it's best for everyone involved, including Sam, if I take some time before interrogating Thomas. I thank whatever deity is listening for their understanding and patience. Especially Amanda, because I know how incredibly troubled she is by not hearing from her brother. It's all she can do not to reveal her worry to their parents. Instinctively, she knows it's best to wait before telling them anything. Sam is an adult, after all, so he didn't need to check in with his parents, and they had no reason to worry. Yet.

I take off my hunting gear and step into a steaming shower. I try to scald away the pain, then scrub at it to no avail. The ache in my chest isn't going anywhere, and I start to wonder if it's because of the stake in Thomas or my heartbreak over Sam. "*Kill me and you will never find out what happened to your precious love.*" Those were Thomas's words. Not "you'll never find him" or anything else that could give me hope. I try to comfort myself by thinking that, of course, Thomas would make it sound like the worst has happened. He wants me off-balance. He wants me weak. Unfortunately, it's working.

With a sigh, I drop into the chair near my bed, draping my towel over my head. I leave it there for a minute, trying to hide from the big, bad truth under its cover. The thought makes me laugh bitterly. Even my cover can't hide me from this truth. I scrub fiercely at my wet hair, towel-drying it so thoroughly it's almost dry when I finish. I take a deep breath at the scent that is approaching my door, appreciating the fact that, though different, it carries a hint of the familiarity of Sam's scent.

"One moment, Amanda," I call out before she can knock. I quickly pull on some comfortable lounge pants and a fitted t-shirt. One good thing about never aging is that everything stays perky, so I don't think about putting on a bra. I comb my hair with my fingers before opening the door.

Here." Amanda holds out a bottle of blood to me, waiting until I take it before she comes in and makes herself at home on my king-sized bed. "God, this bed. I mean, how do you get out of it every morning? I just want to bury myself in the covers and never leave."

"Something wrong with your bed?" I ask, taking a swig of the Hunter-laced blood. I feel a portion of my strength return as the red liquid coats the back of my throat, soothing me.

"Not so much, no. But yours just seems, I don't know, fluffier."

"Perks of being the owner," I murmur and settle back into my chair. "Thanks for this."

Amanda lifts a shoulder.

"We all thought you could use it." She studies me for a moment, until I start feeling a little uncomfortable under her gaze and begin to squirm. "Will you kill him?"

There is no hint of accusation or criticism; instead, it is a sincere inquiry.

"Yes."

"You don't want to see if the elixir will work on him?"

I tilt my head, studying her this time.

"No," I answer finally.

"Ana –"

I raise my hand to cut her off. I wonder if she would be asking this if she knew what Thomas had told me before I staked him. If she knew that he said "*what happened*" to Sam.

"He is too far gone. There is no redemption for Thomas. Not after everything he has done. To fellow Hunters, to innocents, to Zac...to Sam. Humanity is not something Thomas possesses."

"You loved him once," she says softly.

"I was infatuated," I correct her. "Like I said, that boy doesn't exist anymore. Sam does." I hope. "I love Sam. Thomas means nothing to me."

Amanda appears to consider this briefly before she nods. "Will you let Zac kill him?"

"No. I will kill Thomas."

Chapter Fourteen
"Please don't leave me."

My Hunters line up against the glass that separates me and Thomas from them. I had Amanda lock us in, knowing that if Thomas somehow got past me, he wouldn't reach them. I try not to look at them as I prepare to take the stake from Thomas. They are all so nervous that it feels like it radiates through the unbreakable glass. I am already jittery enough, not knowing what I will learn about Sam.

Taking a deep breath, I curl my fingers around the stake and struggle to decide whether to pull it out or leave it in. If I don't, and Thomas can't tell me that Sam is hurt—or worse—then it won't be true. Of course, I don't have to be over 600 years old to know that's not how the world works, so I scold myself for delaying and yank the stake out.

I watch with disinterest as Thomas cries out in pain even as my own dissipates moderately. I know firsthand how painful it is to awaken after being staked, particularly if you're staked with a silver splintering stake - which I purposefully used with Thomas.

"Thirsty," he grates.

"Too bad."

His eyes snap to me, but he becomes paler at the gesture, if that's even possible since he's about the color of a sheet of paper.

"Blood," he tries again. "If you want answers, *Anala*, give me blood."

Fury makes red—the very color of what he desires—dim my vision. I immediately feel the change, welcoming its sting and power.

"Ana, no. Think of Sam."

Amanda's soft words soothe my anger like water dousing a flame. I loosen my fists - which I didn't realize I was clenched - and take a deep, calming breath.

"This is not a negotiation, Thomas. You will tell me where Sam is."

I feel his rejection of my command as if it were tangible. I walk up to him, placing my hands on both sides of the chair, and lean in close.

"Let us see how strong you are after you have not fed. You may be able to resist me right now, but that will not last, Thomas. You will tell me where Sam is."

"You expect me to tell you so you can just kill me?" he spat.

"You are dead either way, Thomas."

"How long do we have to wait?"

Amanda is pacing nervously, and it reminds me so much of Sam that I feel a pang in my chest.

"He is used to feeding whenever he wants. Being deprived of it for even a couple of hours will have a tremendous effect on him."

My hands tremble as I run them through my hair. I clench my fists, trying to regain some control, but until I know what Thomas knows about Sam, I don't think that will happen. I don't even notice when Amanda stops pacing, but when I look at her, I see she's watching me closely.

"What?"

"Do you need blood?"

"I'm fine, Amanda."

"Ana, I'm worried about you almost as much as I am about Sam."

"Focus on Sam." It comes out a little harsher than I intend, and I immediately regret it. I sink heavily into the wingback chair near the floor-to-ceiling window. "I am sorry. I am not used to these feelings, Amanda. I haven't been human for so long that I'm not sure how to handle these human emotions."

"I can't imagine that you haven't had human emotions all this time."

I flinch when Jenna walks into the room. I should have sensed her, but I allowed myself to be consumed by this fear for Sam. I could only stare as the rest of my Hunters followed her in, surrounding me with their concern and care.

"I have humanity," I explain to Jenna. "But after losing my parents, I shut myself off from feeling anything for others. It hurts too much." I don't stop the tear from sliding down my cheek.

"What made you let Sam in?" Emily speaks quietly, as usual, but her curiosity is loud and clear.

"I didn't let him in, Emily. I just couldn't stop it. It surprised me as much as I think it surprised the rest of you."

"He'll be okay." Eric places a gentle hand on my shoulder, which brings on more tears.

"Right, I'm sure this Thomas jackass is just holding him somewhere to make you crazy."

Jeremy's attempt to make me feel better doesn't quite hit the mark, but I appreciate the effort. Once they finish trying to soothe me, they turn to Amanda, giving her the same treatment. I'm grateful for that as well, since I'm not doing a great job at helping her. Some best friend I am.

I get up abruptly. "I need blood," I mumble, and walk away feeling ashamed.

"Ana!" Amanda jogs to catch up with me.

When I turn suddenly, she almost runs into me.

"I'm sorry."

She waves away my apology. "It's fine. I mean, I'm the one who was running after you..."

"No. I'm sorry I'm not here for you. I feel so incredibly selfish. You're Sam's sister, and I know you are scared." I grab her and hug her fiercely. "I will find him. I promise."

She hugs me back, and I feel her composure slip a bit as she clings to me. "I know you will," she whispers, then pulls away. "Listen, we've been talking."

She gestures behind her, where the others suddenly appear again. Their stealth skills are definitely improving.

"Thomas has obviously been feeding live," Amanda continues. "We think you should, too. I mean, it can only help you when you go up against him."

"What are you saying?" I ask wearily.

"Choose one of us, or all. We're willing to help you."

"No."

"Ana," Jenna steps forward. "You can't afford to be stubborn now. We know you feed from Sam, what's the difference?"

"The difference is I'm in love with Sam." They all stare at me, and I know they don't understand. I drag a hand through my hair, not wanting to explain this to them. It just feels like I'm betraying something special between me and Sam. But with all their expectant eyes watching me, I don't think I have a choice. "Look, when I feed...unless the intent is to kill or change someone, feeding is...intimate."

"Oh." Amanda's eyes widen, and I know she understands exactly what I mean. "*Oh*. That's why you and Sam..." Her voice trails off, and she blushes.

"What?" Jenna looks from me to Amanda and back again. "Oh. Never mind."

"Besides," I continue, a little embarrassed by the conversation, "I think this could be my advantage over Thomas. He is accustomed to feeding on live prey, which gives him strength. But I have spent centuries learning to control my hunger. I don't *need* live blood to make me stronger. Not having it won't decrease my power as it will Thomas's."

"So, we wait him out? You drink the blood we've prepared for you, and he gets nothing. He won't be able to fight you then?"

I nod at Eric's assessment. I know they've been using their blood to boost my supply of bottled blood. The extra strength it provides me, even in those few drops, is incredible and deeply appreciated. I don't think I could ever find the words to truly express my gratitude toward my... family. The word and the feeling behind it bring tears to my eyes again. Damn it. Becoming a blubbering mess would not be very helpful at the moment.

"Hungry, Thomas?" I take a swig from my bottle of blood, licking my lips with a smirk.

Thomas follows my movements, the pain of hunger visible in his eyes. I can feel his hunger even as mine is satisfied. Of course, it will never be as satisfying as feeding live, which leads me to think of Sam, and then to other things. I shake myself mentally and refocus on Thomas.

"Where is Sam?"

"Give me a drink."

"You want this?" I hold the bottle out to him, shaking it as I tease him before bringing it to my lips and draining it. "Oops."

"Bitch." Thomas's voice is a harsh whisper. Rough and grating like a new Hybrid. Interesting.

"Where is Sam?" I repeat, opening a new bottle of blood. I'm full, but that won't stop me from provoking Thomas.

"Give me blood, Anala. I am hungry."

"Tell me what I want to know."

"I don't know where he is."

"I don't believe you."

"Blood!" he roars, and I deliberately take a drink from my bottle. "He is alive."

The relief that goes through me almost brings me to my knees. But it is short-lived.

"At least I think he is," he continues with a cruel smile.

"What does that mean?"

"Give me blood."

I am done. My fear for Sam, my hatred for Thomas, my sorrow for the boy lost centuries ago—all of it from the past 600 years rises to the surface, and I struggle with every ounce of my willpower not to rip Thomas's head off. I barely succeed as I walk up to him and grab his chin, forcing him to look me in the eye.

"I tire of this, Thomas." I say, shifting and using that power, channeling it into my words. "Tell me where Sam is. What did you do?"

Thomas's eyes cloud over, and I realize he's finally weak enough that he cannot resist my pull.

"They were ordered to hurt him, not kill him."

My heart contracts painfully.

"Why?"

"To torture you. Distract you."

"To what end, Thomas? What do you hope to accomplish?"

"His wounds should be enough to kill him. I want you to know what it feels like to be too late to save him. I wanted to get to the rest of them, but they were never alone. You were supposed to split them up. You were supposed to choose which one to save."

"Why, Thomas?" I look into his eyes, searching for the boy I used to know. But there's nothing there—no emotion, no love, no humanity.

"Because you are supposed to be mine. Without them, you would be."

"You did not think this through, did you? Did you really think I would be with you after you killed those I care about?"

"You cannot care. But whatever it is you think you feel for them, it would be destroyed by having to choose whom to save. You pretend to have humanity, but in the end, Anala, *you* are like me."

"And, yet you claim to care about me."

"No. You just belong to me. You were meant to be mine a lifetime ago. My father told me. Now, we will finally be together. It is what it is supposed to be. Be rid of these... humans."

Thomas's eyes are still glazed over, and I know he's speaking his truth. I can't imagine what he's talking about when his father told him we should be together.

Papa would never have just handed me over to anyone. He knew I would never accept that. But that was then, and now I have this to deal with.

"These *humans* are Hunters. *My* Hunters. They are who I belong with. Not you. What you did to Zac, and just the fact that you ordered Sam to be hurt, is enough to make me want to kill you. We do not belong together, Thomas. We do not even belong here. But I would trust my life with them way before I trust you." I let go of the power I hold over him and change out of my Cursed state. "I am not like you, Thomas."

"You are," he sneers.

"Ana?"

The fear in Amanda's voice makes me whip my head around so quickly that I almost get dizzy.

"Mom called." She holds her cell phone out, and I see it shake in her hand. "They found him."

My knees buckle from the tears in her eyes and almost give out when the others gather around Amanda and offer support.

"Is he?"

"Alive. Barely. Please, we need to go," Amanda says, glancing at Thomas, then back at me. "He's in bad shape, Ana. Mom could hardly speak."

Rage, despair, and pure hatred surge through me as I turn to Thomas. The sinister smile on his face at the news pushes me over the edge. There is no fighting it any longer. I lack the willpower to stop myself. I accept the change, even though it offers no relief from the pain this time. With a guttural growl that even shocks me, I take Thomas's head in my hands and twist, ripping it from his shoulders in one swift motion.

My Hunters - my friends – are shocked into silence. I don't blame them, really. They just witnessed me murder Thomas with my bare hands. I stand there for a moment, watching as Thomas, the boy that I had feelings for so long ago, dissolves into nothing but ashes before me. And I feel nothing. No remorse, no guilt. Nothing. It is the thought of Sam that brings me to my knees, and I release a wail of emotion from so deep it shakes me to my very core.

I finally gather myself and turn to face the others, ready for their scrutiny. While they are shocked, they don't turn their backs on me. Even their shock at someone as far gone as Thomas doesn't bring out remorse in me. My only thoughts are with Sam and what I will find when I reach him.

The only one who doesn't seem shocked by what I've done is Amanda. I can only imagine she wanted to do it herself. Her eyes are puffy and red, but she maintains her composure as we drive to the hospital, where Amanda's parents told her Sam was. I'm grateful that Eric offered to drive because I can't focus on anything except the pain in my heart. I faintly feel Zac in my mind, wondering if I'm okay, knowing what I did. I know he felt it the moment I killed Thomas. I just don't have the time or desire to reach out to Zac.

The silence in the car is almost deafening, but I can only stare out of the window, blindly watching the buildings and people go by. I am stunned by my first thoughts about the humans we pass. I want to sink my teeth into them. Lose myself in the euphoria I feel when I feed live. But I don't want to stop. I want to drain them until their life force fills me, making me feel alive again.

I mentally shake the thoughts from my mind. That won't help me or Sam. So, instead, I try to think positively. Of course, that's easier said than done when Amanda's words keep echoing in my head. "He's in bad shape, Ana." No matter how much I want to believe he will be okay, I can't help but imagine the worst. I almost wish Amanda's parents had told her what to expect so we could be prepared, but they limited the details. Unfortunately, that only makes my imagination run wild. I'm not even sure if I'll be allowed to see Sam. The thought makes me panic, and my entire body trembles. Apparently, Amanda feels it too, as she takes my hand in her cold, trembling hand.

"Okay?"

I squeeze her hand lightly and nod. "You?"

"I don't know," she answers, and I see in her eyes that it's a genuinely honest reply. "He's my big brother, and he's always been so strong. I mean, I don't know what to expect when we get there."

I don't know what to say to make her feel better, so I stay silent and hope that the small comfort I can give by gripping her hand tightly is enough.

Eric drops us off in front of the hospital, and I follow Amanda as she rushes to the nurses' station.

"Sam Logan?"

The nurse, dressed in bright pink scrubs, glances up briefly before typing on the computer. I assume she's checking Sam's room. If she's not, I'm going to be really angry, and I think we've already established that being an angry vampire isn't a good thing.

"I'm sorry," the nurse begins, and my legs threaten to give out. I vaguely feel Amanda grab onto my arm, and I know she feels the same way I do. "Only family is allowed for visitation."

The relief is palpable. I can almost see the tension drain from Amanda's body as she exhales.

"I'm his sister."

The nurse looks at her. "You can go back. Room 216." She turns to me. Clearly, I am not related to Sam. "You will have to wait in the waiting room."

"She's his girlfriend," Amanda states before I can say anything.

"But they're not married?"

"Please? Just let her back."

"Hospital rules."

Oh, screw this. I am not going to let anyone keep me away from Sam. I lean forward, locking eyes with the nurse.

"I am family. You see nothing wrong with me going back."

She nods slightly, pointing down the hall.

"Handy trick," Amanda murmurs as we take off, searching for room 216. I know she's trying to stay brave, but when we get close to Sam's room, her step falters, and she turns to me. "Ana, if he's...you have to help him."

"Please, Amanda, do not ask that of me."

"Too late, Ana. I'm asking."

Before I can respond, she squares her shoulders and pushes through the door. I hesitate, hearing her slight gasp. I still hesitate as the sound of her walking quickly to her mother and father drifts out to me. They're hugging, and her mother is crying softly. Then I hear her father sniff, and I know he's crying too — my resolve to go in and face what Thomas has done to Sam because of me wavers.

"*Ana?*"

Amanda's quiet whisper makes my feet move of their own accord. Whatever was in my imagination did not prepare me for what I saw.

"*Oh my God.*" I don't realize I've spoken the words out loud until the other three people in the room turn to look at me.

"Ana?"

I turn to Mrs. Logan, nearly breaking down from the sorrow visible on her face. I quickly go to her, wrapping my arms around her.

"I'm so sorry," I whisper, pouring all my guilt into those three words.

"Thank you, honey." She squeezes me gently before releasing and stepping back. She nestles into her husband's arms as he wraps them protectively around her.

"I'm glad you're here for Amanda, Ana. I'm just surprised they let you back," Mr. Logan says quietly.

"She's here for Sam, Daddy."

My eyes snap to Amanda's. She can't seriously be thinking about telling her parents about me and Sam. Not now. Amanda's eyes flick to Sam, then back to me, and at that moment, I don't care about anything else. I turn to Sam, taking everything in. His face is swollen, his eyes black and purple, shut. I don't need to be a doctor to know his nose is broken. As my eyes travel down, I see the casts on his arms and legs. His body is badly broken, and I can feel the rage growing deep in my belly.

"Go to him," Amanda whispers, placing a hand on my shoulder, which calms me just a little. I don't think about Mr. and Mrs. Logan then. I don't think about what they will say or how they will react. I do the only thing I can do: I go to Sam, leaning in close and lightly kissing his lips. I imagine the soft gasp from behind me is from Mrs. Logan, but I don't turn around. I don't want to answer questions right now.

"Sam? Baby, can you hear me?" I lean in close to Sam's ear, desperately hoping he can hear my words. "I love you. Please don't leave me."

CHAPTER FIFTEEN

"YOU DON'T DESERVE HIM."

"D o you want to tell us what the hell is going on?"

Mr. Logan paces the hallway outside Sam's room. Clearly a family trait. His words are soft, but I can hear the disapproval as clearly as if he'd shouted them.

"Daddy, please calm down."

"Calm down? Ana just told Sam she *loved* him!"

"So?"

"So?" He looks at Amanda as if she had lost her mind.

"Yeah. So? Why does it matter if Ana loves Sam?"

"She's a - a —"

Okay, I honestly think - for one split second - that he's going to say I am Cursed.

"*Child!*" he finishes.

"She's eighteen, dear," Mrs. Logan interjects.

"Eighteen is a child!"

"Russ, please. If Sam loves her, maybe she can help."

Mr. Logan looks at his wife before shifting his gaze to me. He narrows his eyes, as if trying to figure out my angle. I meet the scrutiny without flinching. I have nothing to hide. Well, besides being a vampire, over six hundred years old, and a Hunter—okay, I have a lot to hide. But I have nothing to hide when it comes to my love for Sam.

"How long?" he asks me.

"A couple of months now."

"And it's already 'love'?"

Yes, I can actually hear the quotes he puts around the word, even though he doesn't actually make the gesture.

"I know this is a shock to you, Mr. Logan. Frankly, it was to me, too. But, yes, it is love."

My stare never wavers as I keep looking into Mr. Logan's eyes—eyes so similar to Sam's that it makes me sad. He nods slightly before turning away and heading back into Sam's room. I want to follow, but Mrs. Logan steps in front of me, replacing her husband. She silently cups my cheek with her palm, and my eyes start to fill. A single tear slides down my cheek, and she catches it with her thumb.

"I wish I could have seen you two together." Her voice is barely above a whisper, but I know Amanda hears it when she looks sharply at her mother.

"Mom, you're talking like he's already gone."

"I'm sorry, honey. The doctors don't give us much hope." Mrs. Logan's voice cracks, and she clears her throat. "We need a miracle."

Her eyes search mine, for what, I don't know. Answers? Solutions? I don't have any—none that I am willing to give. Unable to hold her gaze any longer, I look away first. Mrs. Logan lets out a small sigh, pats my cheek before dropping her hand, and walks away. I realize then that she was searching for a cure. But that makes no sense. She doesn't know what I am. Right?

"Amanda?"

"I have no idea." She interrupts my question about her mom, knowing full well what I am going to ask. "I didn't tell her, and I'm quite certain Sam..." Amanda's words trail off as she turns to look into Sam's room. "Please, Ana?"

"You do not know what you're asking of me." I start pacing myself, running a tired hand through my hair. Please, please, please don't ask me to turn him. But my silent plea goes unanswered as Amanda turns to me.

"Yes, I do. It's what he wants. It's what my family needs. The *only* one against it is *you*! You claim to love Sam, but you refuse to help him!"

"Turning him into a...a monster like me is not helping him!" I whisper harshly.

"You're hardly a monster," Amanda scoffs.

"You have no idea what he will be like," I argue, ignoring her comment. "Zac is taking up all the elixir for humanity. I have no idea how close Blaise is to having the Blood Orchlips. What you're asking of me is impossible."

Amanda looks at me with eyes full of blame and anger. I notice the others approaching, but they obviously sense something is terribly wrong, so they stay back. I don't bother pretending to care how they got here when it's supposed to be just family. That's not my concern. Right now, my primary focus is convincing Amanda that turning Sam isn't in his best interest.

"It's not impossible. You're just too selfish to do it," she spat.

"Selfish! *If* I turned him, *that* would be selfish! This is not any kind of life. Why would I want to put him through this?"

"You seem to be doing just fine."

"You didn't know me before! You have no idea what I went through! Six hundred years is a hell of a long time, Amanda. I may have figured a few things out, but you still have no idea what it is like to be Cursed. It is the loneliest life, filled with sorrow and death. Just not your own. Never your own."

Amanda's eyes soften just a bit. Yeah, she's still pissed at me. "He will have you."

"And he'll watch you, your parents, and everyone else around him die."

"Help him. Then let him make that decision."

"Save him only to ask him if he wants to be saved?" I ask sarcastically. Not the smartest move when Amanda is scared and angry.

"It certainly wasn't his decision to be beaten to the brink of death because of you!"

The words make me take a step back, as if I had been slapped. Honestly, I'd rather have been slapped. It would hurt a hell of a lot less than the guilt tearing my soul—if I even have one—apart.

"Amanda, *Dios*, it is not Ana's fault."

Amanda turns on Sara. "Who the hell are you to have an opinion about it! You're not even a part of this group, really!"

"Amanda, stop," Jenna whispers.

"She's right," I say quietly. "It's my fault."

"Damn right it is. Now fix it or get the hell away from us. You don't deserve him." Amanda spins on her heel and stomps back into Sam's room, leaving me to stare after her.

"Ana," Emily lays a gentle hand on my shoulder. "She didn't mean that. She's just scared."

Emily's words and kind gesture do little to soothe me. Wasn't it Emily who blamed me for Zac? Am I not to blame for my parents? For Thomas? For the deaths of humans caused by Thomas's hand? I look at Sam's door, feeling the intense unwelcome radiating from within. I feel my beating heart slowly breaking, bleeding... shutting down. Without a word to the others, I run.

I pull my hood low over my head, hiding my face completely. Hybrids are all around me as I perch on a branch of a coral tree. Without Thomas to guide or keep them in check, I've noticed large groups of Hybrids hunting for prey. Well, they will get me instead. This is where they found Sam, in the bushes of a small park next to the Sunset Strip. I found out by using a bit of persuasion with Sam's lieutenant. After getting the information, I stopped by the estate to change, grab my gear, and come out here to wait. I will kill every last one of them, as I did after my parents were murdered. But this time, I will not leave anyone behind. That includes Zac... and me. It will truly be over.

Can you be sure, Anala? How will you know you've killed them all? You thought you did centuries ago. You were wrong then.

I push the nagging voice in my head aside when I spot a trio of Hybrids closing in on me. I drop silently from the tree, landing just behind them. They hear the faint crackle of grass beneath my feet and turn with matching snarls. They begin to circle me, but I am not in the mood to play tonight. I release my swords, spinning as one of them lunges at me. I drag my blade across the neck of one Hybrid as I cartwheel over another incoming attack. I plunge my sword through another Hybrid's forehead, lifting him off the ground as I raise my arm to split his head in two. As he falls back down, I slice my blade through his neck, not bothering to watch him turn to dust as I focus on the last of the trio. I take a moment to think about the fear on the Hybrid's face before shrugging and using both swords to cut off his head.

They were too easy, and I found the killings unsatisfying. It did nothing to alleviate my guilt or rage. More, I think. I need more. So I hunt.

Fifty-three. That was my last count. Fifty-three Hybrids, and I still don't feel satisfied. Even knowing that some of those I killed might have been the ones who hurt Sam, I feel no satisfaction. Sam is still dying.

"Dude, they found him."

My ears perk up at the distant conversation. I don't know what pulls me in, but the urge to listen is overwhelming. So, I slow my pace as I approach the corner of the building from which the voice came.

"So? They ain't gonna know we did him."

"He was a cop, man. If he wakes up, he'll be able to identify..."

"He's not gonna wake up. Did you see what we did to him?" A harsh, human laugh sounds. *"If that cop wakes us, ain't no way he'll remember anything."*

Humans. Innocents. I silently follow the conversation, creeping closer to them. Instinctively, I know they're talking about Sam. That's why Sam didn't fight back. Or couldn't. The code prevented him from hurting them. I resist it.

I truly do. I fight it with every ounce of my humanity to walk away and call the police. *You don't deserve him.* That's the last clear thought I have before I face the two of them. Big. Larger than Sam. One of them still has brass knuckles, and Sam's bruised, swollen face flashes through my mind. To hell with the code.

Brass knuckles guy notices me first and lets out a whoop of laughter.

"Check this out, dude. Little Red Riding Hood."

"Cape's black, man."

Brass knuckles shrugs, still chuckling at his lame joke. "Don't matter. Whatchu want? Come to play with the big bad wolf?"

They both laugh out loud, slapping their knees, so confident in themselves and so indifferent to the life slipping away at a nearby hospital. I take my hood in both hands and lift it from my face.

"Yes. But I want to be the wolf," I say, baring my teeth with a growl.

"Shit! What the hell?" Brass knuckles stumbles back, tripping over his own feet. Dude must feel confident enough that I'm focusing on Brass Knuckles, because he foolishly tries to run past me. I lift my cloak, enveloping him inside, and crushing him against me. I drag Dude along as I go after the other. He's running full speed now, glancing back at me every once in a while, checking on my progress. I let him run for a minute. *Let him think he can get away,* I think with an invisible smirk. Then I see him smile. He doesn't even care that I have his "friend" as long as he's faster.

I pick Dude up easily, judging the distance between me and Brass Knuckles. With a flick of my wrist, Dude sails through the air, smashing into his friend's back. If I cared, I might find the cracking of bones, the slap of heads hitting pavement, and the moans from both of them sickening. I simply don't care. I take my time moving toward them. They're not going anywhere, and the look of pure terror on their faces entertains me.

"What are you? Why are you doing this? Whaddid we do to you?" Dude asks wearily, blood dripping from his mouth and nose.

"You tell me." I grab his chin roughly, making him look me in the eyes. "You tell me what you did to the cop."

CHAPTER SIXTEEN
"REMEMBER THE CODE."

"What if he don't come, man? We still gonna get paid?"

"Relax, dude. The weird Irish guy said he'd be here, so we wait."

"I just wanna get paid. Gonna take my girl out," he says with a grin.

"Yeah? Where to? Burgers at In and Out?"

"Shut up, T. I know how to treat my woman."

"Oh yeah, Malik? She puttin' out, yet?"

"You're an asshole, Trey. How 'bout you do this job yourself? See how far you get."

"Calm down, dude. I'm just jokin' with ya. Hey." Trey bumps Malik's shoulder and points. "That's him."

"Finally. Let's get this shit over with. I don't like messin' with cops."

"They deserve it, dude. Come on."

They do their best 'I-ain't-gotta-care-in-the-world' stroll by the cop. They eye each other at the strange look they get from the cop, like he knew what they were about to do. Trey spins around quickly, swinging his arm, immediately connecting with the cop's face.

The cop drops to his knees, shaking his head, before Malik kicks him hard in the stomach. The cop coughs, spitting out the blood the first blow produced.

"Humans," he whispers harshly.

Trey and Malik look at each other in question again.

"Did he say 'humans'?"

"Think so." Trey laughs. "Of course we're humans, what else would we be? Zombies?" he asks before slamming his brass knuckled fist against the cop's temple. "Remember, don't kill him. Just enough to make him wish he were dead."

Kicks, punches, and elbows to the face and back of the head continue. Damn, it is hard not to kill this son of a bitch cop. Lord knows, if it were legal, all the cops would be killin' them.

"Enough!"

My head pounds at the thought of what these two did to Sam. And my heart dies just a little more hearing how they didn't care that they were essentially murdering someone. Someone I love. I reach down, grabbing Trey - aka Brass Knuckles - by the throat. I lift him effortlessly, my grip making it almost impossible for him to breathe. He claws at my hand, trying to free himself, but I'm not budging.

Kill him. He hurt Sam. Kill him.

Is it my brain or my heart that is telling me to kill this human?

Human, Anala. Remember the code. You are not a murderer.

A growl escapes from within me as the battle rages inside.

"Please. Let me go," Trey gasps, trying to bring in more air.

"You do not think I should do to you what you did to Sam?"

"Who's Sam? I don't know no Sam! I swear!"

"The cop you beat. His name was...is Sam."

"What's it to you? He was just a cop! One less cop ain't gonna hurt anyone."

Wrong answer. And, just like that, the scales of my inner battle tip to "kill him".

Amanda Logan

"Where is Ana, honey?"

I walk past Mom without saying anything and sit next to Sam, taking his hand in mine.

"Amanda? Your mother asked you a question."

"I don't know. Somewhere out there," I reply with a flick of my hand toward the door. "It doesn't matter. I don't want her in here anyway."

"What happened?"

"It doesn't matter, Mom. Let's focus on Sam."

"Honey, Sam needs Ana now."

I turn my head and study Mom's face. It's so familiar that it feels like looking into a mirror at what I might look like in another thirty years. Her hair isn't as light as mine, but I bleach mine. Mom doesn't even color her gray hairs, which is uncommon here in California—the land of Botox and plastic surgery. But her eyes are like Sam's: as golden as her hair used to be when she was younger, and now completely unreadable.

"What do you mean by that?" I ask carefully.

"They love each other, don't they?"

"I thought she loved him," I mutter, turning back to Sam. How could Ana do this? How can she refuse to help the man she claims to love so much? Her excuses might have been valid, but in the end, they were just excuses. She has the chance to spend the rest of her days with someone she loves. Why would she pass that up?

Because Ana doesn't believe she should be alive. My inner thoughts need to stay out of it, and let me be mad. I don't need them trying to rationalize Ana's decisions while I sit here and watch my brother die.

"Don't you think this is hard for her, Amanda?"

Mom's voice quiets my inner thoughts, and I feel mad all over again.

"It's hard for us all, Mom."

"But she has seen so much death already. She's lost everything. You shouldn't be mad at her. Whatever she did or said, I'm sure she didn't mean it." I feel my mom's hand on my shoulder. "She's scared."

Well, I can't very well argue with my mom about things she knows nothing about. Sigh. And now I feel bad about what I said to Ana. I told her that what happened to Sam was her fault. Crap. She already feels responsible for her parents' deaths and what happened to Zac. Double crap. She has to understand I'm upset, too. I mean, I wouldn't have said that stuff if ...crap.

"I'll go get her," I sigh. I place a swift kiss on Sam's cheek, and with a glance at Mom, I try not to shuffle my feet in shame as I go to apologize to Ana.

"What do you mean she left?"

"She ran out of here after you said those things to her," Jenna scolds. "Did you expect her to hang around when you told her she didn't deserve Sam?"

Crap. I didn't actually say that, did I?

"And you just let her leave?" I look at all of them with disgust. But really, I am disgusted with myself.

"Do you think we could stop her?" Jeremy asks with a short, mirthless laugh.

I spy Sara sitting quietly behind the group, and she won't look at me. Double crap. Have I always been such a bitch? Or does it take a special circumstance to bring that out in me?

"I'm sorry, Sara."

She shrugs slightly. "It isn't me you should apologize to."

"Well, if I knew where Ana was, I'd apologize to her, too," I reply sharply.

Sara stands and faces me but doesn't approach.

You've read all the journals. Journals that Ana wrote. You've read about the devastation she faced. I'm sure you've even noticed that she is very reproachful of herself. All of this," Sara says, flinging her arms out, "is Ana's fault."

"That's not true!" Jeremy cries.

"You know that," Sara says quietly. "I know that. But does Ana? No. And Amanda just reminded her of how much she is to blame. How much do you think her humanity can handle, Amanda?"

My mouth drops open. Not because I am being reprimanded by the newest member of the group, but because of the truth in what she said. And the fear that I might be the one to cause Ana to lose the humanity she still has. Triple and quadruple crap.

"I have to make a call. Meet me at the estate in twenty minutes. Be dressed in your hunting gear."

"Who are we hunting?"

"Anala."

"Okay, Blaise said some of the Blood Orchlips are ready. She'll drop them off here. Zac, you were good at chemistry. Give the formula a try. And take some of it."

"I'm going with you."

"I don't think that's a good idea."

"Amanda, I'm bonded with her. I will be able to find her."

I hesitate, weighing my options. If Ana has lost her humanity—which, God, I hope hasn't happened—will that affect Zac? Or, what if Ana goes on another killing spree of Cursed Ones like she did after her parents were killed? Again, Zac would be in danger. But he was right. He is bonded with Ana. We could be searching forever. Then, there's the matter of the elixir. What if Ana lost hers? We would need the elixir to give her and pray that it works. But that leaves none for Zac. God, how does Ana do this? All these decisions and consequences are maddening.

"Are you finding it's not so easy being a leader?" Jenna asks. I consider knocking her out, but then I realize she's not joking; she's genuinely concerned. I nod and raise my hands; palms open in surrender.

"Help me. I know this is my fault because of what I said to Ana. But, please, help me. Tell me what to do."

"First, I think we should stop with the blame. We can't blame Ana for all of this, and we can't blame you for being emotional," Eric states with conviction. "Who knows what each of us would do if we were faced with your predicament?"

Eric and Emily lock eyes for a moment, and I know they just communicated something to each other. I feel a pang of jealousy. Sam and I were close. Not close enough to communicate mentally, but sometimes we understood what the other was thinking without needing to ask. Oh, Sam. Please be okay. Then my thoughts turn back to Ana. I was so hard on her. Mom was right, Ana has seen so much devastation—more than Mom could even imagine (I think). I just made it worse for her.

"Plan. We need a plan. I mean, we can't just go out there all willy-nilly."

"Willy-nilly? Ana would never use those words."

Okay, now Jenna is making fun of me. Again, I consider knocking her out, but Jeremy must have seen my expression because he steps between us.

"Zac needs to be out there. We still have some of the humanity stuff left, right? We'll take what we have with us and work on more when we get back here. We might not even need it."

"True, but we must be prepared," Sara adds.

"Right." Jeremy looks at everyone. "If it's necessary, let's make sure we don't use a splintering stake on Ana."

"Oh, God," I groan. I do *not* want to think about having to stake Ana. "Fine. Good. We're all set? Got the elixir, Jeremy?"

He gives me a brisk nod and checks his stakes diligently.

"Then let's go find our leader." I turn to Zac. "Think you can find her?"

"Yes. And she's struggling, Amanda."

The concern shows on his face, which makes me nervous. If he can sense Ana's struggle, we might be too late to help her.

"Let's hurry."

CHAPTER SEVENTEEN
"YOU HATE ME."

Anala

*K*ill him.

    The thought echoes like a mantra in my mind. I feel like two different people are fighting for control - or maybe the monster within me is trying to dominate the human side. I still hold Trey's neck in my hands, and my foot is pinning Malik to the ground. Although I doubt he can get away, since I'm fairly certain his leg is broken.

Oh, how my teeth ache to sink into Trey's neck flesh. My mouth waters at the thought of drinking the warm blood, alive with Trey's life force. My heart begs to seek revenge. And it fears losing itself. How can one part of me want two opposite things? But isn't that how it always was? Part of me wants to die, to be done with this long, long life. The other part wants to give in and do what Amanda asked—to turn against Sam. To have him in my life—part of me—forever.

The thought of Sam, lying helpless and broken in his hospital bed, brings back the rage, and I bare my teeth, ready to give in to my hunger and need.

"Ana, no!"

My head snaps back at the sound of Amanda's voice. I shake it, knowing she wouldn't be here. She hates me and blames me for Sam. I bend my head toward Trey again.

"Anala, please? He's an innocent. This isn't you."

I'm startled when Amanda comes into view. I furrow my brows in question and tilt my head.

"He is not an innocent." My rough voice unsettles me; I can only imagine what it's like for my Hunters. No. Not my Hunters. Not anymore. "These two are the ones that hurt Sam."

A collective gasp sweeps through the group, and I can almost see the same struggle in their eyes that I feel inside.

Amanda shakes her head, then walks over to me, resting a hand on the forearm of the hand holding Trey.

"It explains why he couldn't fight back. He would have killed them if he had. It wasn't what he wanted." She squeezes my arm. "This isn't what Sam would want, Anala."

"It is what I want."

"Think of your humanity, Anala. If you do this, you could lose yourself."

"Sam is gone. You hate me. I have already lost everything."

"I don't hate you. Please, release him. We'll call the cops. That's what Sam would want."

My grip loosens slightly, but I don't let go of Trey. I fix my gaze on Amanda, trying to determine if she's truthful or if I'll see the hatred I saw earlier.

"I don't hate you, Ana," she whispers. "I am so sorry for what I said to you."

I glance at the others, seeing nothing but concern and understanding in their eyes. It's as if they expected this from me. Am I the only one who didn't realize how dangerously close I was to losing control?

"We have the elixir here." Zac eases his way toward me, clearly trying not to make me feel threatened. Or maybe he knows that my plan was to eliminate all of us Cursed Ones. He's wise to be cautious. I'm not sure I've changed my mind about that. "Take it, Anala."

I shake my head, declining the bottle. There is only a little left, and I have no way of knowing if the Blood Orchlips are ready. Besides, if I want to carry out my plan, I certainly don't want my humanity to get in the way.

"Anala, this isn't you." Zac forgets about being cautious and walks up closer to stand in front of me, next to Amanda.

"Perhaps it is, Zac."

"No." Jenna joins them, followed by the others.

It strikes me as a bit strange that I still hold the man responsible for Sam in my grasp, while my Hunters gather around me, trying to tell me this isn't me.

"Listen to them, lady!"

"I would keep my mouth closed if I were you," Amanda snaps. "I mean, I'm debating whether to let someone else hurt you, just not Ana."

"Ana?" Trey manages. "He mentioned you."

Brass Knuckles Trey is either incredibly stupid or believes that by engaging with me, I might let him go. Unfortunately for him, telling me that Sam mentioned me while he was being beaten did not make me want to free him. My fingers tighten, and Trey gurgles as I effectively crush his larynx.

"Ana, stop. I'm begging you. Sam is dying. You should be there."

Amanda's words cut me deeply, and depression takes hold. Too exhausted to try anymore, I let go of Trey. He sputters and tries to scramble away, only to be caught by Zac.

Do you want me to kill him?

Zac's voice echoes in my mind, somehow piercing through my despair. I pause for a moment, meeting his stare. Finally, I shake my head almost unnoticed. Yes, I want them dead, but I can't risk Zac's humanity, as I feel it's barely hanging on.

"Ana?"

I face Amanda, noting the sadness that matches my own. She reaches out for my hand, but I can't take it. I know I'm letting her down. But how do I reconcile creating something I am sworn to defend against? And that's just a lie I am telling myself. Truth is, I'm scared. What if I change Sam, and he turns out to be like

Thomas? If I have to kill Sam, it will devastate me. I won't be able to live with that.

Amanda tilts her head and studies me. If I didn't know better, I'd think she could read my mind or sense what I'm thinking as much as Zac can.

"You're scared, aren't you?"

Startled, I just stare at her. I remind myself that she can't read my mind, but she's close enough to guess what I'm thinking.

"Yes."

"Afraid he'll turn out like Thomas?"

Again, her astuteness astounds me.

"Yes."

Amanda takes my hand, this time not giving me an option. "I can understand that. I promise you, if it turns out to be that way, I...I will be the one to correct it."

"You cannot do that."

Relief flashes across Amanda's face, and I assume it's because the roughness in my voice before was fading somewhat. Maybe my humanity isn't lost after all.

"I can. If I can ask you to do something like this, I can make that promise to you."

"You think he will be fine."

"I hope." She squeezes my hand. "It's all I have, Ana. If you let him die, I will not only lose him. You will not be able to live with his death. You will want to die, as well. Don't do that to me," she finishes in a whisper.

I can't do this. That thought runs through my mind, and it makes my feet stop just before I reach Sam's door.

"Amanda, I don't think I can do this."

Amanda's shoulders fall. She was so sure I was going to do this that my hesitation now is deflating.

"Is there something else you're scared of?"

"I've never willingly turned anyone before. I don't know what I'm doing."

We'll be here with you, Ana," Emily says softly, touching me briefly. The others nod in agreement, and I realize they all hope I will help Sam. We've become a close family, and the thought of losing one of us is almost impossible to accept. I should have been ready for this possibility after they refused to let me kill Zac.

I lift my chin towards the room. "Are your parents still in there?"

Yes, but I can persuade them to go to the cafeteria with me. They haven't eaten anything since..." Amanda looks at me expectantly. "Will you?"

I pause, but only for a moment. I know I'm going to do it. I'm not sure if I want to, but I will. Will he still be the Sam I fell in love with? Will he resent me? I know Sam and I touched on the subject, but we never discussed it in detail. I'm not confident that his claims of wanting me to change him were genuine, or if it was just because he was jealous of Zac's bond with me. Taking a deep breath, I square my shoulders.

"Yes."

"Ana, you're back." Mrs. Logan approaches me with open arms. She wraps me in a warm hug, and I am surprised by how fragile she looks. It's as if she's trying to channel all her energy and life into Sam.

"I'm sorry I ran, Mrs. Logan."

"I understand, dear. You've been through so much. I imagine this is difficult for you."

"That doesn't excuse my behavior."

Mrs. Logan waves her hands in dismissal. "You're here now, and that's what matters."

"Mom, why don't you and Daddy come with me to get some food. You haven't eaten or rested for a while now."

"We want to be here, Mandy girl," Mr. Logan offers Amanda a sad smile.

"I know, Daddy, but Mom needs some food. And I think it would be nice if we let Ana have some time with Sam."

Mr. Logan narrows his eyes at me. Apparently, he still doesn't think that Sam and I are a good idea. I'm starting to doubt he's going to give me any time alone with Sam.

"Russ, darling, let's go with Mandy. I could use a little time away from the room."

Mr. Logan's reluctance disappears at the look in his wife's eyes. "Of course, dear." He begins toward the door, but suddenly stops and approaches me. "I was surprised to discover you and Sam were together. But, well, I trust Sam's decisions, and if he chose to be with you, I'm sure there's a reason. Sometimes even I forget how young you are." He places a hand on my shoulder, and it trembles slightly. "You're good for him."

With that, he extends his hand to Amanda and Mrs. Logan. Amanda takes it, looks at me once, then follows him.

"I'll be right there," Mrs. Logan calls after them, then comes to Sam's bedside, leaning down to kiss him motherly on the forehead. She turns to me after patting him on the cheek. "I trust you," she whispers. "Don't let him leave us."

"Mrs. Logan?" I call after her, knowing she sees the question in my eyes. She only smiles and walks away. Damn. Could my lover's mother know what I am? And could she really be okay with our relationship and what I plan to turn her son into? I shake my head, not wanting to delve into that particular thought before doing what I came here to do. Silently, I close the door and walk to Sam's bedside.

Chapter Eighteen
"WHY WON'T YOU LOOK AT ME?"

"**I** have no idea what I'm doing, Sam," I whisper close to his ear. "If this isn't what you want, please forgive me. Don't hate me."

I'm almost afraid to touch him. His face is so badly beaten that I hardly recognize the man I love. I wonder if he feels pain. Can he sense my presence? Does he have any idea what's about to happen to him? He's in a coma, and many believe that those in a coma can hear you if you talk to them. I'm not sure I believe that, but I hope Sam can hear me.

Once I turn him, his appearance will start to shift back. He shouldn't be here when that happens. The hospital staff will never understand that. Damn it. I should have thought this through more carefully. How am I going to get him out of here without raising suspicion? We're on the third floor of the hospital. It's entirely possible to go out the window, but that won't explain Sam's disappearance. And what about his parents? Do we let them believe Sam died? Would Mrs. Logan accept that? For all I know, she might already know exactly what I am and expect me to help Sam. All these questions are overwhelming me even more than I already am. I slump heavily into the chair next to the bed.

"Ugh. What do I do, baby?" My quiet question is, unsurprisingly, answered with silence. It is so quiet that the buzz of my phone startles me.

We didn't really think this through, did we?

I almost laugh at Amanda's text because she must be going through the same questions I am.

No. I don't know if I can MAKE everyone forget Sam was here.

Technically, I *could* compel anyone who came in contact with Sam, but that's time-consuming.

Can you compel my parents? Make them forget anything happened to Sam?

Well, there's a solution. I smile at Amanda's suggestion, wondering why I didn't think of that.

I could, yes. But I think your mom knows something.

Amanda takes longer to answer this time. I wonder if she's freaking out or asking her mom. Surely, she wouldn't do that.

Are you serious?

Okay, so she's not asking her.

Yes. She told me she trusted me. And not to let him leave us.

Holy sh*t!

I chuckle at that. Amanda isn't one to cuss. Apparently not even through text.

What do I do? And, why didn't we discuss this before?

Because we're stupid? And desperate.

Sigh. Well, I can just do it, and then deal with whatever we're faced with. I texted Amanda that exact "plan".

Guess that's how it'll have to be. I'll tell the others to prepare. Then another text comes through immediately after. *Does Dad know?*

I take a moment to consider what Mr. Logan said to me. There was nothing to suggest he knew what I now almost definitely believe Mrs. Logan knows.

I don't think so. Prepare the others. It will be done soon.

I slip my phone into my back pocket and concentrate on Sam. Standing, I take Sam's face in my hands.

"Please don't be like Thomas." I kiss him gently on his swollen lips, then turn his head to expose his neck. With a deep breath, I change, feeling the familiar ache in my eyes and teeth, then sink those teeth into Sam.

This sensation is unlike any other time I have fed from Sam, even though the intimacy remains. I feel a sudden pain in my head, arms, and legs, and I realize I'm absorbing Sam's injuries and pain. Then comes the intense connection, as if our souls are merging. I briefly wonder if that's really happening before the fierce protectiveness over Sam floods through me. My hands grip his shoulders, holding on as a wave of pure love washes over me. This can't be what happens to everyone who is turned. I can't imagine Thomas feeling this way about those he has turned. It must be because I was already in love with Sam.

The entire process of biting Sam and initiating the change takes no more than a minute. However, it feels much longer than that. To me, it seems as though my teeth were connected to Sam for hours. I step back in wonder when I finish, watching the transformation begin immediately. Bruises fade, and with my heightened hearing, I can hear bones snapping back into place. Sam stirs, and I hold my breath. This is the moment of truth. When he opens his eyes, I will know the full effect of this change.

Before I can understand what is happening, the door crashes open, and Zac is there with a feral look on his face. He locks that violent stare on Sam, and I automatically move to protect Sam.

"Zac!" I hold my hands out to block an attack. Something must be done fast. It wouldn't be good to draw attention to Sam's room now. I'm sure the nearly breaking down of the door was enough to raise concern. "Do something!" I hiss at the others who ran in after Zac.

Jeremy tries to restrain Zac, but he's knocked away like an annoying gnat. Jenna, Eric, and Emily try again and manage to turn him away from Sam, but only for a moment. When he turns back to pounce, Sara steps in front of him and drives a stake into his chest. He drops immediately, and the only sounds are the heavy breathing of the others in the silence.

"What the hell was that about?"

"I don't know," I say, looking at Jenna, whose eyes are so wide they resemble saucers. "Get him out of here before someone comes in and finds us like this. I have to figure out what to do with Sam."

Jenna gasps then. Emily covers her mouth in disbelief, and Jeremy, Eric, and Sara all stare. I'm almost afraid to look at Sam, because that's who they're staring at.

"Anala?"

I close my eyes at the sound of Sam's voice. My heart is pounding painfully in my chest, and I force myself to stay calm.

"Go," I tell the others quietly, and wait until they're gone before turning. "Sam."

"What... am I? Did you?"

He is understandably confused, but I can't resist the wide smile spreading across my face. His voice is... well, it's Sam. I can only nod in response, unable to trust my voice. I realize I'm avoiding his eyes, looking everywhere else instead. I can't bring myself to look directly at him yet.

"I don't know if I feel different. Are you sure?"

I'm sure.

His breath catches at the sound of my unspoken words. A distant noise from the hall pulls me back into the perilous situation.

"We need to get you out of here. We'll never be able to explain your...miraculous recovery."

"I don't feel any pain." Sam lifts his hand to his face.

"Sam, baby, we can talk about this all you want *after* we get out of here. But, right now, we *have* to go." I look around quickly, trying to find something that Sam can wear. But he wasn't supposed to recover, so, of course, there are no clothes. "Come on."

I grab his hand, and though I want to kiss him, hug him, and just make sure everything is really okay, I resist and pull him towards the door. I sense someone coming, no one familiar, and I push Sam against the wall next to the door.

Stay quiet.

He nods, and I wait for the stranger to pass or enter the room. Naturally, they are heading to Sam's room, probably to check on the commotion caused by Zac's confusing outburst. I step into the hall to greet the uniformed man. Security. Perfect.

"Good evening," I greet sweetly.

"Ma'am."

I judge him to be in his thirties, and he kind of stumbles on the word as if unsure whether 'ma'am' is the proper term for me.

"I was called to come and check out a disturbance." He points to Sam's door.

"Oh? No disturbance here. He's in a coma. Are you sure it was this room?"

His brow furrows, and he pulls out a small notebook from his shirt pocket. He flips it open and examines it.

"216," he reads, glancing at the number next to the door. "This is it." He steps forward, and I place a hand on his chest.

"Like I said, there was no disturbance here," I reiterate, putting power into the suggestion. "Go back and tell them everything is fine."

"Right." He turns back the way he came and disappears down the hall.

It's clear. Come out and follow me. Keep your head low.

Sam steps out, squinting at the brighter light. I steal a quick glance at him but keep my eyes away from his face. I'll handle the changes I know I'll see in him when we're alone. For now, I just wish I had time to find scrubs or something else to replace the hospital gown.

"Let's just hurry," he murmurs, and I realize he knows what I'm thinking. I grab his hand and rush toward the staircase. No way we're risking the elevator.

I grope for my phone as we rush down the stairs, making sure to listen for others. I pause when we reach the ground-floor exit.

We're almost out. I'll come back to fix things here once he's safe. Bring your parents to the estate.

I put my phone back, not waiting for an answer, grab Sam's arm, and tentatively open the door.

We're going to make a run for it.
You're faster than I am.

His thought makes me smile.

Not anymore.

I estimate the distance to the hospital exit, considering the number of people at the nurses' station - three that I can sense. I'm glad it's late. If we time it right, when the nurses are busy talking or doing something else, we can dash by unnoticed.

Ready?

Sam squeezes my hand, which rests on his arm. I interpret that as a yes and pull him along, as we become nothing but a blur, fluffing up papers and making it seem like the doors are opening on their own.

We don't stop until we reach the shadows of the trees lining the side of the hospital. I push him against a tree and turn back to check if we've been followed or noticed.

"If you're going to keep pushing me against things, I'm going to insist you do something more to keep me there."

The seductiveness of Sam's voice startles me, and honestly, if I could blush, I would be beet red right now.

"Hush."

His deep chuckle makes my lips twitch.

"Why won't you look at me?"

I feel his fingers thread through my hair, and he tugs lightly to get me to face him.

"Not here. Not yet. Please?"

I hear the desperate plea in my voice, so I know Sam does, too. He stops tugging but keeps his fingers tangled in my hair, resting his hand on my shoulder.

"What now?"

"Now, we make our way to my...damn it!" I shove away from Sam, realizing only now that I don't have my car here. When the others found me, I had returned here—reluctantly—with them. They already left, hopefully heading back to the estate with Zac. "I'm going to have to call someone to bring my car. You'll go back with them while I fix things here."

"I want to stay with you."

"You can't, Sam. You're supposed to be in a coma, broken and dying. If you're seen walking around without a scratch on you... Well, there's no explaining that."

"I'll stay here. In the shadows."

"Too risky," I say, pulling out my phone again. "Go back to the house and wait for me. Then we'll talk."

"And, you'll look at me?"

I hesitate as I tap the call button. "Yes. Then I'll look at you."

CHAPTER NINETEEN

"WIPED."

It takes longer than I expected to completely remove any trace of Sam from the hospital's system. And a vast amount of compelling. Doctors and nurses who were aware of Sam's case needed to be "wiped." I just hope that anyone else who had briefly seen Sam wouldn't remember or think that the poor, beaten man had died. My next stop is the station where Sam works. I managed to convince his superior that it wasn't Sam who was found severely beaten, but someone who had stolen his wallet. An email is sent out to inform Sam's colleagues of the mistake and that the suspects have been caught. Obviously, I would have felt much better if the "suspects" had met an untimely and especially brutal death. But apparently, my humanity matters more.

I hope, damn it, that my efforts are worth it. It might have been easier to let everyone believe Sam had truly died. But Mrs. Logan's pleas not to let Sam leave us stop me from making that choice. Besides, I'm genuinely curious about what she knows.

Wearily, I walk through the front door of my home hours after Sam drove off with Eric and Jenna. They had driven my car there for me, then took a reluctant Sam back with them. But even when he wasn't there, I could still feel his pull. It was almost as if he were still standing right beside me. I would catch myself looking around to make sure he hadn't ditched Eric and Jenna and come back to me—such an odd feeling, but almost comforting too. For the first time in my long life, I feel like I belong to someone. I no longer feel alone in this world.

Being in the same house as Sam intensifies those feelings tenfold. All I want is to find him and make sure he's really okay. But I have Zac to deal with. I don't understand why he suddenly lost his mind—or his humanity. With a deep sigh, I step away from the door and head toward the holding room where I assume my Hunters have put Zac.

You're home.

Sam's voice in my head causes me to stop my course to Zac.

Yes.

I am in your room. Come to me?

It's not a demand, but an almost uncertain question, and suddenly, I want nothing more than to go to Sam.

After everything Sam and I have shared, I find it hard to believe that I am actually nervous to see him. Six hundred plus years of living have prepared me for almost anything. Except this. I've never been in love, and I've never intentionally changed anyone. Damn it. *Just go in there. What are you expecting?* Well, that's the thing, isn't it? I don't know what to expect. What if I can't look Sam in the eye? I know his eyes will be different. They won't be the beautiful golden brown I've grown to love. No, now they'll look like mine, and every time I look into them, I will remember how Sam lost his life because of me. Yes, he's still here, but this isn't really living. He won't be a detective much longer because he won't be able to stay in one place for extended periods without drawing suspicion. And he won't be able to grow old, have children, or grandchildren. What have I given him? Immortality? A false promise. It doesn't really exist. He can still be killed. Cravings? Oh, yes, that's something to be proud of. He'll yearn for blood, and it will hurt if he doesn't get it. What I have given him is a life full of death. A life of watching everyone he loves die around him, until he completely shuts himself off because it's just too painful to do otherwise.

You've given me a life with you, Anala.

Sam's voice in my head startles me. I've been standing outside my bedroom door for the past five minutes, trying to talk myself into going in. With his words, I gather my courage and walk in.

"And, one hundred, two hundred, *five* hundred years from now, do you think you'll still be happy with that? Will you be content living your life with *only* me?"

"Yes," he answers simply.

Easy for him to say now, just a few hours into being Cursed. Does he really think that a life such as this suddenly isn't lonely because of *one* more person?

"We have Zac." He's in my head, and I have no idea how or if I can keep him out. I wonder if I will be able to read his as he is reading mine. I wonder if I'll ever find out, because I seriously cannot, for the life of me, stop my mind from just blubbering on.

"Zac doesn't want to live like this. Now that Thomas is dead..."

"Thomas is dead?"

Oh. Right. Sam doesn't know everything that transpired while he was... missing.

"Yes. I killed him."

He reaches for me, curling his fingers around my bicep. "Are you okay?"

"Yes." I avoid eye contact — I still haven't found the courage for that — but I can feel him watching me. "I felt nothing, Sam. Not for him."

Sam is quiet for a moment, and I can "hear" him contemplating my words. This will definitely be interesting in the years ahead. No way we'll be able to hide anything from each other. I suppress a laugh, thinking couples everywhere probably wish they could read each other's minds. That is, of course, until they hear something they really didn't want to know.

"Will you look at me, now?"

He stands in front of me, gently placing a finger under my chin and lifting it. I let him do so, not resisting, but keeping my eyes closed until I feel him stop. Slowly, I open my eyes, realizing I am so close to Sam, our breaths mingling. I force myself to look into his eyes, managing to hold back a gasp at what I see reflected back at me.

"I'm so sorry." I reach up and stroke his cheek with my fingertips. He peers down at me, his eyes as translucent as mine, the blood red border a sickening contrast.

"I'm not."

"Sam, you don't know..."

"I know what's important," he interrupts. "I'm going to be with you."

I pull away from him, running a frustrated hand through my hair.

"You'll resent me for that."

"No, Anala, I won't."

I turn back to him, studying him. "Anala?"

He shrugs. "That's how I think of you now."

I recall that Zac had said the same thing to me. I guess it makes sense. The cursed part of me is the one they are bonded to. Surprisingly, though, I'm not sure if I like Sam calling me Anala.

"You will resent me, Sam," I repeat. "Years of this, of being Cursed, will wear you down."

"You seem to have handled it just fine."

I ignore his words and concentrate on his voice. Sam sounds perfectly normal. I can't get over it. His humanity still seems fully intact. It makes me wonder why his humanity remained that way, while Zac continues to struggle. And that thought takes me back to Zac's outburst at the hospital.

"What happened? With Zac at the hospital?" Sam explains, noticing my questioning look.

"Sam, I love you. I do. But can we make a deal that you will stay out of my head unless I invite you in?"

Sam gives me a slight smile. "I can't exactly control it, baby. But I'll work on it. I promise."

I nod, unable to stop the smile forming on my lips. "Zac lost control. Tried attacking you."

"Why?"

"I don't know yet. We staked him." I pause, letting Sam absorb that. He's going to have a lot to deal with in the next few hours. I can't imagine it will be easy. "We'll have to handle him later. I'll text Blaise and see if the Blood Orchlips are ready before we... wake him. Right now, we need to focus on your parents."

I chuckle at Sam's muttered expletive. It's definitely not a laughing matter, but the look of pure terror in his eyes when facing his parents is somewhat amusing. He's scared of *that*, not of being a monster.

"How the hell are we going to explain *this*?" He asks, gesturing at himself.

"Compulsion? At least for your dad."

"What does that mean? Did something happen to mom?"

"No! No. She seems to be more...knowledgeable of what I am."

"Impossible."

"I would have thought that, too, if she hadn't basically told me to 'fix' you." Sam plops heavily onto the bed. "You're kidding."

"Nope."

"They're here?"

"Yes. Amanda has them in the parlor. She texted me to hurry because your mother apparently wants a tour of the place."

It's Sam's turn to chuckle. "Sounds like Mom. How did Amanda get them to leave the hospital?"

"Let's go find out."

"Your father is going to need some...help with this, Amanda."

"Yes, ma'am."

I hear Amanda pause, and I know what her next question is going to be. Since I am curious about that myself, I slow down, grabbing Sam's arm to keep him with me. I put my index finger to my mouth, signaling Sam to keep quiet. Okay, so technically I could have told him telepathically; I just need to get used to all of this.

"Mom, what do you know?"

"Enough."

"That's not an answer. Please, Mom, I need you to tell me exactly what you know."

"Amanda, honey, I've read the journals."

Whether the gasp I hear is mine, Sam's, or Amanda's, I can't tell.

"You went into my room and read... my journals? What happened to privacy?"

I barely hold back a laugh that bubbles up. Amanda is more upset about the invasion of her privacy than her mom knowing I am a vampire. Priorities.

"You and Sam have been acting so... odd lately. You won't discuss it with me. I needed to do something."

"So, you read my diary?"

"Technically, aren't they Ana's? Or does she go by Anala?"

This time, I know it's my gasp.

"Why are you so nonchalant about this? I mean, we're talking about vampires." Amanda whispers the word. *"What makes you believe all of this?"*

"I... don't know, really. I think I've always known there was something different about Ana. She certainly doesn't strike me as a typical eighteen-year-old. You and she are completely different."

"Thanks a lot," Amanda mutters.

"Oh, honey," Mrs. Logan laughs. *"I didn't mean that as a bad thing. I want you to be a kid. Somehow, I don't think Ana had that opportunity. And, now, you seem so much different than just weeks ago. It makes me sad."*

"Don't be sad, Mom. I finally feel like I'm doing something worthwhile. It's about more than just me. Ana has...helped me find me."

"I can see that. But this is so dangerous. Just look at what happened to your brother."

"Mom, Sam is a cop. This could have happened to him with or without whatever is going on out there."

"Of course you're right. I just hope Ana can help him."

And that's my cue. I motion for Sam to stay put until I can gauge the situation.

"Mrs. Logan?"

"Ana." Mrs. Logan turns to me, and I notice a hint of apprehension in her eyes. She wonders if I succeeded in helping Sam, I'm sure. "Please, I think we're past formalities. Call me Donna. Besides, I believe it is you who is my elder if I am to understand the journals correctly."

I flick a glance at Amanda, then offer a smile to Mrs. Logan. "Donna. I must say, you're quite calm about all of this."

"Well, I was just telling Amanda…"

"She knows, Mom. Ana can hear from miles away."

"Amanda is exaggerating," I say at Donna's surprise. "A little."

I take Donna's arm and guide her to the floral print settee, gently encouraging her to sit down.

"Donna, are you sure you understand everything that's happening? Are you certain you're ready to understand?"

Donna nods, but the look in her eyes is anything but confident.

"Where is Mr. Logan?"

"I persuaded him to take a nap. Ana, I don't think Russ is ready for… this. I read in the journal that you can do things to make people forget?"

As much as Donna wants to believe what I am, her brain is still telling her that it's too impossible to be true.

"I can make Mr. Logan forget what happened to Sam. In the same way, I managed to make the hospital personnel forget. And the police." I take Donna's hand in mine. "Do you want me to make you forget as well?"

"No," she answers immediately. "You helped him?"

"Yes."

"Can I…see him?"

Sam? Are you ready?

I think so.

I nod at Donna, glancing at Amanda. I wonder if she's ready to see Sam this way. Well, we're about to find out.

Come in.

I can feel Sam's hesitation. But then he walks into the room, straight to me. I'm not sure he is ready for his mother's reaction. Frankly, I wasn't.

Chapter Twenty

"Oh my God!" Donna makes a move towards Sam, then stops and turns on me. "I thought you were going to *heal* him!"

"I-I did." To say I am confused by her reaction is an understatement. I did as she asked. She has her son.

"You didn't heal him, you *changed* him!"

"Mom."

Donna spins around, fixing her glare on Amanda. "Did you know about this?"

"Of course I did. Mom, you said you understood."

"What I understood was that Ana was going to heal Sam. With her blood. I read in the journals that her blood is a healing agent. She *turned* him into a...a monster."

"Mother, stop." Sam's voice is low, but not menacing. He didn't want to scare her. "I am not a monster, nor is Anala."

"It's okay, Sam. I understand her concern." I take a breath and face Donna. "Mrs. Logan, Sam's injuries were too extensive for just a drop of my blood. I did what I had to do."

She stares at me, and I wish I could read her thoughts. Perhaps she hates me now. Maybe she regrets trusting me with her son.

"Is he... what happens now?"

Sam steps forward gingerly, not wanting to scare his mother. I should have thought to give Sam Papa's elixir that would restore his eyes to normal, or at least closer to normal. It's definitely next on my list. Especially when Mr. Logan is ready to see Sam.

"Mom, I'm still me. Anala didn't do anything that I didn't want. I love her. I want to be with her. Forever. I'm not sorry she did this."

I feel as if a boulder has been lifted from my shoulders at that moment. Sam hasn't seemed upset by my decision to change him, but hearing the actual words did wonders for my guilt. Hearing the truth in those words meant the world to me.

"But...I guess I just don't understand what you will do now. Your eyes..."

"I have something that will help with that," I try to reassure her.

"Will it work before Russ sees him?"

"Yes. It's instantaneous. I should have thought to give it to him before you saw him."

"No. I think— I think I needed to see him like this." She takes an audible breath and tentatively lifts a hand to Sam's face. "I miss your eyes."

I know exactly how she feels. Tears gather in my eyes when Sam closes his eyes, takes his mother's hand, and places it over his heart.

"My eyes may be different, but in here, I have not changed."

A small sob escapes Donna as she hugs Sam tightly. I glance at Amanda and see that she's openly crying. Quietly, to avoid disturbing Sam and Donna's moment, I move toward Amanda.

"Are you okay?" I whisper.

She nods. "I didn't think about his eyes. It's kind of creepy." Her hand quickly goes to her mouth, as if she just realized what she said. "I didn't mean anything by that."

I laugh softly. "It *is* kind of creepy. Imagine seeing your own eyes like that for the first time." I glance at Sam, and he catches my gaze for a moment. "I'm not sure he's looked in a mirror yet. It may hit him hard."

"He has been looking into yours for a while now; maybe he'll be used to it."

"It's not the same," I smile. "But I hope it helps."

"What are we going to do about Zac? I heard what happened."

Sigh. "I don't know. I wish I knew what happened. I can't feel him, though that may be because he's...not awake. I need to call Blaise."

"I did. She has a few Blood Orchlips ready. I was going to pick them up in the morning."

Surprised, I turn my full attention to Amanda. She shrugs and blushes slightly.

"I thought we were going to need it with you after what I said."

"What did you say?"

Sam's question surprises us both. I didn't realize he was paying attention to us.

"It doesn't matter, Sam."

"It matters to me. What did you say, Amanda? Did you hurt Anala?"

I feel Amanda bristle beside me, and I reach out to take her hand.

"She was scared for you, and I deserved it." I shoot Sam a look that stops any response he might have and turn back to Amanda. "Don't take it personally. Our bond is much stronger now. He has an innate need to protect me."

Amanda shrugs again, but I can tell Sam's accusation hurt her. He's her brother, and they were close. But now his connection with me is stronger than we ever thought possible. Sam clearly saw Amanda's bruised ego and wrapped his arms around her.

"I'm sorry, Mandy bear."

My lips twitch at the nickname. I've never heard Sam use it before. In fact, the first time I heard anyone call Amanda Mandy was when her father said it at the hospital.

"It's okay. I shouldn't have said what I said. I was wrong, and I can't apologize enough," she finishes in a whisper, glancing at me.

"Do I want to know?" Sam asks, looking first at me, then at Amanda. Donna, I notice, hasn't said anything else. She just keeps watching Sam silently, as though he might, at any moment, attack her or Amanda.

"No," Amanda and I say simultaneously.

"Mrs. Logan..."

"Ana, dear, I thought we were past the formalities."

She works so hard to make her voice sound normal, but the subtle crack doesn't go unnoticed by me.

"Right, I'm sorry. Donna. I'm going to take Sam and give him something that will change his eyes. If you're ready, you may bring Mr. Logan here to the parlor. I'll come in and...visit before bringing Sam in."

"Will it hurt him?"

"No. I would never hurt him. Or you."

She looks at me for a long moment before she nods. "I will bring him."

With that, she turns and walks away without saying another word.

"This isn't going to be pleasant, baby."

We're in the bathroom, opening the cabinet where I hide my stash. I unlock the box filled with vials and select the one I need. When I turn around, I notice the smile on Sam's face.

"What?"

"I like it when you call me baby," he answers quietly, his voice holding a hint of flirtation.

"Hush."

He chuckles softly, reaching up to stroke my cheek. "Why haven't I noticed how embarrassed you can get? It's adorable."

"You haven't noticed," I say, playfully pushing his hand away, "because you never used to be this... seductive."

Sam's eyebrows shoot up. "Seductive? Hmm. I suppose I do feel a bit..."

"Stop!" I laugh as I put my hand over his mouth. I know exactly what he wants to say. Hell, I feel the same way. We just don't have time to explore those feelings. "Later. For now, I need you to take this," I murmur, handing him the vial.

Sam looks at the liquid warily. "This stuff has to be way past its expiration date."

"Is that a dig at my age?"

He laughs heartily, and I admit I'm happy to hear it. Not only does it confirm his humanity is intact. It's also sexy as hell.

"Of course not, baby. Just a comment."

"Mmhmm. Drink."

I step back, knowing this will be the first time Sam will change. And it hits me that he hasn't been hungry. In fact, he was very calm and in control with Amanda and their mom.

"They gave me blood," he says softly.

This time, my eyebrows shoot up. "They did?"

"Yes. Well, they showed me where it was, then sort of disappeared. I haven't seen them since they dropped me off."

"I'm sure they're just giving you space to get used to all of your changes."

"Or they're scared of me." He smiles, but I notice a hint of sadness.

"They're not afraid of you. They've been okay with Zac. But they also realize it's a big change. Zac isn't managing it as well as you seem to be. They're just being cautious."

"I suppose you're right."

"So, you fed?" I ask cautiously. I'm a little disappointed, wishing I could have been there for him the first time.

"Actually, no." His eyes soften, clearly having read my thoughts. "I'm hungry, and I did open a bottle. But I was afraid of what might happen if I actually...drank it. So I waited."

"And yet, you still didn't feel an urge when you were around humans?"

"I believe I did. But the fear in Mom's and Amanda's eyes made me feel that all I wanted was to reassure them I wouldn't hurt them."

I think back to when I was changed and the turmoil I felt. The pain of hunger, the need for blood. Even the sensitivity of my eyes and feeling nauseous. I study Sam. He's obviously much stronger than I was. He's definitely taking this extremely well.

"I think it's because I've been anticipating it."

Again, he speaks to my thoughts, and I narrow my eyes at him. "What did we say about being in my head without my permission?"

"Sorry." He grins sheepishly. "Still have to work on that." Sam takes a breath, eyeing the vial again. "Bottoms up," he says, tossing the liquid down his throat.

He grabs the counter, hissing in pain. His grip is so tight that the granite flakes onto the bathroom floor.

"Jesus," he grunts. I know his eyes are burning like hell. His teeth are throbbing, and he feels as if he's burning from the inside out. I wish I could take his pain away—pain that I can feel myself, though not as harsh as he feels it. But he has to go through it and let the elixir do its job.

Sam bares his teeth, and a growl from deep within him comes to the surface.

"It will be over soon, I promise."

"It...hurts."

"I know, baby. Just a little longer. Hold on."

Perspiration dots his forehead, and he breathes deeply. In through the nose, out through the mouth. His heart is pounding so hard in his chest, I can hear it. I see the vein in his neck pulsing, and I try to will the elixir to work faster.

"It's...getting...better."

Each word seems like a struggle for Sam, and I desperately want to reach out to him. But he needs to get through this. I reassure myself and him that he will be okay. Finally, his heartbeat slows, and I see him lift his eyes to look in the mirror. He stares at himself, seeing himself as Cursed. Instinctively, I know this is the first time. Then, he begins to change back. Sam's eyes shift to a warm, golden brown, leaving behind the translucent eyes of a Cursed One. They're not exactly the same, but they're close enough to make me smile.

"There you are."

He looks at me through the mirror, the corner of his mouth tipping up. "Now, I'm hungry."

I consider making Sam wait until after his meeting with his dad to eat, but then I quickly decide that's probably not the best idea. If he's hungry now, especially after the change, it's better to feed him. I scold myself for not thinking to feed him before he used the elixir, and I hope it won't interfere with the effects.

"Ready?"

"Yes. It's something I will have to get used to, right?"

I nod, handing him the bottle. I hate this part. I hate knowing that Sam will now be dependent on blood.

"Go slow," I say as I watch him bring the bottle to his lips.

"Smells good," he states, then looks at me. "That's one thing I really enjoy about this change."

"The smell of blood?"

"No. Your scent. It's...intoxicating."

I can't resist moving closer to him. "Now you know what your scent does to me," I whisper.

He clears his throat, but I see his eyes darken. Interesting that desire can still have an effect, even on Cursed eyes. And, of course, that leads my thoughts in a very specific direction.

"If you want me to feed and then meet with dad, you have to stop thinking that."

Sam's voice is hoarse with longing, and I struggle to resist the urge to focus only on us.

With a deep breath and extreme willpower, I back away.

"Feed."

With his eyes still on me, he tips the bottle, tasting the blood for the first time. Both of us were prepared for the change this time, and he heeds my warning to go slow.

"Will we be able to feed from each other?" he asks before taking another drink.

Again, if I could blush...

"I don't know." And I don't. I'm almost nervous to find out. If feeding on Sam was intimate before, I can't imagine what it will be like now. Or what it will be like to feel him feed from me. Hell, we may very well kill each other.

Sam laughs and drains the rest of the bottle. "It'll be fun finding out, don't you think?"

"Out of my head, pal."

"Mr. Logan, it's nice to see you again."

"Ana." He studies the room around him before looking at me again. "Quite a place you have here."

I shrug. "Family estate," I say simply. "How are you feeling?"

"Guilty." He smiles sadly at my questioning look. "My son is lying in a hospital bed, and I came here to take a nap."

"Russ, dear, you needed to rest."

Mr. Logan pats Donna's hand but says nothing. Donna looks at me, pleading for me to help ease her husband's guilt. I nod slightly and shift my focus to Mr. Logan.

"Russ," I begin, using his first name to show familiarity. "Sam was never in the hospital. Nothing happened to him. It was a case of mistaken identity. Someone stole Sam's ID. But your son is fine."

I notice Mr. Logan's eyes glazing over. His exhaustion makes him more vulnerable to my compulsion.

"You are here to visit with your kids," I continue, "who are both alive and well. Do you understand?"

He nods and smiles.

"*That's it?*" Donna whispers to Amanda.

"*That's it,*" Amanda whispers back.

Sam?

At my beckon, Sam walks in. Donna's smile is broad, and she looks at me.

Thank you, she mouths. I nod, then watch Sam and his dad hug and slap each other on the shoulder. The rest of the Logans' visit was a blur. I am exhausted, and I can only imagine how the rest of my Hunters feel. Especially Amanda. But she is a trooper, and the others made it a point to give us space. I send up a silent thanks for their intuitive absence. Their time with the new Sam will come soon enough, as will having to deal with Zac.

But what am I most afraid of? Being alone with Sam, without anything demanding our time. I wasn't joking about possibly killing each other with our desire.

Sam chuckles from across the room and raises his eyes to meet mine.

Out.

He laughs again and winks.

CHAPTER THIRTY-ONE
"WE CALL OURSELVES ENFORCERS."

"**A**re you really afraid to be alone with me?"

"Sam, we *really* need to discuss boundaries."

Sam approaches me, stopping just before making contact.

"We're not going to hurt each other."

"And you know this because of the extensive experience you've had being a vampire and making love with another vampire?"

Sam blinks and then bursts out laughing. He doubles over, holding his stomach, gasping for air.

"I'm glad you find this so very funny," I mutter.

"Baby, I have about as much experience as you do. But I'm willing to give it a try." He wiggles his eyebrows mischievously. He grins, taking my hand. "Look, I know this is new for both of us. So, we'll take things slow. In fact, we don't have to do anything."

"It's not that I don't want to... be with you, Sam. It's just that we have a lot going on at the moment. I don't know if I can deal with..."

"It's okay, Anala. I understand." Sam kisses me lightly on the lips, and it literally takes all my willpower not to deepen the connection. "And I agree."

A feeling of relief—and disappointment—falls over me. Of course, I'm glad Sam understands. And, yes, I'm overwhelmed by everything happening. But, damn, I really want to know what Sam and I are going to be like now.

Soon.

Sam's voice inside my head makes me smile and shake my head. Add to the list: have Sam meditate and learn to stay out of my head.

"These are beautiful."

Amanda places the Blood Orchlips on the table next to me, sticking her face in them to give them a sniff.

"Careful," I murmur. "They're poisonous."

Amanda immediately steps back. "Nice of you to tell me." She rubs her hands on her jeans, glaring at me.

"You're fine," I laugh. "As long as you haven't eaten any."

"But, if they're poisonous –"

"To humans," I clarify. "Of course, when the medicine men used them back in the day, whatever they combined them with counteracted the poison. In turn, the poison became somewhat of an antidote."

"Like using snake venom to counteract the effects of a snake bite?"

"Exactly."

We are in the kitchen, and I've made a makeshift lab with all of the ingredients Papa used for the humanity elixir. Sam and Amanda's parents left long ago, and the others have ventured out of their respective rooms. I know they're curious about Sam, not having spent much time with him the night before. But, to their credit, they don't ask questions; they simply wait.

They all surround me now, even Sam, and it is incredibly...normal.

"We still have some elixir. Can't we wake Zac up with what we have?"

I raise my eyes to Jenna. "You saw what he was like at the hospital. Do you honestly believe that what we have is enough?"

Jenna looks chagrined, and I know she thinks I am dismissing her.

"No, Jenna. I'm asking for your honest opinion."

She blushes slightly with embarrassment as the others look at her. "Oh. Um." Jenna considers her response, glancing at the others. "No. I suppose not. He was pretty...irrational."

"You call that irrational?" Jeremy laughs. "He went insane."

"I'm inclined to agree with Jeremy's description," Eric adds. "His eyes went completely wild before he crashed into Sam's room."

Sam is sitting at the table, quietly listening to everyone. At Eric's words, he stands up and walks closer to me.

"Did he want to hurt me or Anala?"

I realize then that I never questioned who Zac was after. I just assumed that he was after Sam, and I instinctively moved to protect him. I know the others are wondering the same thing now, as they all look to each other for answers.

"We're not sure," Eric says finally. "It all happened so fast, we just reacted."

"I don't want you near him," Sam states matter-of-factly. When I look at him, I realize he is talking to me. The absurdity of that almost makes me laugh out loud. But it is Jenna who speaks up before I can say anything.

"Sam, I'm sure Ana is more than capable of handling Zac."

Sam glares at Jenna, anger flashing in his eyes. Awesome. I need to step in before things escalate. I put my hand on Sam's forearm.

Don't. Then aloud, "You're right, Jenna. I can. But I'm also afraid of hurting him." I turn to Sam. "And I'm terrified that the two of you will kill each other. So, *I* don't want *you* near him."

"Then how do you want to do this?" Amanda asks, ignoring Sam's low growl.

I mix the ingredients, following Papa's instructions carefully, while glancing up at Amanda briefly.

"He is my responsibility." I raise my hand to stop Sam's disagreement. "I won't argue with you about this. Not only am I Zac's true Maker, but I'm also his leader. *Your* leader. It is my responsibility to do everything I can to keep you all safe. Or make the tough decisions if your safety is at risk."

"Ana, you don't have to be the only one those decisions fall to," Emily interjects. "I think we've proven that we can handle..."

"Emily, I have no doubts about your abilities. *Any* of them. But if I have to decide to...end Zac's existence, I don't want you to have a part of that."

"Why shouldn't we?" Amanda asks quietly. "He's our friend, Ana. He's not just your Hunter, or you Hybrid."

I look up from my task and observe them. When I was out hunting—losing myself and my humanity—they stepped in. "You're right. We should all make this decision together. I will administer the elixir and remove the stake. After that, we will see what we need to do."

I shake the vial, hoping it works. I'm definitely not a chemist, and the one of us who was good at science is currently staked. My nerves threaten to take over. If this doesn't restore what little humanity Zac was holding onto — well, I don't want to think about the consequences.

I watch my Hunters through the thick window of the holding room. "I will give him the elixir now. Then, we'll wait before removing the stake. Hopefully, that way it'll give the liquid time to absorb into the bloodstream, and he won't be able to fight it."

"Do you think he would? Fight it?" Emily asks, her gaze never leaving Zac.

"I don't know. But I'd rather not take the chance." I tilt Zac's head back, wishing I had an IV bag or something that would make this easier, even though his skin would make it impossible for a regular needle to penetrate. Sigh. Well, back to pouring it down his throat.

"Do you need help?"

I consider turning Sara down but change my mind. I nod and wait for her to come in. I catch Sam's eye, noticing the concern.

It's okay. We won't remove the stake now. We'll be fine.

With Sara's help, I pour the elixir into Zac's mouth, coaxing it down his throat. At least he's not conscious to feel the pain the elixir causes, I think. I watch, ensuring all the liquid has gone where it needs to go.

"Now, we wait."

"For how long?" Sara asks.

"We'll give it the night. Tomorrow, we'll take the stake out and see...what awaits us."

Sam wraps his arms around me, pulling me close. It's our second night together, alone, and we're still sticking with our agreement to wait. With Zac's future uncertain, we can't justify exploring the depth of our...bond. Of course, we're taking a risk just sleeping in the same room, but Sam seems to think we're strong enough to resist the urge. Feeling his arms around me, his heartbeat beneath my ear, I'm not sure I agree. I feel his body shake, and I know he's laughing.

"Sam," I warn.

"I haven't had time to work on how to stay out, baby. Sorry."

He clears his throat, and I sense his hesitation.

"Is something wrong?"

"I talked to Amanda. Actually, I talked to all of them today."

"And?"

"They're very...accepting."

"Did you expect anything less?"

"I-I'm not sure. I guess I expected Amanda to at least look at me differently."

Our fingers are entwined, and I allow myself a moment just to feel the connection.

"They know me, Sam. They've gotten used to seeing a...vampire among them."

"You, yes. But...I'm Amanda's brother."

169

I think about that and how Sam is handling his transformation. He's unlike any Hybrid I've ever seen, including myself. He's not consumed with thirst, nor is he in pain. Hell, if I hadn't seen him change before my eyes, I would think he was completely normal. Maybe that's why the others are finding it easier to deal with this. They were scared when Zac was changed, but they begged me not to kill him. Still, their guard was never down when around him. His fragile grasp on his humanity kept that in check. But their interactions with Sam are, dare I say, comfortable—like they can sense he's not a threat.

Still, I wonder if the other proverbial shoe will eventually drop. I just don't understand why Sam is so...different.

"Maybe it's you," he says quietly.

"What do you mean?" I ask, ignoring his trip into my mind. He's right; he hasn't had time to learn how not to do it, so I will have to be patient with him.

"You turned me." He shrugs as if that is the answer to everything, and I should understand what it means.

"Yes, darling. I do recall that," I say sarcastically.

He smirks, and I hear the word 'darling' rolling around in his head.

"I'm just saying, maybe my humanity is still intact, and I'm...fine, for lack of a better word, because you love me. You didn't turn me to make an army, or even just to create another one like you. You turned me to save my life. We're in love." He shrugs again. "Maybe that's the difference?"

It's definitely an intriguing theory, and I haven't had any experience with it. I make a mental note to talk about it with Amanda tomorrow.

She has definitely grown a lot, hasn't she?

"Yes, she has," I reply to Sam's silent question. "More than I ever imagined. I don't know what I would have done without her."

Sam tightens his arms around me, pulling me closer. Honestly, sticking to the 'take it slow' agreement is extremely difficult. Sam, of course, reads my mind and lifts my lips to his.

"Maybe we should..."

CHAPTER TWENTY-TWO
"I MAY JUST STAKE YOU."

"Ana!"

The intense panic in Amanda's voice wakes Sam and me right away. I'm glad I'm wearing something decent to bed because I don't think to change. I just run to Amanda with Sam right behind me.

We rush into the training room just seconds after Amanda screams for me. Yes, screams. I've never heard her sound so terrified before. Not even when she was yelling at me while Sam was in the hospital. We find her and the others standing next to the holding room, and my steps falter. A flood of thoughts races through my mind in a split second, with the most dominant being: I messed up on the elixir and killed Zac. I force myself to keep going, suppressing my doubts.

"Amanda, what's wrong?" I keep my eyes on Amanda, not looking in the room. I will hear it from her first.

"Z-Zac is gone, and Emily..." her words trail off as she points into the holding room.

I steel myself before following her aim. Emily lay in front of the silver chair that Zac once occupied. Blood is drying on the side of her neck, and her heartbeat is faint.

"Is she?"

"She's alive." I touch Jenna briefly on the arm as I pass her.

"But if she's been bitten..."

"Zac is a Hybrid, Jeremy. He doesn't possess the power to turn anyone."
I kneel next to Emily, and though I can hear her heart beating, I check for a
pulse. "The fact that Emily is still alive tells me that Zac hasn't entirely lost
his humanity."

"How can you say that?" Eric yells. "My sister is lying there, dying!"

"She's not dead, Eric. That's how I can say that. If he had been lost
completely, she would be dead."

I pick Emily up easily. I believe that even if I weren't cursed, I could still
lift her; she's so tiny. And that's what worries me. Zac may not have drained
her, but it was close. The others follow me into the parlor, where I gently
place Emily on the couch.

"Can you heal her?"

"She needs blood," I say absently as I examine her neck.

"But I thought you said she wasn't turned!"

I turn to Eric, my brows furrowing in confusion. Oh. He thinks I mean...

"No, she needs a transfusion."

"Can't you just give her some of your blood?" Jenna asks.

"It is not my blood she needs. Zac drank quite a bit. She needs to
replenish that blood."

"So, what can we do?" Eric asks, his voice quiet again.

I weigh my options quietly. If we wait for her blood to replenish naturally, it could take weeks for Emily to recover. A transfusion, however, would
shorten that to hours. That means I would have to go to the hospital for
equipment and blood. Still, Emily might be able to tell us if Zac said anything
to her, or maybe why she decided to remove the stake in the first place.

"Transfusion," I decide aloud. Sam nods in agreement as the others look
at me questioningly. "It's the fastest way for her to recover and tell us what
happened."

"Okay, but how do we go about doing that?" Amanda asks. Her body
still trembles. Sam must have noticed as well, so he went to her and put his
arm around her.

"I'll go to the hospital and get the supplies. We'll set it up here where we can keep an eye on her."

"Do you know how to do that?"

I smile at Sara. "You learn a thing or two after a few centuries. Especially if your father was a chirurgeon."

After my trip to the hospital, which I had to convince Sam not to accompany me on, I have everything I need to set up a transfusion drip. Eric watches me intently. He doesn't know the technicalities of what I am doing, but he seems to approve of my ability.

"How long will it take?" he asks over my shoulder. Eric is so close, his breath tickles my ear.

"A little room, please?" I murmur, as I continue my preparations. "It'll take a couple of hours."

"What should we do while we wait? Look for Zac?" Jenna asks. She gathers her blond hair, twisting it back into a ponytail. The gesture gives me a good look at the expression on her face, and I note the sincere concern.

"We wouldn't know where to start. If we could wait until Emily wakes up, maybe she can give us some insight."

I finish setting up the drip and brush Emily's ebony hair off her forehead. *I'm so sorry.*

"Anala, this is not your fault," Sam says softly.

I stand and face Sam, guilt and anger battling for the lead in my mind.

"If not mine, then whose?"

"Bernard is the one who brought them here. Blame him." *Or your father.*

My eyes widen, and I gasp at his silent claim. "Are you saying Papa should have killed me?"

"Sam!" Amanda exclaims, instinctively knowing he said something to me that the others could not hear.

"No! Of course, that's not what I'm saying, baby! But he did... create Cursed Ones," he finishes in a whisper as if he's sorry he has to say it.

The anger dissipates at Sam's genuine shame, but the grief remains. I'm quiet for a long moment, considering my next words.

"I don't know if I believe that," I finally say, cutting through the uncomfortable silence.

"But Bernard said..."

"Bernard hated my father, Jeremy. I can't believe anything he said."

"Ana, your father's own journals say the same thing," Amanda reminds me.

"I know that's probably what he thought." I gesture to the sitting area next to the colossal, marble fireplace. "Let's talk about this."

I wait for the others to settle in around me. Part of me wants to go out searching for Zac, hoping with everything I am that he isn't doing anything foolish. Like killing people. But I know our best option is to wait for Emily. So, we'll discuss my theory.

"I have known Hunters my entire life," I begin. "People who were incredibly talented at what they did, who were born with this innate power. I never once questioned it, as I thought it was a normal thing. I was born with it. Why would I question whether others were? However, reflecting on it now, people who came from other countries were the same age as Papa. If Papa had been the one to create Cursed Ones, how were these Hunters born with this power? Wouldn't it stand to reason that Cursed Ones had been created long before Papa?"

Amanda stands suddenly. "Wait!" She rushes out of the room, and I listen carefully, expanding my hyper-hearing to follow her. I hear her rummaging around her bedroom, whispering 'Got it' before hurrying back. She flips through the journal she brought with her until she finds the page she wants. "I think you may be right, Ana. I didn't think much about this before you mentioned it. But here, your father writes about using a common mixture among other medicine men. If that is really what caused someone to be Cursed, maybe it had been used before?"

"Exactly my thoughts. It helps explain why we had Hunters coming from everywhere. Like your family, Sara, who traveled from Spain. Thomas and his family arrived from Ireland. All ages, all stages of training."

"But why did they flock to your parents?" Jenna asks.

"That's what I'm trying to figure out," I admit. "From the time I was born, my parents were the leaders. I knew nothing different. Unfortunately, my parents were murdered before I learned that story."

"I may have a theory," Amanda interjects shyly.

"Please."

"Wasn't your father seen as something of a magic man? Like a wizard?"

I smile. I fleetingly wonder if Amanda had put as much effort and interest in school, she would be graduating at the top of our class.

"Yes. However, I didn't learn that until after I had been turned. I heard Mum and Papa talk about using magic to cure me. And you think that's why people flocked to them?"

"Well, I think your father was working on a... cure before you were changed," Amanda flips through another journal. "He says, 'Having Anala with Cursed Blood now will perhaps give me more success with the cure.' Maybe word got out that he was... magic? You also said that he and your mom had unmatched abilities. Of course, there's you. We all know that you were immune to the worst side effect of being Cursed."

"I'm not immune." I look her in the eye, knowing she remembers just days ago when I almost lost that battle. "And your theory is good, but at this point, we may never know what the truth is. The more pressing issue now is determining if there are indeed more Cursed Ones out there. I may have eradicated all of those in my land - that I knew of - but I never wondered if they existed anywhere else."

"Did Bernard's journals say anything about others?" Jeremy asks, and we all look at him in surprise. "He's the one who brought Cursed Ones here. He must have known where Hunters were?" he shrugs.

"The journals list all Hunters who were under Henry Geil's leadership. If Bernard brought them here to locate the Cloaked One, he could have traced the lineage of those closest to the family, which would have led him here," Amanda responds. "However, there are no other places mentioned."

"So, we try to find them ourselves," I announce and turn to Sam, who has been quietly watching— as always. "Can you check the databases of various authority organizations and see if there are any similar cases you would consider unexplainable?"

"Other police departments, maybe, but I wouldn't have clearance to go any deeper than that."

Sigh. He's right. And I want to avoid raising any red flags, so direct questioning is out.

"Anyone good with computers?" I mumble, wondering if I can find someone discreet to hack into government computers.

"I am," Jenna says softly.

I blink at her, unsure whether to laugh or scold her for not taking this seriously.

"You don't believe me, do you? What? You were expecting maybe Eric or Emily?"

My eyes widen, completely surprised by both her accusation and genuine hurt. Although I have to admit, I did expect the Asian stereotype over the bimbo cheerleader. God, I'm terrible.

"I'm sorry, Jenna." I flick a glance at Eric. "I did expect Eric over you."

"I know nothing about computers," Eric admits. "Well, other than social media."

I turn my attention back to Jenna, giving her an apologetic smile. "Forgive me?"

She shrugs, but I notice the faint grin. I take that as a yes, since I'm about to ask her to do something highly illegal. Damn. I hope Sam forgives me as well.

"Are you good enough to hack into government systems?"

She raises a blonde eyebrow. "I suppose I deserve a bit of doubt, since I haven't been exactly forthcoming with everything. But, after this, if you ask me again if I'm good enough, I may just stake you."

CHAPTER TWENTY-THREE
"GOOD LUCK."

I laugh outright at Jenna's statement. "Deal. What we will be looking for are any crimes that, basically, defy human logic."

"Can I pop my gum while I'm hacking?" she smirks. "Or will you fire two warning shots - at my head?"

I laugh, again. "Got some culture, did you?"

"I watched the movie," she answers without even a flicker of a smile. But I see the amusement in her eyes.

"If you find us a trail, you can pop your gum all you want," I grin. "Do you have everything you need?"

"For systems that complex, I may need something more than what I have."

I nod. "I'll give you my credit card. You can shop for what you need."

Jenna's eyes brighten.

"Do *not* go clothes or shoe shopping," I warn.

"I'll go with her," Jeremy volunteers. "I won't let her buy anything she doesn't need."

"Who says I don't *need* new shoes?" Jenna mutters. "What's the limit on the card?"

"There is no limit. But still, don't go crazy. Get what you need and come back. Jeremy, watch her carefully."

I shake my head at both of them, noticing a hint of shyness when Jeremy glances at Jenna. Seems like spending so much time together is bringing my Hunters much closer than I thought possible.

I send them off and leave Eric with Emily. Sam, Amanda, Sara, and I head to the training room.

"So, if there are other Cursed Ones out there, does that mean there are more of us?" Sara asks, then looks at Sam and me. "Hunters, I mean."

"It would stand to reason."

"It's so strange to think there are more of us out there." Amanda walks over to the weapons cabinet and opens it. "I wonder if they're as well trained as we are."

I take a moment, just a small one, to feel pride at Amanda's statement. True, we haven't had much time together, and training was rushed. However, I am more than impressed—and completely happy—with their progress. It's almost unbelievable how quickly they picked up skills that some Hunters took years to learn. I also wonder if there are others out there and if they have been training for much longer.

"Is that why you wanted to train now?" I ask Amanda, distracted by my thoughts.

Amanda snaps me out of my reverie by hurling a sword at me as her reply. I'm grateful for my quick reflexes, catching it just inches from my face. She grins at my raised eyebrow, daring me to retaliate. Oh, she wants a fight? She'll get one.

"Where is my other sword?"

"What's wrong, Anala? Do you need two swords to compete with me?"

Both Sam and Sara snort with laughter, and my mouth twitches, but I hold back the smile. Instead, I give Amanda a mock scowl, releasing my sword with one hand, while inviting Amanda to fight me with the other.

She crouches, contemplating her moves. Unfortunately for her, I notice the nearly imperceptible glances to my left and right. Even more unfortunate for her, I can read Sam's thoughts, and I realize the three of them are signaling for a group attack. I nearly crack a joke about how I can't have two swords, but she can have three people, but that would ruin my advantage. I stay focused on Amanda, but my ears catch every move Sara and Sam make behind me. Do they truly think they can move quietly enough that I won't hear them? I hear Sam chuckle softly, and I figure out their plan. He's trying to read my next move so he can somehow relay it to Amanda and Sara. Pssh.

Good luck.

The three of them lunge at me. At that very moment, I jump to the rafters above me, swinging my legs up and over until I am standing on the five-inch-wide board. To my surprise, Sam followed me up and is now standing in front of me, balancing quite easily.

Think you can beat me?

Sam smiles mischievously.

You have to admit, I have a better chance now. And perhaps it'll help us release some of this pent-up...energy.

My balance wavers slightly at his seductive words. Damn him, he's playing dirty. It isn't the first time, and I highly doubt it'll be the last. He tries to exploit my wobble, but I'm already in motion, flipping backward on the beam and landing smoothly on my feet.

Ah, ah, ah. You've tried that before. Fool me once...and all that.

Sam laughs out loud, and Amanda grunts below us.

"Sam! You're supposed to be helping *us,* not playing inside her head!"

I hop beams, dropping lightly behind Amanda. "Boo!"

"Damn it!" Amanda pivots, swinging her sword towards my head. It takes a backbend worthy of the Matrix to avoid the blade, but I do it. Thankfully.

"Is this a training session, or are you really trying to rid me of my head?"

"Sorry! That was totally instinct!"

"Mmhmm." I smile at Amanda's expression of shock. "It's fine, you did very well." I bump her shoulder when she continues to pout. "Let's keep training. Sam, you spar with Sara."

Don't pout. We'll spar again... soon.

I wink at Sam and focus back on Amanda.

"How is she?"

After sparring and a quick shower—without Sam, because I really don't trust myself in that situation—I check Emily's IV. Two bags are gone, and she still hasn't woken up.

"No change," Eric mutters. "You're sure this will work?"

"Yes. Her vitals are stronger. Resting is good for her." I place my hand on Eric's shoulder, squeezing lightly. "Talk to her. Let her know you're here."

He nods sadly and begins murmuring softly to Emily. I step back quietly, giving them their space. Jenna and Jeremy should be home soon with whatever equipment Jenna needs—and probably a lot of gear she doesn't. Note to self: think twice before giving a teenage girl a credit card without a limit. I stop thinking that way when I realize I'm underestimating Jenna again. I'll wait until she gets back to judge her.

I don't have to wait long, as Jenna and Jeremy waltz in with boxes of equipment.

"Grab Sam, we could use some help," Jenna calls over her shoulder as she sets boxes inside the door and heads out for more. Great. Can I start judging her now?

Sam? I need you.

About time.

Down tiger. I just need your hands... arms... damn it, I need you to help bring in the boxes.

Even in my mind, I can hear Sam snickering. Fantastic. I hope we find Zac soon, because taking it slow with Sam is becoming increasingly difficult every day.

"My thoughts exactly." Sam smacks my ass on the way out the door, making me yelp.

"*I made it more than 600 years without someone smacking my ass,*" I mumble, and follow him out. I try to block him out of my head when the thought that I enjoyed it stubbornly fights its way out. There's no need for him to know that. Yet.

"You really *needed* all of this stuff?"

Jenna pops her gum deliberately and looks at me. "Yes," she responds with a bored and annoyed tone.

I wonder if Jenna invented 'bored' mixed with 'annoyed.' It seems to be her go-to. Let it go. Let it go. Let it go. I repeat this to myself, reminding myself that I need her to do this for me. I'm having her set up the system in the den, which I haven't used in years. Oh well, a little dust won't hurt anyone. It really is a great room, I think, as I look around. One expansive wall features built-in bookshelves filled with books I've collected over the centuries. Some are first editions of classics that are priceless. And, of course, there are some that will never be classics, but are great entertainment. A colossal stone fireplace is the focal point of the room. The beautiful mantle made of reclaimed wood holds trinkets from around the globe, but no photos. In fact, there are no photos at all in my home. I do not need pictures to remind me of those I have lost.

The massive mahogany desk is more than sufficient for Jenna, even with all the monitors she insists she needs. The rest of the den is sparsely but tastefully decorated with a buttery-soft, taupe leather couch and a plush cream rug that I used to love sinking my bare feet into when reading.

"It's nice in here."

I turn to face Jenna, noticing the sincerity in her eyes as she looks around. "Yes."

"Why is it closed off all the time?"

"It's not closed off; it's just not... used."

"But, why?"

"There's no special reason, Jenna. But you're in here now. Use it to its fullest. Just be careful with some of the books in here. They're priceless."

Jenna sat in the high-back leather chair behind the desk, spinning once. "Yeah, sure. Great chair."

"How long do you think it will take you to get some information?"

Jenna shrugs. "Depends. I can hack into the systems pretty quickly, but the actual search might take longer. I'm going to assume you want me to sift through everything we know couldn't possibly be a vampire."

"Yes. We'll be looking for drained victims—whether it's a broken neck or other bones. Full bloods are usually more discreet, but if Hybrids are involved, the killings will be especially gruesome."

"Got it. And I'm looking all over the world?"

"Yes. Anywhere you can get in."

She gives me an arrogant smirk, letting me know without words that she can get in wherever she wants.

"I'm going to check on Emily to see if she's awake yet. Let me know if you need anything. If we get a lead on Zac, I'd like you to stay here and keep working on this."

"Fine with me. I don't relish the idea of having to watch Zac being staked again."

I leave Jenna without telling her that I'm not sure if staking Zac will work this time. Zac is determined to die. If his humanity has been as compromised as I believe it has, I may not have any other choice but to kill Zac.

CHAPTER TWENTY-FOUR
"COME HOME."

"Zac? Where is Zac?"

Emily's already soft voice is now a mere whisper, but I can hear the panic as clearly as if she were yelling.

"Emily, what do you remember?"

She studies the IV in her arm, not answering me right away. Then, as if she suddenly had a revelation, she whips her head around and glares at me.

"What did you do to him?"

"Emily, Ana saved your life," Eric tells her softly. "Zac almost killed you."

"He wouldn't do that."

"He did," Eric reiterates harshly.

I step up, placing my hand on Eric's shoulder and giving it a gentle squeeze. The last thing we need right now is for the talented brother-sister duo to be fighting.

"You took the stake out?" I ask Emily, knowing the answer but needing her to go through what happened.

"Yes."

"Why?"

"Because it's not right to keep him like that!" she spat.

"I was doing it for his own good, Emily. Do you think I wanted to do that?" I try reigning in the ire I feel creeping up to the surface.

"You gave him the elixir. He was fine."

"Was he? Is that why we found you almost drained of blood and Zac missing?"

She blanches at my grim words. "He's missing? You didn't...kill him?"

I meet her gaze, noticing the fear and regret.

"We found you unconscious, and Zac gone. Do you remember anything at all?" I ask, purposefully ignoring the last part of her question.

"I just remember taking the stake out, and he looked at me." She hesitates as if she's trying to remember. "Then he just lunged at me. I don't remember anything else."

"Why didn't you stop him?"

I know my words sound accusatory, but I believe Emily could have easily stopped Zac.

"I couldn't hurt him."

"Jesus, Emily, he almost *killed* you!"

The others stand quietly, listening to our exchange. They know better than to get in the middle of this.

"He didn't," she answers, lifting her chin in a challenge.

"You're lucky," I retort. "And you were incredibly stupid."

"Ana."

I pierce Eric with my stare. "It's true and you know it, Eric."

"How do you expect us to kill one of our own, Ana? She hesitated. You would have, too."

"No. I wouldn't have. The *only* reason Zac is alive is because all of you begged me."

"Then why did you turn Sam?" Emily sneers. "Or is it only your feelings that should be considered?"

I can almost feel my blood beginning to boil. Even with my anger, I know what she's saying is justified. I did change Sam. I can tell myself I did it for the team, but I know deep down it was a selfish choice. Guilt, anger, worry, and 600 years of repressed emotions hit me all at once. I feel the change taking over without my permission.

Anala, calm down.

Sam's voice in my head does nothing to stop the change that I can't seem to control. Eric stands in front of Emily, who is still lying on the couch. Amanda, Jeremy, and Sara follow suit, ready to protect Emily from me if needed. Only Sam comes to me, reaching for my hand. I can feel his calmness flow through me, even as I sense the change happening in him. He would fight with me, not against me, despite the fact that he would be fighting his own sister. The thought is incredibly sobering. I look at my Hunters in utter shock.

"*I am sorry,*" I whisper, before running.

Knock. Knock. Knock.

Yes, I'm being a coward and hiding in the meditation room. I'm trying to pretend that I'm using this time to connect with Zac, but honestly, I can't concentrate. I can't believe I lost control. I haven't had trouble controlling my change since I was first bitten. Sigh. There have been too many damn changes lately.

Knock. Knock. Knock.

"Go away."

"Ana, let me in."

"Go away, Amanda."

I hear whispering, but other than the fact that I know it's Sam out there with his sister, I block out the words. Since I don't want to deal with what's going on out there, I turn my thoughts inward. I focus.

Zac?

Although there's no answer, I can feel him resisting. The same way Thomas did.

Zac, enough of this. Come home.

No home. Comes the rough reply. It startles me enough that I nearly break the near meditative state I am in. What's left of his humanity is fading quickly. If I can't reach him soon...

Too late.

A sense of dread washes over me at Zac's words.

What have you done, Zac?

I will him with everything I have to answer me.

Kill me.

Shit. That is not the answer I want to hear. If he has hurt an innocent, I cannot allow him to live.

Where are you?

Zac doesn't answer me directly, but I sense his surroundings. A familiar place, and if Zac gets what he wants, perhaps it is the most appropriate place.

"I know where he is."

Sam is immediately at my side when I open the door.

I heard.

I give him a nod, then turn to the others. To my surprise, Emily and Eric are there.

"I am sorry. I would love to say I would never have hurt you, but I could not even control the change."

Emily approaches me, and I notice her color has improved, but she still appears weak.

"I don't believe you would have hurt me," she says matter-of-factly. "Just as I don't believe Zac would have."

"But he did." I remind her. "The only way we know that he still has an ounce of humanity is that you're alive."

"That's something, right?" Sara asks hesitantly.

I feel Sam's hand on the small of my back, and I draw strength from the gentle gesture.

"I wish I could say yes. But I have heard him. His humanity is…" I meet Emily's scared eyes. "He is losing," I finish softly.

"Has he…has he killed someone?"

"I do not know."

"So there's still hope." It isn't a question, and Emily puts every ounce of conviction she can into the statement. Unfortunately, it isn't as optimistic as she hopes.

"We shall see. Get dressed and meet me in the training room. Emily…"

"I'm not staying away."

"You are not well. You need to rest."

"I'm going, Ana. If you have to…I want to be there."

She can't bring herself to say the words she knows she needs to say. She wants to be able to say goodbye if necessary. I cannot take that away from her.

"Fine," I nod. "But you stay in the background. Do not make me worry about you."

After changing and checking in with Jenna to let her know where we will be, we all pile into the van. It's so reminiscent of our battle with Thomas that I can't help the shiver that runs through me.

Are you okay?

I squeeze Sam's hand in response. Of course, I'm not okay, but this is just how my life is.

Jeremy is driving, so I raise my voice enough to include him in the conversation.

"Are you all clear on what we're going to do?"

I watch them all nod wistfully. It may feel like *déjà vu*, but this time, our opponent is someone we're all close to.

"I know you all want to be close, but please, let me try talking to him. I'm hoping that our bond will help with whatever he's going through."

"Ana, what if he has Hybrids?"

I turn to Amanda and immediately wish I could make this all disappear. These kids should be focused on graduating next week - damn - not on the possibility of having to kill one of their friends.

"He cannot change anyone, remember? And my...rampage earlier either seriously depleted the number of Hybrids, or I got rid of all the ones Thomas created."

"So, he'll be alone? And we'll be ganging up on him."

Emily's voice is dripping with disdain. Her sudden changes in attitude are seriously beginning to give me whiplash.

"We're not ganging up on him, Emily. *You* wanted to be here, remember? The others deserve the same opportunity." I pause to take a deep, calming breath. "We're not here for a battle." I just hope it doesn't end in death.

Just then, Jeremy stops the van and lets out a whoosh of breath. It's the only sound he has made since leaving the estate. "Jenna should be here," he mutters.

While I agree with Jeremy, I offered Jenna the option to come with us, and she declined. I even explained what the possible outcome might be, but she still refused. Jenna made it seem like she was too busy doing something important to make the trip, but the sadness in her eyes told me she wasn't sure if she could handle it. I respect her decision. If I could skip this trip, I definitely would.

We step out in front of the faux Colosseum that Thomas used as his hideout. The same place Zac became who he is now. A full circle.

"Are you ready?" I don't ask anyone in particular, and no one answers me. They're not ready, but they'll do it. I take a deep breath and go inside to face the destiny that awaits beyond.

Chapter Twenty-Five
"I HAVE NO CHOICE."

B y silent agreement, all my Hunters stay a few feet behind me. My anxiety is through the roof, and I am hoping against hope that things won't be so bad. I already heard the evidence when I heard Zac in my head. But I still insist on ignoring my gut feeling.

"Zac?" I call out, not really expecting an answer. I hone in my hyper-sensitive senses, listening intently, trying to get Zac's scent. However, the smell I catch makes my stomach roil. *"Jesus."*

Oh, God. Is that...

Sam's voice cracks even though he says nothing out loud.

Yes. Stay back.

An eerie growl echoes through the ruined space. Zac steps out of the shadows, his face twisted with feral rage. He is in full Cursed mode. His face is covered in blood, and the red ring around his irises seems to pulse with each heartbeat.

"Zac, what have you done?"

Another growl responds to my question, but Zac is not looking at me. Instead, he's watching Sam with a look that makes my heart jerk painfully in response.

"Zac!" I try to bring his attention back to me, and it works— for all of two seconds. With his unnatural speed, he turns around and disappears inside a doorway behind him. Just as I go to follow him, he reappears, carrying a limp body with him. I don't want to believe what I am seeing. I don't want to see what

189

Zac has done. And, most of all, I don't want to do what I know in my heart needs to be done. "*Oh God.*" I reluctantly release my swords, never taking my eyes from Zac.

"Ana, no!" Emily grabs my arm, struggling to turn me away from Zac. When she realizes she can't move me, she lets go and runs halfway up the stairs between me and Zac. It's a stupid thing to do, and it definitely grabs my attention.

"Emily, stay back! He won't let you live this time. It's too late." With wide eyes, I watch as Emily draws her sword, then releases the blade and goes on guard... with me. She will fight me to save Zac. Unfortunately, I notice two problems in just seconds. First, Zac is about to attack her, and second, she is no match for me. But getting Emily out of the way before Zac reaches her will be difficult, since she's clearly willing to face me. I let instinct take over, hoping they won't let me down. I bend slightly at the knees and jump.

Zac must have taken his attention off of Emily long enough to read my actions, because he jumps with me, releasing his sword in midair. Our swords met in a violent clash, but my superior strength gives me enough of an advantage to have Zac flying backwards into the plaster of the fake wall of the faux Colosseum. He isn't hurt, but it gives me a spare, yet all too brief, moment to deal with Emily.

"He is not Zac, Emily. Do not fight me."

"I won't let you kill him!"

"I have no choice." I hear Zac coming back, and I push Emily towards the others. "If you cannot keep her in check, take her out of here."

"You have to give him a chance!"

"Emily, he *murdered* innocents!" Amanda hisses. "He's gone."

"And when Sam does the same thing, will you be just as eager to kill him?"

I stay alert, listening for more movement from Zac while hearing Emily's argument with Amanda. If I had a moment to try to reason with Emily, I would. But I have to trust my Hunters to handle their friend. I feel Zac's presence rather than noticing his approach, and I relax my stance, inviting him to attack me. I will do whatever it takes to distract Zac from the others, especially Sam.

I tense up just before impact, pulling my body into Zac's as he crashes into my stomach. The force of the blow sends us both tumbling into the Styrofoam boulders, shattering them on contact. Zac is snapping at my neck, trying to sink his teeth into me.

Anala!

Stay back, Sam! It's you he wants to kill, not me.

I'm not sure how I know this, but I am certain it is true. I also don't think Sam will be able to kill Zac, even if it means saving his own life. I use my legs to launch Zac up and over me, away from the others, then do a kip-up. He's on me again before I have fully regained my balance. His hand is around my throat, pushing me against the wall, and I allow it. I want the close proximity. I need to give Zac a last chance to prove he has at least *some* humanity left. Hell, I need that for myself. Killing Zac will be excruciatingly difficult. Even more so than Thomas. I raise my hand to stop the others' advance, who are still struggling with Emily.

"Zac, look at me." Briefly, I contemplate compelling Zac to stop what he is doing. But that won't help. He won't be Zac, but just a shell of the person he used to be. Fake humanity. I'm not even sure it would work, and if it did, I can't begin to know how long it would last. So, instead, I search his angry eyes, trying to find any semblance of Zac. I find none as his hand squeezes harder around my throat. "Stop this. Don't make me hurt you. Please."

His smile, if you can call it that, is evil. He thinks he has bested me, and it makes him bold. Either that, or the loss of his humanity has made him believe he's invincible.

"Kill Sam," he snarls, his voice unrecognizable. But it's not his voice that makes my blood run cold. It's the words—and the fact that I can't tell if he's telling me to kill Sam, or if he's planning to do it himself.

"Will you stop this if I kill Sam?"

"Emily!"

Amanda's shriek and Emily's question cause Zac to turn and loosen his grip on me. He tilts his head, seemingly considering Emily's... offer.

"Will you? Will you stop killing innocents if Sam isn't here?"

Sam is staring at Emily as if it's the first time he's seen her, and he's unsure if he can trust her. I don't blame him. She's negotiating with his life—something I cannot, will not, allow. I see Sam step back, letting go of Emily as if touching her burns him. When his hand drops from her arm, she immediately reaches for her sword.

"Emily, don't!" Eric's shout makes Emily twitch, but she keeps reaching. Shit.

She's compelled, Sam. Get away from her.

As soon as Emily releases her blade, Sam jumps from his spot to the second landing of the building. How has Zac managed to compel Emily before almost draining her? I have to snap myself out of my shock-induced stupor and take advantage of Zac's brief distraction of watching Sam. I grab his arm, spinning him around until his back is to me. I twist his arm painfully behind his back until he drops to his knees.

Emily screeches, wrenching her arm free of Amanda's grasp. "Leave him alone! Let him go!" She stops abruptly before climbing the stairs to us. Her eyes glaze over as she stares at Zac.

"Kill all. Kill you."

I can see Emily gripping her sword tighter, but she hesitates. I know she's fighting him, but I don't think she's going to win. She trusted Zac. And she has feelings for him. Those two factors make compulsion stronger.

"Emily, you are released!"

Her eyes snap to me, but I can't focus on her properly for my command to work. As I keep my attention on Emily, I don't immediately notice when Zac reaches for my sword. It's out of my hand and headed toward my neck in a flash, and I barely manage to block it by raising my own sword. The clash of silver against silver draws everyone's stunned attention.

I am going to kill him.

Sam, stay where you are.

I take a quick glance at Emily and see that the others have surrounded her in a non-threatening way. They want to show her she's still one of them, but they'll also do what they must to save themselves... and me.

"You just tried to kill me," I growl at Zac. "I am your Maker."

"His!" Zac roars back, and I know instinctively he's talking about Sam. Something happened with Zac the moment I turned Sam.

I push him roughly, and he skids across the dirt and debris. "You tried to *kill* your leader!"

"Deserved!" He yells and charges me.

I deflect his unpredictable swings with ease, but he's becoming increasingly frustrated with each miss.

"Enough of this, Zac! I do not want this!"

His response is just to snarl at me, glance up at Sam - who is practically dancing around, begging me in my head to let him come down and fight - and turn toward the others. "Kill them!" His thunderous voice echoes throughout the space, and Emily struggles in the grips of the others. It's taking my Hunters everything they have to keep Emily from hurting them, without hurting her. They grapple even harder when Zac begins to chant his order repeatedly.

Anala!

Stay, Sam. Please!

I hope against hope that I can forgive myself for what I'm about to do. Emily is struggling more and more, and I can smell blood - Amanda's and Eric's - knowing they won't be able to hold her much longer.

"Zac!"

He spins around, his eyes lacking any humanity, and charges at me. I block his swing by grabbing his wrist with a straight arm and twisting it. His wrist snaps, causing him to howl and drop the sword.

"*Forgive me*," I whisper, using his arm to spin him around. I stab my sword into the ground beside me and pull him into an unbreakable embrace, keeping his arms pinned with one hand and wrapping the other around his neck. "Bring her closer."

Amanda and the others bring the struggling Emily closer.

"Look at me." I wait until Emily's eyes meet mine, and I tighten my grip on Zac so he can't command anything more from Emily. "You are released."

Emily immediately stops struggling and slumps in Eric's arms.

"*Thank you,*" Eric mouths.

"Turn around. All of you."

"Ana..."

"Turn around, Amanda." I wait until they obey, then force Zac to his knees. *"I tried, Zac. I wanted to save you. I care about you, and I am sorry for failing you."* I force myself to wrap my hand around my sword, force myself to bring it up. And force myself to slash it across Zac's neck.

Chapter Twenty-Six

"**B**aby..."

"Not now, Sam. I need some time."

"Away from me?"

I see the hurt in his eyes, and part of me wants to do whatever I can to take it away. The other part is too devastated by what I've done to be comforted by Sam.

"Not away from you, just time. Please understand."

"I do. I know you're hurting, baby. Let me help you."

"Let us help you," Amanda says softly. "He was ours, too. You should have let us..."

"What, Amanda? What should I have let you do? Watch me kill Zac? Would that have made you feel better?" My words sound harsher than I intend, but I'm just too emotionally drained to hold back.

"You should have let us be there with you," Amanda finishes.

"You were there."

"You know what I mean. You took that on by yourself, and you shouldn't have had to."

"It was my responsibility."

"Oh, fu –"

"Ana." Jeremy interrupts Amanda's expletive, laying a soothing hand on her shoulder. "We know you are our leader, and Zac's true Maker, but we are not just a society of Hunters. We are a family. You're not alone."

195

"Oh! Hey, you're back. I –" Jenna stops in mid-sentence when she sees everyone's forlorn faces. She looks at each of us, glances at the holding room, and then I see her shoulders slump. "Oh God."

Jeremy immediately goes to her, wrapping his strong arms around her. For once, Jenna doesn't resist the affection. She holds on as she meets my gaze. I know the sorrow in her eyes is mirrored in mine, and she closes her eyes, mouthing *'I'm sorry.'* Then, just like that, I see her square her shoulders, adopting the tough façade she usually wears.

"I've found something," she announces. Her voice holds only a slight tremor, betraying her composure.

I watch her for a moment, appreciating the fact that she's trying to be strong. For me, for the others, and most likely for herself as well. Unfortunately, I'm just not ready. I know I'm not being the best leader, but I've just killed a friend. I'm doing my best.

"Tell the others. I need some time to myself."

Sam Logan

"Sam, we should really wait for Ana to be here."

I know Amanda is right, but Anala isn't even talking to me. Not that I blame her. I watched her eyes as she killed Zac. I saw the light go out, and I wish with everything inside me that I could have taken her place. I only hope I can bring that light back.

"I know, Amanda. But she needs some time, and we need to give it to her." I squeeze her bicep, effectively cutting off any other arguments. She watches me for a moment and then nods. Finally, I turn my attention to Jenna. "So, what do we have?"

"Is this cool for you to see? Like, you're not going to arrest me or anything, right?"

Jenna pops her gum at me, and I finally see what Anala finds so annoying.

"Right, Jenna. Let's get to it." I force myself to pay attention and not let my mind wander to Anala. I'm trying to give her the space she needs, no matter how much I want to go to her.

"Fine. I've compiled a couple of lists. One has the top matches for the criteria Ana wanted. The others are possibles."

I'm impressed, but I'm smart enough to keep that to myself. I doubt Jenna would appreciate my surprise.

"Where are they located?"

"Everywhere. Seriously, like, all around the world." Jenna turns back to the computer and taps the keyboard. Three monitors came to life, scrolling with information. "I went back five years just for a reference point. The weird thing is, the attacks, while still happening, have declined each year."

"Possible Hunters?"

"Could be," Jenna shrugs. "But, if there are, they're not as good as we are. Either that, or they are letting Cursed Ones live amongst them."

"Why do you say that?" Amanda asks.

"Well, because the killings haven't stopped. Only declined. So, either they haven't found all of them..."

"Or they've come to an understanding," I finish for her. She shrugs again and turns back to the computer.

"I've categorized the areas. The ones in red have the most killings, yellow has fewer, and green has only a few that are *possibilities*. Meaning, I can't determine whether these killings are what we're actually looking for."

"Can you print the list out for us?"

"Um, yeah." Jenna pauses. "Does this mean we're going on a field trip?"

"Where are the most killings?" I ask, ignoring her question.

"Ireland."

"The land of our ancestors," Amanda mutters, and I know she's thinking about Thomas. I wonder if Bernard took Thomas back to his homeland so he could start building his army. It's something we'll need to discuss with Anala. I just hope she's ready for this. I can't imagine what she's going through, but I want to be there for her.

Please let me be there for you.

"Yes. I guess Anala and I will be going to visit the Emerald Isle."

"Wait. Why only you two? We're Hunters, too." Jenna whines.

"I agree," Eric chimes in. "It can only help to have us all there."

"I wouldn't mind going to Ireland," Jeremy states, plopping down on the couch.

Sara says nothing as she observes the monitors from behind Jenna with interest. I briefly wonder what has captivated her before turning to Amanda.

"I suppose you want to go, as well?"

"Of course. You are newly turned, Sam. I mean, yeah, you're doing exceptionally well with all of this, but it's better to be safe than sorry. And Ana...she shouldn't have to deal with this by herself."

I raise my eyebrow. "She wouldn't exactly be by herself, Amanda."

"I know that, Sam. But I think she needs all of us now."

"I know. Let's just hope she feels the same way." I can already see Anala trying to take all of this on herself, not wanting to put any of us in danger. I don't think she will survive losing another one of us. But I can't allow her to be reckless. If there are other Hunters out there - even if they have an agreement with Cursed Ones - I can't see them letting Anala live. And I'm terrified she will use that to her advantage. I feel Amanda's hand resting on my forearm, bringing me out of my reverie.

"You don't think she would try..." Amanda's voice trails off, and I realize she is thinking the same thing I am.

"Of course not."

I pray that's the truth.

CHAPTER TWENTY-SEVEN
"I WILL BE STRONG, PAPA."

Anala

I have secluded myself in the meditation room, trying to calm the anger in my heart and mind. I'm afraid the only thing I've successfully kept out of my thoughts is Sam. I haven't heard him since I left him with the others. That was - I check the clock, which provides a calming tick in the room - more than two hours ago.

"*Mum, Papa, help me.*"

Nothing in my training or my years of living has prepared me for the despair I feel. I've killed many Cursed Ones without a shred of remorse. But this is different. I trained with Thomas. I spent more than three years by his side, much of that time harboring an infatuation with him. Zac and I had spent the better part of the past two years flirting with each other. I can't help but think of the night we kissed. I was going through changes I didn't understand at the time, and I wanted to hurt him, but he meant that kiss. I knew he had feelings for me before he confessed. I didn't share those feelings, nor did I feel the same infatuation I had for Thomas, but Zac was still special to me. He was my Hunter, my responsibility... mine. Even though I had been so far removed from Thomas, believing he had been long dead and hating him for what he had become, taking his life was hard. But taking Zac... how do I forgive myself for that?

"*How?*" I close my eyes and lose myself in the ticking sound of the clock and the aroma of lavender that fills the room.

Anala, age 7

"*Anala, do you know why the rules exist?" Papa asks me as he passes me a biscuit.*

My hand pauses in mid-air as I think hard about the answer. I want to please Papa, so I need to get this right. But I just do not know. I frown and bite my lip. I hear Mum chuckle, and I glare at her. It is not funny!

Papa smiles at me and puts the biscuit in my hand. "We need the rules in order to know what to do when we are faced with difficult decisions."

"But, Papa, why would the rules tell me to kill family?"

"Anala, once someone is turned, they are no longer the person they used to be. Do you know what humanity is?"

"Yes, sir. It is what makes us nice."

"Something like that, little one," he laughs. "But when someone is Cursed, they are not nice anymore, are they?"

"No, sir."

"They want to hurt others. Others who cannot protect themselves. We cannot let that happen, can we?"

I shake my head, taking a bite of my biscuit.

"So, we have rules that remind us of what we must do in order to keep those innocents from harm. Even if it means killing someone we once knew."

"Because they are not human anymore?"

"Because they cannot determine between right and wrong anymore. You were born to help those who are not as strong as you. You must use your strength to get through those times that may be the hardest for you. You must use your strength to

do the unthinkable. Even when you are faced with the impossible to comprehend. Do you understand, young Anala?"

"Yes, Papa. I have to do what others cannot because I am a Hunter. I will be strong, Papa."

"I know you will, little one." He takes my hand in his, then, with his other hand, he holds Mum's. "I believe you are the strongest of us all."

I hope to hell you're right, Papa, because the last thing I feel right now is strong. I should be with the others, finding out what Jenna has learned. I should be with Sam, making sure he's still handling this change well. He's definitely surprised me with how much of his humanity he still has. I'm not sure what to think or believe—whether it's because I love him or something completely unrelated. It certainly wasn't love that kept my humanity intact. Maybe I should just let it go and be thankful. I have more important things to worry about now—like facing my Hunters after I killed their friend. Of course, I know they understand. At least, I hope they do. Zac was too far gone to save. Killing an innocent sealed Zac's fate. And I can't help but think he knew that. He didn't want to live like this, so he made it so that I had no choice. And it pisses me off that he put me in that position.

"Why did you have to kill an innocent, Zac?" I gather my hair up, putting it in a haphazard ponytail. Meditation isn't helping me, so I have to fall back on my usual routine. I head to the gym, ready to lose myself in relentless punching and kicking. Maybe I could get Sam to spar with me, but given how I feel, that probably isn't a good idea.

It's about time you let me back in.

Sam's voice in my head startles me. Apparently, thinking of asking him opens myself to him again.

I've been worried, Anala.

I am fine, Sam. Just needed a little time to myself.

I can feel his disappointment as if it were my own, and I'm sorry for it. I don't mean to shut him out, but I honestly don't know how to handle what I've had to do.

Let me be there for you, Anala. I love you. I am yours in more ways than one now. Let me in.

I close my eyes, unable—and not caring—to prevent the tears from falling. I haven't felt this broken or lost since the day I had to burn my childhood home—with my dead parents inside. Maybe Sam is exactly what I need.

"*Come to me,*" I whisper, knowing Sam can hear me clearly. Within seconds, I hear a gentle tap on the door before Sam hesitantly pushes it open. I feel myself change, but it's different this time. The familiar aches are gone; it just feels natural. I don't have time to think about that, because when Sam sees me, he changes as well. Without saying a word, he walks over to me and wraps his arms around me.

The warmth of his embrace fills me, and I find myself crying for a different reason. I've been alone for so long, especially after losing my family, that having someone is a feeling I'm not used to. I like it. If I'm completely honest with myself, I love it. I feel Sam shift, his lips grazing my cheek before he finds my lips. I've never kissed anyone while in full Cursed mode—certainly not another Cursed One. If I thought it would be awkward, I have nothing to worry about. Just like the change this time, it feels natural.

Sam shifts again, his mouth trailing down to my throat. I can feel his tongue tentatively touching my skin. We haven't been brave enough to do this since I turned him, afraid there would be a force greater than we could control. Either we're no longer afraid, or we've lost control of ourselves. Sam pauses, and his arms tighten around me.

May I?

I nod slightly, not trusting my voice. The only one who has bitten me before is the Cursed One who turned me. But Sam isn't asking just to bite me. He wants to drink from me.

I don't want to hurt you.

I understand his hesitation. He's worried he won't know how to control what the bite does to me. Or to him.

You will not hurt me. Your body will know.

My answer seems to calm his fears, and I feel his teeth scrape against my neck before sinking in.

"Oh, God." My fingers involuntarily thread through Sam's hair, and I clench my fist, holding him tightly against me. It's the most erotic feeling I have ever experienced, and I know Sam feels it too. Our connection, our bond, deepens within us both as we fall onto the mat beneath us.

CHAPTER TWENTY-EIGHT

I left Sam sleeping in my room, where we eventually ended up after our time in the gym. His body knows he doesn't need much sleep anymore, but his mind hasn't caught up yet. And, while my body is sated, my mind can't rest.

I stand on the balcony, gazing across the vast grounds. I chose this spot for the estate because it's secluded and surrounded by acres of lawn and woods. It feels peaceful, especially on a clear, cool night like tonight. The stars shine as brightly as the dew on the grass, and I take a deep breath, hoping to find some calm in the quiet of the night to soothe the unrest in my soul.

"Are you afraid of me?"

I hear Sara gasp, clearly surprised that I know she's there.

"Should I be?"

I glance at her as she stands beside me. "I'm not sure anymore," I reply softly.

"I wish I felt it," Sara says softly, as if she doesn't want to disturb the peace around us. "I didn't know Zac well, so I can't understand what you're feeling."

"Perhaps that's a good thing," I murmur.

"You did what you had to do. They understand that."

I'm not sure if I believe that, so I remain silent. Yes, I did what I had to do. That doesn't mean I like it any more than the others do. I wouldn't blame them for not trusting me.

"How did you know I was here? Vampire," she answers herself when I shrug. "What will we do next?"

The complex answer is for when we are all together, so I give her the simple answer.

"Graduation."

"Something so trivial."

There was a hint of disapproval in her voice, and I fought to keep the anger out of mine.

"Trivial or not, it is not my intention to prevent these kids from being human."

"They are Hunters. *We* are Hunters. There are other Cursed Ones out there. *No podemos hacer nada.*"

"We're not 'doing nothing'," I retort. "Graduation is in a week. During that time, we will form a plan. But these kids, my friends, will graduate. It is the least I can do for them."

Sara gazes at me briefly, then turns sharply and walks away. Clearly, she disagrees with me.

"Do you and your brother make it a habit to eavesdrop?" I ask Amanda, who steps out of the shadows with a slight grin.

"I know your abilities. I would hardly call it eavesdropping when you know I'm there." She lifts her chin toward the spot where Sara stormed off. "She doesn't think graduating is important."

"It doesn't matter what she thinks."

"She's right, you know. After everything that's happened, I don't think any of us are really looking forward to it. I mean, Zac won't be there," she says softly.

"Which is exactly why you should be. All of you." I look back out over the yard. "I've taken too much away from you. Do something normal. Get away from here, from me, for at least a night and be a teenager."

"We all agreed to this, Ana. You didn't force us," Amanda sighs when I say nothing. "It's your graduation, too."

"I have graduated many times. High school, college. It means nothing to me."

"You would be with us this time. I mean, that has to mean something."

I nod. She's right. All the other times, I graduated with acquaintances, not friends. I never let myself get emotionally involved with anyone. When I moved here two years ago, I couldn't resist the connection I felt with Amanda. Maybe it would be good for me to be 'normal' for just a little while.

"What do you have degrees in?" Amanda asks, surprising me.

I look at her with a sheepish grin, feeling good just smiling a little. "History."

We gather in the dining room, with Chinese take-out containers spread across the large oak table. We avoid talking except for murmurs of 'pass the lo mein' or 'toss me an eggroll.' It's understood that heavy topics, like Zac or Thomas, are for another time. We will discuss plans about what happens after graduation, but nothing more emotional than that.

I immediately catch Sam's scent, and an involuntary smile crosses my face. Not only that, but memories of our time together earlier flash through my mind. I have never been more grateful that I can't blush than right then. Sam chuckles as he leans down, kisses me on the cheek, and then heads to his usual spot at the other end of the table.

"*If those smiles are any indication, I'd say...*"

"Stop." I gently kick Amanda's shin under the table as she chuckles, much like Sam.

"As I told Sam and the others earlier," Jenna begins, plopping a dumpling in her mouth. "Most of the odd occurrences are happening in Ireland."

She seems like she wants to say more, but our silent agreement keeps her from speaking. She avoids mentioning Thomas, and I appreciate it.

"Hmm. And, you found others, correct?"

"Yes. All over. But, not as concentrated as the ones in Ireland."

I notice Sam pushing his food around his plate with his chopsticks. I know he must be full after our prior encounter, but he still needs to try for normalcy.

Eat something, baby.

Sam's lips twitch, and he can't hide the smile at the endearment. He lifts a piece of chicken kung pao from his plate, deliberately placing it in his mouth. With a flick of his tongue, he licks the sauce off his lips, then winks at me when he sees I'm mesmerized by the show.

Mmm.

"I, um," I clear my throat, tearing my eyes away from Sam. "I think we should talk about next week."

"Do you really think it's necessary?" Emily asks, refusing to look my way. She's the only one who doesn't seem comfortable around me. The others are understandably subdued, but they didn't seem to... hate me. I'm not so sure Emily will ever get over what I did.

"Ana said we should do something normal. I agree. Not only for us, but for Zac, too," Amanda responds.

"I agree, too," Eric says, placing his hand over Emily's. I notice she ever so gently pulls her hand away, and I give Eric an apologetic smile.

"Let's just get this over with, then we can focus on the real problem," Sara grumbles. I want to be offended by her use of the word "problem" since she is talking about the likes of me and Sam, but I can't. She is a Hunter. And, honestly, if there are others out there like me, it is a problem. But her blatant disrespect is what upsets me. And, apparently, Sam as well.

"You will regard Anala with respect. She is your leader." His voice is steady, but his look is commanding, causing Sara to shrink back in her seat.

It doesn't take her long to recover, though, and she straightens her shoulders. Her bravado is a facade, but I don't call her out on it when she looks at me.

"So, *Leader*, will you change the code?"

"The code is in place for a reason, Sara."

"It was. But obviously, things have changed." Her eyes shift to Sam, then back to me. "Or are the rules not for you?"

"You are out of line, Sara!" Believe me, no one is more surprised than I am when Jenna stands up, glaring at Sara. "You are new to this group, so I don't think you have a right to have an opinion like that."

"She is a Hunter, Jenna," I say softly.

"So? She's been a Hunter for what, ten minutes?" Jenna snaps her fury back to Sara. "You don't know what we've been through! You have no *idea* what Ana has endured! So, yes, things have changed. And, until you've experienced even a fraction of what we've been through, keep your mouth shut and either follow Ana or get out!"

With that, Jenna tosses her chopsticks on the table and storms out, leaving us all in shock.

"Well. That was..." Amanda begins.

"Weird," Jeremy finishes, then looks at me. "When did Jenna become your champion?"

"Hell if I know," I respond, but I can't help the satisfied smile that forms.

"Emily?"

She stands at the weapons cabinet, her fingers trailing over the stakes. I wonder, briefly, if she wants to use one on me.

"I don't know if I'm ready to talk to you, Ana." Emily's tone isn't cruel, but sad. I know we're going to have to talk this through if we're going to hunt together. We need to be able to trust each other.

"I understand how you feel..."

"I don't think you do."

I hold in a sigh, but my gaze never wavers. "You really think that? Do you not think I cared for Zac? Do you not think what I had to do hurts me immensely?"

"I've known Zac for years, Ana. We had become close." She takes her sword from the case, releasing the blade with a push of a button. Instinctively, my body readies itself for combat. I also feel the tension of the others in the room. I raise my hand, silently telling them to stay back. If Emily needs this, I will give it to her.

"I've known Thomas for centuries," I remind her. "I've known Zac for the past two years. And, for the past few weeks, we were bonded. How can you not think this affects me?"

Emily turns to me, twirling her sword in her hand. "I'm not sure if you can feel what we humans feel."

Quiet gasps fill the room, but no words of protest are spoken. I hear Sam's thoughts. He wants to yell at Emily. He wants to tell her how wrong she is for speaking from her heart. I shake my head and know he's disappointed, but he remains silent.

"You don't believe I have humanity?"

"You have humanity. I just don't know if it's the same thing."

I intentionally glance at her sword, then lock eyes with her again. "Do you want to use that on me?"

Emily briefly lowers her eyes, then lifts them again to look at Eric.

"Don't do this, Emily," he pleads softly.

"I have to," she replies just seconds before swinging the blade toward my head.

I duck just in time, but she immediately follows up with a low backswing. I twist my body, my feet leaving the floor just in time to dodge the razor-sharp edge. My biggest advantage is that Emily is fighting with emotion, not her usual precise discipline. Unfortunately, that's also my biggest disadvantage. Her movements are erratic, and I'm struggling to anticipate her next attack.

Emily, being as agile as she is, counters my evasive maneuvers with acrobatic jumps, flips, and spins of her own. We both leap simultaneously, and without my swords, I have to rely on my arms, hands, and feet to deflect deadly blows. Her blade slices through my bicep with enough force to bring me to my knees.

"Emily, stop!"

From the corner of my eye, I see Amanda and Sam running toward me.

"No! Leave her!" I deflect another potentially deadly blow and get to my feet just in time for Emily to push her sword into my chest. She doesn't stop until it's buried up to the hilt. I release a guttural moan from the pain and momentarily think it was pure luck that she missed my heart by mere inches—until I look into her eyes. They're filled with tears and deep remorse. I realize then that she missed on purpose.

"I'm sorry," she cries, then sinks to her knees as sobs wrack her body.

I extract the blade, which is also extremely painful, by the way. I change, relieving some of the agony and speeding up the healing process.

Are you okay?

"I'm fine," I answer aloud for everyone to hear. "Leave us."

"No way," Jenna protests. "She just tried to kill you!"

"Leave us. Now." I don't bother to look at them, but the authority in my voice leaves no room for argument. They go, reluctantly, and I focus on Emily. I crouch down next to her and wrap my arms around her. She resists only for a second before allowing me to comfort her.

"Why are you doing this?" she asks between hiccups. "Why aren't you throwing me out?"

"Because you are one of us."

"I tried to...I tried..."

"You tried to alleviate your pain. Pain you believed I caused. You understand now, don't you?"

"Yes." She lifts her tear-streaked face to me, not even flinching at the sight of me in full Cursed mode. "Maybe you're more human than all of us."

I chuckle, feeling tension drain from both of us. "I don't know about that." The smile leaves my face as I change back to Ana. "But I do feel pain, Emily. My heart aches for what I had to do to Zac. It hurts for what I've done to Sam. It hurts for all you've been through because of me." I pause. "And my chest hurts from being impaled by your sword," I tease.

"I'm so sorry."

"Don't be. As long as you feel better now, it was all worth it."

CHAPTER TWENTY-NINE
"GRADUATION."

"**W**hat will we tell people about Zac?" Amanda dries the glass I hand her with a towel, placing it in the cupboard above her. The medial tasks of eating together and doing the dishes give my Hunters a sense of ordinariness. How ironic that something as mundane as chores would be welcomed by teenagers after a hard day of training.

"I will leave that up to all of you," I respond, handing her another dish, and dry my hands on her towel before turning to the others. "Emily? What would you have me do?"

Emily's head whips up in surprise.

"I-I don't know." She looks to the others for ideas, but they say nothing. "I've been in contact with his mom," she says hesitantly. "Texting as Zac," she explains quickly. "She thinks he's just being difficult. I don't have the heart to tell her..."

"Do you want me to compel her?" I ask as her voice trails off.

Again, Emily looks to everyone else. Eric steps up, wrapping his arm around Emily's shoulders.

"Maybe that would be better than reality," he suggests.

"If it were me, I would want my mom to think I was still alive," Jenna weighs in.

"Me, too," Jeremy agrees.

"Very well," I agree. "I will visit her tonight. As for the rest of you, go home. Get ready for tomorrow." I pause to consider their plans for the future. What they will tell their parents. During this time with me, they have been giving their family one excuse after another, saying they have after-school activities or just hanging out with friends. Now, they've decided to go 'backpacking' across Europe before starting college. "Spend time with your family. I don't know when you'll be back."

They all look at each other solemnly. We have no idea what lies ahead for us in Europe and beyond. The only certainty is that we are trained, and now there are two Cursed Ones on the Hunters' side.

My only hope is that other Hunters are not protecting Cursed Ones. If we must dispose of vampires, I'd rather not have to go through Hunters to do it. Another potential problem? They will sense Sam. I don't want to hurt innocents, especially other Hunters. But I will do whatever I must do to keep Sam safe.

I sit alone in the back of the private plane. Even Sam has agreed to give me space for now. Of course, I must call him immediately when I want company. Thinking about the past few nights leaves me a bit unsettled. I did what I agreed to do—visited Zac's mom. She was understandably upset by Zac's 'defiance' and his going off on his own right before graduation. But with a bit of help from me, she saw the reasoning behind it and is even happy for him. I sent her strong, peaceful, and happy thoughts of Zac living a full and successful life. That's the least I could do for her after being the one responsible for taking Zac away from her. It doesn't help ease my guilt, but if she can find peace, that's all that matters.

Graduation was . . . normal. Zac's mother informed the school that Zac would not be attending. They would mail his diploma. I can't help but feel sad about that. As for the others—part of them was excited about graduating, about finishing this chapter of their lives. And part of them couldn't keep their minds off Zac. I went through the motions, even though I was finally among friends at one of these events. I clapped for my classmates, walked across the stage, and accepted yet another diploma. Throughout it all, I silently grumbled about the speeches being endless and dull. Like I usually do when I attend a new high school, I don't bother vying for awards or scholarships. I don't need that stress; I just want this to be over. I decide then and there that this is definitely my last graduation. Ever. At least my inner thoughts kept Sam entertained during the ceremony.

Which brings us to now, with us on this private plane heading to England—my home. I hate not knowing what we're facing. I would have preferred to do some recon before dragging my Hunters into whatever danger awaits. But they wouldn't listen to reason. As much as I like to fancy myself as the leader, this group really does challenge me. I smile. I wouldn't have it any other way.

I unbuckle my seatbelt and walk up the aisle to join my friends.

I missed you.

I give Sam a subtle wink, slip into the seat next to him, and squeeze his hand as he intertwines his fingers with mine.

"Swank ride, A." Jeremy leans his seat back a bit, acting like a boss. I feel Sam shaking beside me, laughing, and I join in with the others. It feels like the first time we've laughed since Zac, and I won't begrudge them that.

"How does an 'eighteen' year old, with no job, afford something like this?" Jenna asks, using air quotes when she mentions my age.

I laugh again and scan my surroundings. The plane really is 'swank,' as Jeremy described it. A total splurge, but one I firmly believe is absolutely necessary. After all, we can't carry weapons on commercial flights. There is no explaining swords, daggers, and stakes. The Gulfstream 650 provides luxurious travel, with plush, ivory leather seats and state-of-the-art electronics. But it also gives us the ability to bring whatever we need to fight whatever may come.

"An eighteen-year-old doesn't," I respond to Jenna's question. "But a 600-year-old vampire with extensive connections and a sharp mind for finance finds it easy to have something like this at her disposal."

"Tell the truth. You compelled someone to give you this sweet ride, didn't you?" she teases.

"Jenna, if I could compel everyone I meet to give me what I want, you would never chew gum again."

Everyone laughs, including Jenna. Well, almost everyone. Sara sits by herself, a few chairs away from everyone. Brooding. Brooders get on my nerves. Sam nearly died and is now an immortal, blood-guzzling vampire. You don't see *him* brooding. Sam laughs out loud, and everyone turns to look at him as if he's lost his mind.

"What's so funny?" Amanda asks, her eyes twinkling with amusement. She probably figured out that Sam had read my mind.

"Nothing," he answers her with a wink.

"No fair that you two can talk to each other without speaking. It's like speaking a language none of us can understand," Jenna whines.

"You don't complain when Emily and Eric do it," I counter.

"Yeah, well, they don't do it unless we're in combat," she grins. I have to admit, getting along with Jenna is much less frustrating than verbally sparring with her.

"Is this how this works?" Sara asks, not looking at us. "You just joke around, not talking about real plans? You haven't even told us why we're going to England when it's clear most of what you're looking for is in Ireland."

"You know, I'm really getting tired of your sh..."

"Jenna." I try to placate Jenna with a sincere smile. "Sara, if you want answers, ask questions. We have eleven hours together on this plane. We've been on here for exactly," I check my watch, "one hour and thirty-two minutes. Do we have to spend every moment discussing strategy to satisfy you? Or can we be human for a little while? And," I hold up a hand before Sara can make some stupid retort, "I know I'm not human, but humor me."

A light blush creeps up Sara's neck, and I'm almost sorry for embarrassing her. Almost. She swivels in her chair, finally facing us. "Why England?"

"Because I don't know what we're up against," I answer honestly. "England seems to be the least active place that Jenna found. I think that's the logical place to start in order to get to know something about what we're about to face without walking straight into the fire, so to speak."

Sara's blush grew even brighter then. I don't believe she truly thought I had a credible reason. I need to remind myself that she hasn't been with me long enough to see me as a leader. I'm hoping to influence her a little more during this flight. It would be extremely helpful if we could trust each other.

"Are you nervous?" Amanda asks me when Sara remained quiet.

"About what we will find?"

"No, about being in England again."

Both Amanda and Sam know I haven't been back to England since I fled centuries ago. I admitted as much to them when I told them where we were headed first. But am I nervous?

"I don't know if nervous is the right word," I respond softly. "It's not something I'm particularly looking forward to, but it is what it is. It must be done."

"Because of your *familia*?" Sara asks, and I'm surprised to see that her tone is genuine. I nod, and she lowers her head, her mouth moving. Her whispers are faint, but I can clearly hear her reciting the Lord's Prayer in Spanish. My attitude toward her shifts slightly at her willingness to say a prayer for my long-lost family.

I feel Sam's fingers tighten around mine. I glance at him and offer a small smile. He's worried about me. When we were together last night, after learning our destination, he was especially affectionate. And, while I appreciated that from him—last night—I don't want my Hunters to think they will be compromised at any moment because of my emotions.

"Look, I want all of you to understand that while this may be difficult for me, it will not stand in my way from doing what we need to do. I lost my family centuries ago. I won't allow it to put you in danger. I promise."

Five hours into the flight, with plans discussed and then discussed again, everyone has gone about their own business. Amanda sits with Sara, perhaps trying to make Sara feel more comfortable with me as her leader. They study the journals and write notes about Jenna's findings during her search. Jeremy is sleeping, snoring quite loudly, with earbud headphones in his ears. I can clearly hear the music from my seat, three rows back from him. How he can sleep through techno music pounding into his head is beyond me.

Eric and Emily sit quietly together, playing chess. I watch them for a moment, wondering if they cheat by trying to use their ability to anticipate each other's next move. Their matches don't seem to last very long, as they are already on their third game.

Sam is sitting beside me, reading the case report about his beating. I didn't want him to relive that day, but I couldn't very well tell him no. Of course, the official report doesn't mention Sam's name because, in the minds of the investigating officers, Sam wasn't the victim. The 'official' victim had died. I can hear Sam's thoughts as he reads through the list of injuries, and I feel his temper rising.

Baby, stop.

We're in an enclosed space, 41,000 feet in the air. If Sam suddenly decides that now is the time to lose his humanity, it would *not* be a good thing. I reach over and pluck the folder out of his hands. His eyes flash with anger, but I hold his gaze without wavering. He struggles for a moment, then the tension leaves his body as his face softens.

Sorry.

I shake my head, leaning over to kiss him softly on the lips.

"It's okay to be upset by what happened to you," I say lightly, making sure our conversation is private. "You just need to control what it does to you."

"You're afraid for me, aren't you?"

"I'm not sure what to think, Sam. You're not reacting the way I expected you to. It's all been so normal and easy. Maybe I'm afraid of a delayed reaction?"

He laughs softly. "Delayed reaction, huh?" Sam leans closer, his lips near my ear. "*You handled the change pretty well. Why is it so hard for you to believe I would?*"

"*That's not entirely true,*" I whisper, trying to ignore the shivers his breath on my ear causes. We definitely aren't in a place to explore *that*. "I had a terrible time adjusting to the change."

"But, the difference is, baby, I have you to help me." He kisses me gently on the cheek, then settles back into his seat with a smile. "It makes me feel safe." Sam closes his eyes, and with a quick listen, I notice he's meditating. He's doing everything he can to help me help him, and I love him for it. Sam's smile widens, making me shake my head. I hope I get used to having him know my every thought.

I change my thought process, glancing at Jenna, who is sitting in the back of the plane, tapping away at her computer. After a moment of hesitation—brought on by our tumultuous relationship—I get up and walk over to her.

"May I join you?"

Jenna looks up, pulls an earbud out of her ear, then tilts her head, studying me for a moment before nodding. Maybe she's just as cautious about talking as I am. There's no way to know how it will turn out.

"I've been compiling a list of places to visit when we get to England. They're separated by how often an incident occurs and the intensity of the crime." Jenna sighs, sitting back and crossing her arms. "You know, you don't have to look so damned shocked that I have a brain."

I close my mouth, knowing my jaw was practically sitting on the table in front of me.

"I'm sorry, I know I'm not being fair to you." Although, to be fair to myself, Jenna hasn't given me much to work with. Of course, I'm not going to tell her that. I reach for the sheet she printed out on the portable printer and study it. The areas are not concentrated. In fact, they're spread out over the entirety of England. "Wow."

"Exactly. If we're right about this, and all of these killings are vampire-related," Jenna glances around us, looking at each of the others, "we're not going to be enough."

CHAPTER THIRTY
"WHO ARE YOU?"

England

"What? You don't have a fancy castle here that we can crash at?" Jenna rolls her suitcase across the expansive foyer of the rental villa, looking around. It's not as big as my estate in California, but it's still not your average home.

"Is this too small for you, Jenna?" I tease.

"It'll do, I guess. Too bad there's no room service." Jenna gives me an amused look before rushing up the stairs, calling 'dibs' on picking her room first.

"Leave the master bedroom for me and Anala, please," Sam calls after her.

Jenna pauses briefly with a smirk, then disappears down the hall. I glance toward the others, noting each of their knowing smiles, and all I can do is shake my head. So glad I can't blush.

"Have I been presumptuous in thinking we would be staying together?" Sam asks softly.

I see the apprehension in his eyes, and take his hand, tugging him toward the master bedroom. "No, not presumptuous. Perhaps just a bit too revealing with the others."

"I'm pretty sure they know we're sleeping together, Anala," he chuckles.

"I'm sure they do. That doesn't mean we need to say it out loud." I smile to lessen the harshness of my words. "I think I miss you calling me Ana," I say suddenly, surprising both of us.

Sam tugs my hand, stopping me. "You don't like that I call you Anala?"

"It just reminds me of how different things are now," I shrug.

"I can call you Ana."

He actually hesitates before saying 'Ana,' as if he has to force the name out.

"I want you to call me whatever you're comfortable with, Sam."

"Okay," he pauses, a slow, mischievous smile forming on his beautiful face. "Baby."

"That'll work," I laugh, as I head to our bedroom.

I'm amazed by the weather today. It's one of those rare occasions in England when the sun is shining bright, there are no clouds in the sky, and the temperature is absolutely perfect. It should've been enough to make me happy. Unfortunately, as I stand out on the terrace, looking out at the green meadow, I can't help but think of my parents. Images of Mum and Papa form in front of me, laughing and teaching the younger version of myself. It occurs to me then that we were happy. In spite of everything that was happening around us at that time - the Black Death, Cursed Ones - our little family was happy. Mum and Papa were very much in love, and they loved me unconditionally. Even when I became what I am, they never stopped loving me.

"Ana?" Amanda stands next to me, placing her hand on mine and squeezing before letting go. "Are you okay?"

"How long have you been standing there?" I ask, confused by her presence. I didn't sense her or catch her scent. Clearly, I was more absorbed in my reverie than I realized.

"Not long. Do you want to talk about it?"

"Did your brother ask you to come and talk to me?" I laugh lightly. I can sense Sam's concern, but he knows I'm not open to discussing how being here makes me feel.

"No," Amanda answers a little too quickly. "Yes. But I wanted to check on you myself. I mean, I can't imagine what this is like for you."

"My reasoning for letting Sam know that I don't want to discuss this is that I can't have any of you worrying that my emotions will compromise our mission."

"Oh, Ana, please. You're hum..."

I raise my eyebrows and grin at her. "Human?" I finish, sarcastically.

"You are to me," she answers softly. "And emotions are normal. Especially the emotions you must be feeling here."

I turn to Amanda and wrap my arms around her. "*Thank you.*" I pull away, noticing tears in Amanda's eyes. Nudging her, I give her a quick, reassuring smile. "I *am* fine, you know." I lift my chin towards the open grassy area before us. "I saw them."

Amanda follows my gaze. "Saw them?"

"My parents. I know that sounds crazy," I add quickly.

"No, it doesn't. It's not crazy at all. Are they happy?"

Amanda doesn't realize that what I saw was the past, but her question makes me stop and think. The scene I watched in the shadows of the trees, shining in the rays of the warm sun, was one of pure happiness. I hope that's true for my parents.

"Yes."

Jenna rolls the map out onto the large dining table. It reminds me of the maps used for strategy sessions during wars back in the day.

"This would be less time-consuming if we had some superior technology."

"I'll keep that in mind, Jenna. For now, what do you have for us?"

She smooths out the edges, placing weights at the corners to hold it down. Jenna points at the areas circled in red. "These are the areas that we need to concentrate on."

But I can't keep my focus on Jenna. My eyes keep going to a small area on the map that isn't circled in red. In fact, the entire area surrounding it is clean. Without thinking, I reach out to touch the territory.

"Ana?" Amanda's soft voice brings my attention back to them.

"This is where my village was," I explain quietly. The closest red markings are at least 300 kilometers from the land where my village once stood. Whether the village, or any semblance of it, is still standing, I don't know. "There's no activity around here."

"I don't think that's a coincidence," Eric states. I give him a questioning look, but it is Emily who elaborates.

"You eradicated Cursed Ones in that area. The Cloaked One put fear in that village and the surrounding areas. Would you risk going back?"

"Even 600 years later?" I ask, almost to myself. I shake myself, refocusing my attention on the areas that need our help. I focus on a small cluster of towns that have the fewest killings. "We'll start here."

"Shouldn't we start in the more affected areas first?" Sara asks, watching me closely.

"No. First, we still need to determine what we're up against. If Hunters have Cursed Ones working for them, forcing them to kill for them, it needs to be stopped. Two, Sam is Cursed. I'm not sure if they will be able to sense him. The smaller the group, the easier it'll be for me to protect Sam."

"I can protect myself, Anala." Sam is embarrassed and quite annoyed with me.

"Sam, I'm not questioning your abilities. But you are newly turned. I will not put your humanity in jeopardy. I cannot allow you to kill a Hunter, an innocent." I look around, holding everyone's gaze for a moment. "I cannot allow *any* of you to kill an innocent. If this goes bad, it will be my responsibility."

"And what about your humanity?" Sam argues.

I ignore Sam's question. Will my humanity be compromised? I don't know. The only thing I am certain of is that none of my Hunters will have to live with killing another human being.

"You will need to wear contacts," I say to Sam, looking him directly in his eyes. I miss his expressive golden eyes. Oh, they're still expressive. Right now, they're filled with a mix of confusion and lingering annoyance towards me.

"Contacts?"

"Yes. Hunters will know what you are if they see your eyes. So, it's either contacts or take some of Papa's elixir. You already know how that stuff burns like hell."

"Contacts it is, then. What about you?"

"I will use contacts as well. They're more reliable. I picked some up back home." I touch his cheek softly. "I got as close to your original color as I could."

Sam leans into my touch, his stubble scratching against my palm. "What is your original color?" he asks softly.

It has been so many years since I've seen *my* eyes. The eyes I was born with. The eyes that used to remind me of mum's.

"Blue."

"Creepy much?" Jenna mutters.

We're dressed in our hunting gear (minus my cloak, of course), leaving nothing to chance. If we need to fight Cursed Ones, we will be prepared. I glance up, blinking several times to clear the dryness caused by the contacts. The small building is the most central in the town. It's logical to assume this is where the Hunters gathered. We're about to find out if our assumptions were correct, but Jenna is right. It's very creepy. The building itself is in good shape, but it's dark and unwelcoming. Though the paint looks new, it's black. Shutters cover fewer windows than expected for a building of this size, almost as if they're feeding into all the myths about vampires—like they're trying to keep out the sun, making everything dark and gloomy. Scary. In reality, I—being a real vampire—find it utterly silly.

"How trite." Seriously? Could they be any more stereotypical? They are definitely taking this to the extreme. I turn to my Hunters. "Let me do the talking."

"You are the leader," Amanda says with just a hint of a smirk.

"Well, it's about time someone remembered that," I mutter. "Just stay close to Sam. If there's any sign of trouble, I want you to get out of here."

"I'm not running, Anala," Sam growls. Oh yeah, he really does *not* like my instructions. "Not again."

"Sam, we've been over this. I'm not going to compel you, but I'm asking you to do this. For me."

If anything happens to you, Anala...

If I feel I cannot take them, I will get out. I promise.

He nods slightly, and I feel the tension drain from my shoulders. But only a little. This whole situation still feels unreal. I have a deeply unsettling feeling about what we might discover here. I take a deep breath and step toward the massive door that looks out of place on the building. I barely hold back a sneer at the absurd lion's head door knocker and dutifully grasp it, knocking three times.

It creaks open—of course it creaks—and I come face to face with an absurdly muscular bloke. He stands at least six inches taller than my five-foot-nine frame. I assume this is how they try to intimidate anyone who dares to approach. Sadly for them, I see him as a cartoonish parody of a real Hunter.

He leers at me, and I feel Sam's displeasure competing directly with my own. "What?"

Perfect. Meathead has the manners of an unevolved Cursed One. Just the arrogant look on his face makes me want to punch him.

"Are you the head of the Hunters?"

Surprise flashes in his eyes, but I'm willing to bet he's too stupid to know to hide it.

"Who are you?"

"We come from California. We heard about you, and have decided to come here and see for ourselves if it was true."

"Heard about us?"

I can see the light bulb isn't even close to going off in this dude's head. I suppress a sigh and manage to keep from rolling my itchy eyes at him.

"Who is it, Gunner?"

Oh, Jesus. Gunner? Seriously? Well, with biceps like those, why wouldn't his name be Gunner? I look past Gunner and see another man coming toward us. He's dressed in black leather, just like the rest of us, but he doesn't bother to hide the weapons he's carrying, including guns strapped to both hips. This just keeps getting better. Are they even real Hunters?

"Some chick claims she and her friends here heard about us in California."

John Wayne brushes past him, offering what I assume he believes is a charming smile. If it weren't for his arrogance and his yellow, misshapen teeth—never mind. His hair is dyed an unnatural black, and his skin is unnaturally white. Even using my best imagination, I wouldn't find this guy appealing. Sam chuckles softly behind me, and I struggle to keep from laughing myself.

"My name is Malcolm." He eyes Sam suspiciously, and I hold my breath. I don't believe I'm dealing with true Hunters, at least not ones that take Cursed Ones seriously, but I won't take chances where Sam is concerned. Malcolm finally turns his attention back to me. "I run things in this area. And, you are?"

"My name is," I hesitate. For some reason, I don't want to give him my name. I'm not sure why that is, but my instincts have always served me well.

Do not react. Turn to the others. Try to get them to understand without alerting Malcolm and Gunner.

Sam silently agrees, and I feel him turning to the others.

"My name is Ella."

CHAPTER THIRTY-ONE

A small territory in Northeast England

"You say you're from California? But you have an English accent."

Malcolm gestures to a red and black pleather couch. I eye it skeptically but sit anyway—no need to alienate the weirdos. Amanda and Jenna sit on either side of me, with the others standing behind us.

"I was born here," I explain. "My family... relocated to the US." I offer nothing more. Instead, I take a moment to observe my surroundings. What appears to be a building from the outside feels more like a house inside. Yet, it's just as dark and gloomy as its exterior—gothic in style. The decorations include gargoyles, dragons, swords hanging on the wall, and even medieval crosses. Ridiculous, I think again.

"What brings you here, Ella?" Malcolm sits back in his throne-like chair. He's trying to project confidence and authority. I don't buy it, but when others fill the room, it seems to bolster his bravado.

"As I told Gunner, we heard about...others like us. We thought we would come and check it out."

"Like you?" Malcolm smirks as he observes my Hunters. I notice then that the others who have entered the room are all men. The only woman present is a

225

voluptuous blonde dressed in a gothic dress that is way too small to contain all of her...essence. But she isn't one of them. She serves them. Fantastic.

"Yes. You are Hunters, aren't you?"

"Hunters? We call ourselves enforcers." He looks at my Hunters again and focuses on Sam again. "So, I take it you're the spokes...*person* for this little group?" Malcolm asks, bringing his eyes back to me. I guess he feels Sam, or perhaps one of the other guys, should be the leader. My urge to throat punch Malcolm escalates exponentially.

"What do you mean 'enforcers'?" I ask, ignoring his question.

Malcolm shrugs. "We don't hunt unless we have to. Our orders are to keep –" he pauses, then shrugs again. "We keep the vamps in line. They work for us. If we have any that decide to defy us, then we hunt. Make an example of them."

There are so many things wrong with what he said, but I focus on one thing in particular.

"Orders? You're *not* the leader?"

He bristles at my question, scowling as if he has a strong opinion about that. "I rule this territory."

"And, who rules you?" I ask when he offers nothing more.

"No one rules me!" he barks. I feel Sam tense.

Stay calm.

"Fine. Who appointed you?" I try again.

Malcolm scowls again. He obviously doesn't like his leader. I realize then that Malcolm has lofty ambitions. He's not content just "ruling" this territory.

"As of right now, it's someone who really doesn't deserve the description. The *only* reason they have power is because of their lineage. We're working on changing those rules."

His group closes in, a show of solidarity. I wonder if it's a true alliance, or if they have no other choice. Malcolm doesn't seem like the type of guy who tolerates anyone defying him. Maybe that's what the guns are for, since they certainly don't work on Cursed Ones. I also note that he didn't answer my question.

"If I wanted to rule my own territory, would that be the person I would go to?" I ask, trying again to get a straight answer.

"You? Run your own territory?" he laughs.

I lift an eyebrow. "What's funny about that?"

"You're a girl."

"Nice of you to notice," I say dryly.

"You can't rule your own territory," he says matter-of-factly. "There's no way you would be able to handle the vamps."

I rein in my fury. My urge to throat punch him shifts into a desire to make him see just how much I can handle—by smashing his stupid throne-like chair across his big ass head.

"I can see it was a mistake coming here," I say, standing abruptly. Amanda and Jenna also stand, and I can feel their own rage radiating from them.

Malcolm also gets up. "Don't play around with things you can't possibly understand, little girl. Leave the enforcing to those who know what's going on."

Rantings of an angry vampire just got another entry. It honestly takes all of my strength not to rip the arms off this ass and beat him senseless with them. Instead of giving in to my desires, I narrow my gaze and take a deep, cleansing breath.

"Of course," I respond with a sarcastic smile. "What on earth was I thinking?"

I turn on my heel, and although I want to storm out of there, I walk calmly and confidently to the door. My Hunters waste no time in following me.

"Make sure they understand who the boss is here."

That was Malcolm's whispered directive. Since Gunner grunts his assent, I assume we'll be joined by meathead soon.

"We're about to have company. Let me take care of it," I say quietly.

"Yo! I have a message for you."

I stop walking and wait for Gunner to catch up. The look in Gunner's eye tells me he has no qualms about hitting a girl. Lucky me.

Sam, do not *react. He is going to hit me, and I'm going to let him.*

Anala...

Do as I ask. Please.

I can feel Sam's frustration, but I don't have time to dwell on it. Gunner doesn't let me down. He's pretty quick for such a big guy. His hand goes up instantly, and he slams his closed fist into my face. It hurt, of course, snapping my head to the side with force. If I had been human, it probably would have brought me to my knees, because douche bag did not hold anything back.

Unlucky for him, I'm not human. I turn my gaze back to Gunner and let a smile slowly spread across my face. He looks surprised. Surprised that I'm still standing. Maybe surprised that I'm not bleeding.

"Tell Malcolm I said, 'message received'. And be sure to give him my message in return."

Blood gushes from Gunner's nose after I hit him. I admit, I take immense pleasure from plowing my fist into his arrogant face. And, when he falls to his knees, that pleasure turns to euphoria.

"Come," I command my Hunters, turning away from Gunner before I do something I will regret.

"Prick," Sam growls. I take his hand, gently coaxing his fist to relax.

"Yes, it seems to be an epidemic in this *territory*." I shake myself, trying to calm my urges to go back there and show them exactly what this 'little girl' can do.

"Anyone else want to go back and kick their asses?" Jenna asks. I laugh when the others raise their hands emphatically. What I just saw makes me appreciate my eclectic group so much more.

"What was with all the gothic crap?" Amanda makes a disgusted noise. "I mean, talk about going overboard."

"They called themselves 'enforcers,'" Sara reminds us. "Do you think they enforce humans as well as Cursed Ones?"

"Absolutely," Emily answers. "Did you see the girl? No self-respecting girl would cater to guys like that."

I don't want to think about how they enforce humans, especially women. "Wait!"

The urgent whisper halts me in my tracks. I know Sam heard it, but the others look at me, confused. I raise a finger, signaling for them to wait as I turn back toward the petrified voice.

She comes out of the woods cautiously, raising her hands in surrender. It's the young, buxom blonde who served Malcolm and his 'followers.' I tilt my head and study her, then glance over her shoulder to see if she has brought reinforcements.

"No one followed me," she reassures quietly, crossing her arms over her chest as if she's embarrassed by her appearance. I don't blame her, really, since her boobs are pressed so high up she could practically rest her chin on them. She's smaller than me—shorter by at least five inches—and tiny in stature. Well, that is, excluding her pushed-up bosom. Feeling sorry for her, I take off my coat and hand it to her. She thanks me, wrapping it around herself.

"What is your name?"

"I am Tania. Malcolm is my brother."

I don't think I could have been more surprised by that. What brother would treat his sister with such disrespect? I glance at Sam and Amanda, each of whom shows their own surprise and displeasure.

"He is also not the true ruler of this territory," she continues, adding to my confusion. "I am."

Well. I did *not* see that one coming. But this definitely isn't the place to have this conversation, especially with Malcolm's henchmen so close.

"Come with us," I demand, not waiting for her response. I turn and walk away, confident she will follow.

CHAPTER THIRTY-TWO
"PRIESTESS?"

T ania's build is closest to Sara's, so Sara graciously lends her some clothes. Now Tania sits comfortably in front of the fireplace at our rented villa, sipping tea. Out of that terrible dress, hair tied up in a ponytail, and face scrubbed clean of over-the-top makeup, Tania looks to be in her early twenties. Her nearly pixie-like stature contradicts her claim of being the 'ruler,' but I know better than most that size doesn't matter. Emily certainly showed me that when she plunged her sword through my chest.

"Are you a real Hunter?" I ask bluntly.

"Yes. But Malcolm doesn't take it seriously. He's made a mockery of everything Hunters stand for."

"You said you were the true... ruler." Wow, I *really* dislike that word. "If that's true, then why let Malcolm take over? Why let him treat you the way he does?"

"Malcolm doesn't like how things are run. He doesn't believe the Priestess should be in charge. I think you've seen that he has little respect for women, other than what they can do for him, whether in service or... service." Tania shivers with disapproval.

"Priestess?" Everything Tania said about Malcolm I could have figured out for myself. What I'm really interested in is this 'Priestess'.

"Yes, she rules over all Hunters," she states, as if I should already know this. "She only appoints other women as rulers of each territory. Malcolm is trying to overrule that."

I am definitely going to have to find out more about this "Priestess," but first...

"So, you just let Malcolm take over?"

No. He forced my hand. He has killed almost everyone I know and love, including our own parents. The only way I could stop him was to give up control to him. I helped some of my Hunters escape, but I was forced into the role of his servant. He filled his 'enforcers' with friends who share his mindset. I'm not even sure if they're all real Hunters.

"With brothers like that, who needs enemies?" Jenna mutters in disgust.

Tania gives her a small smile before turning back to me.

"I saw what Gunner did to you. You barely flinched. Then you nearly took his head off with one blow." She stares at me, and I don't shy away. "Did She appoint you? Did the Priestess send you to take Malcolm out? Does she know he's planning on attacking her?"

So, Malcolm is planning a coup. As tempting as it might be to "take Malcolm out", I need more information. There's no way I am going to follow the orders of some "Priestess ruler of Hunters" that I have no idea about.

"No. But, if you tell me more about this 'Priestess', we will consider helping you."

Tania looks disappointed, but she knows she has no other choice. After a brief silence, she finally nods.

"I'll tell you what I know, but there are journals that have all the information you seek."

"Where are they?"

"In Malcolm's office."

Of course they are.

"We will need those journals," I tell my Hunters, then focus back on Tania. "For now, tell me what you can. Who is this 'Priestess'?"

"She is a descendant of the greatest Leaders of the Society of Hunters." Wonderment takes over Tania's features. Whomever this Priestess is, Tania holds her in high regard. "Generation after generation, a successor is born. Always a daughter. Sons do not become leaders." Tania smiles. "The Cloak is passed down to the daughter who will reign."

A collective gasp fills the room, including from me.

"Cloak?" It surprises me that my voice sounds calm when I feel anything *but* calm.

"Yes. The Cloak, and the name, is passed down to the firstborn daughter. It is her responsibility to keep peace and integrity among the Society. My...Malcolm's territory isn't the only one that wants things changed. Enforcers were put together by Malcolm, consisting of anyone he could find who wouldn't bow to a woman. They have used brute force, not to kill Cursed Ones, but to use them."

"He plans to use them against this Priestess?" Amanda asks. I'm thankful that she has the presence of mind to ask the necessary questions.

"Yes."

Jenna hands Tania a smaller version of the map that rests on the dining table.

"These areas," she points at the red-circled areas. "Are they with Malcolm?"

"My God. He has more than I thought." Tania grasps the map, examining it thoroughly. "What are we going to do?" She looks pointedly at me.

"We go and see the Priestess," I tell her evenly. "First, tell me who her ancestors are. Does this Priestess have a name?"

"Yes."

Tania smiles brightly, and I feel the hairs stand up on my neck. My skin tingles as goosebumps take over.

"Her name is Anala Lagan."

ΛCKNOWLEDGMENTS

End credits song: Stay a Little While by Amaranthe

We'll get to the original acknowledgements here in a second. First, I want to "acknowledge" that because I'm having the Destined Trilogy narrated by Aven (Tessa Stavers), she asked me to "clean up" the manuscripts for her so she could read them more easily. Now, I was a "baby author" when I wrote these books more than a decade ago, so 'cleaning' these up took quite a while! And it was a bit cringey. My "tense" game was HORRIBLE. Especially in this book. But this has given me the chance to 'revamp' – heh – these books. I've polished them up, given them a new look, and I've dreamt of a new storyline that may continue this "bloodline." To anyone who read these books before the re-edit... I'm sorry. Listen, I did my best back then! We live, we learn, and we do better. I hope this is better! Now onto the original acknowledgments:

I was nervous starting the second book of the Destined series. Mostly because I wasn't sure where it was going, that's probably something a writer shouldn't say, but it's true. I had just finished the sequel to Something About Eve - Flawed Perfection - so, my mind needed a little while to get back to Anala. I did get on track, thankfully, though there were times when 'writer's block' set in. These are the times when having people cheering you on is most helpful.

To my beta readers, Daisy, Wanda, Lisa, and Lee - Your opinions, grammar checks, and enthusiasm were invaluable. Thank you so much for taking the time to read and discuss with me. I can't tell you how much I rely on people like you.

Of course, I'm always thankful for the support of my family - blood and chosen. What I write may not always be what you want to read, but you still support me. I love that about you all.

Book nerds everywhere - Without you, writers would be - well, essentially writing in our diaries and hiding them under the mattress.
(Mine really isn't under the mattress. I promise. ;))

Jim McLaurin (Pops -RIP), thank you for proofreading! I'm sure teenage vampire hunters aren't necessarily your "thing", but that doesn't stop you! Just wait until I come to you with my other books. . . I absolutely adore you!!

As always, to my readers - I can't thank you enough for your support. I hope you're enjoying Anala's story. I hope you will stay interested enough to stay tuned for the third and final book in the Destined series. All my characters hold a special meaning for me. There are more characters to come, and I hope all that I bring to the page will touch you in some way.

ABOUT THE AUTHOR

I've called Houston, Texas home since 2009, where I've been writing novels and building the life I love. The arts have always been part of who I am: music sets the mood, reading sparks my mind, and writing lets me explore the limitless corners of my imagination. I've been writing and imagining stories since I was a teen, but I knew it was truly my passion the moment I finished my first novel, *Something About Eve*.

Books have always captivated me, carrying me into exotic worlds and impossible scenarios where I could live as someone else, if only for a while. That same magic drives me to bring my own characters to life. My greatest hope is that my stories inspire readers—or at the very least, give them a welcome escape from everyday life.

Beyond writing, I founded **Jaded Angels LLC**, a business inspired by my beloved momma. Through Jaded Angels, I merge creativity and heart, offering products and stories that honor her memory. Since her passing from Alzheimer's, I've dedicated a portion of my proceeds to supporting those impacted by this devastating disease. Mourning someone who is still alive takes a toll on the soul and losing them entirely shatters it. Writing has been my anchor through grief, and I carry her memory with me in every word. #endalz

Find out more at:

www.jourdynkelly.com

Follow me on social media:

Instagram: @JourdynK
TikTok: @jourdynkelly
Facebook
(https://www.facebook.com/AuthorJourdynKelly)
Secret Society on Facebook
(https://www.facebook.com/groups/JoKels/)

What you should know:

Anala Geil (Ana Gale)

- Daughter of the Leaders of the Society of Hunters.

- Hunter

- Vampire

- Leader of the New Society of Hunters

- The Cloaked One

- Senior in high school – again (Probably because she gets bored)

- Thomas's true Maker

- Over 600 years old

- In love with Sam

Sam Logan

- Homicide Detective

- Amanda's brother

- Hunter

- Descendant of Thomas Lagan

- In love with Anala

Amanda Logan

- Ana's best friend

- Sam's sister

- Descendant of Thomas Lagan

- Keeper of the journals

- Hunter

- Senior in high school

Jenna Hynes

- Senior in high school

- Hunter

- Mean girl with attitude

- Loves to pop her gum

- Closet geek

- Captain of the cheerleaders

- Crushing on Jeremy

Emily Zhou

- Senior in high school

- Hunter

- Eric's sister

- Fencing expert

- Acrobatic

- Can communicate with Eric via thoughts

Eric Zhou

- Senior in high school

- Hunter

- Emily's brother

- Fencing expert

- Can communicate with Emily via thoughts

Jeremy Trent

- Senior in high school

- Hunter

- Football quarterback

- Crushing on Jenna

Zac Connor

- Hybrid

- Senior in high school

- Turned by Thomas

- In love with Ana

- Crushing on Emily

- Trying to hang on to his humanity

Thomas Lagan

- Cursed

- Was once a Hunter

- Lost his humanity

- Once loved Anala

- Wants Anala to join him

- Created armies of Hybrids

Innocents

- Humans

Hybrids

- Vampires

- Cursed

- Recently turned

- Cannot turn others

- Not as strong as Full Bloods

Full Bloods

- Vampires

- Cursed

- Hybrids that have completed the change

- Can turn humans

Cursed Ones

- Vampires

- No humanity (with a few exceptions)

- Can turn humans

Blood Orchlips

- Man-made flowers created for medicinal purposes

- Ingredient used for Humanity serum

www.ingramcontent.com/pod-product-compliance
Lightning Source LLC
Chambersburg PA
CBHW070816180626
46818CB00001B/290